After The Show

Linda Van Meter

Cover design by Linda D. Van Meter

This book is a work of fiction. Names, characters, places, and incidents either are products of the author's imagination or are used fictitiously. Any resemblance to actual persons, living or dead, events, or locales is entirely coincidental.

Linda D. Van Meter

Printed in the United States of America

First Printing: February 2019

ISBN: 9781795151573

This book is dedicated to the women who share in this accomplishment. They make be a better writer with their sharp eyes, brilliant minds, and valuable input; Michele, Kait and Jean.
Thank you to my readers. Your enthusiasm for my stories fills my heart!

A special dedication to my precious Bristol Blue. Writing will never be the same without your loyal companionship and unwavering love!

Finally, this story is for my forever rock star- Jerry. Your music and love inspire me! Thank you!

Chapter 1

Findlay, Ohio

No matter how big or small, nearly everyone has had that moment of waking up in the morning and thinking, “What have I done?” These were the silent words that Paige mouthed as she placed her phone back on the nightstand. Her alarm, playing Maroon 5’s *Sunday Morning*, startled her awake, and she’d grabbed it and shut it off. The body next to her hadn’t moved. *The body next to her*?

Now Paige sat up and her head screamed in protest. As she attempted to swing her legs noiselessly over to the side of the bed, her stomach lurched. Throwing up in the hotel bathroom was out of the question, certainly the man sleeping would hear. Before the ramifications of him lying there in bed naked took over, Paige focused on the fact that her alarm signaled exactly ninety minutes until she had to be at school. Somehow, she had to get home, shower, and dress within that time frame. A teacher didn’t show up at school in last night’s outfit.

The hotel blackout curtains made it nearly impossible to see, Paige used the screen of her phone as a light. Items of clothes were strewn about. She grabbed her bra, underwear, found her tank top, shirt, jeans. Her boots were together, but only one sock was nearby. After a desperate scan of the floor, she realized one sock would get left behind. Now with arms full, Paige stepped into the bathroom, pulling the door closed silently. Without thought, she flipped on the light. It was attached to the fan, and the noise seemed deafening. She flipped it back off, her heart pounding. Standing frozen, listening for the sound of footsteps, she felt that vomiting was imminent. No movement outside the door, her stomach held.

This time she found the flashlight app on her phone and it gave her enough glow to pull on her outfit, haphazardly. The tall boot felt strange against her bare foot, but it would do. A glance in the mirror, as she pulled on her shirt, showed a glowing, hideous face with mascara below her eyes and her hair standing at odd angles. *Please don't let him wake up and see this!* Dressed, she flipped off the phone and snuck out of the bathroom. Still no movement from the bed. Paige pulled her purse off the table and couldn't help a small smile to escape. *Wow! Last night really happened.*

***

Exactly eighty minutes later, she was back in the car. This time she had clean but damp hair and school attire. Her car Bluetooth signaled a call, it was Laurel. Paige took a breath and hit *Accept.* "Where are you?" her friend hissed.

Deciding to play dumb, Paige casually responded, "On my way to work."

"From where?"

"My house."

"Cut the crap, Paige. When did you get home?"

The jig was up, "An hour ago."

Her friend's high-pitched hoot through the car speaker cut into her hangover headache, "I knew it. Tell me everything!"

"This is all your fault!" though Paige spoke with a voice of attempted anger, Laurel's response was more ear-splitting whoops.

***

The Jack Corey band was a big hit in the eighties and early nineties. They played songs that went from heavy electric guitar to sweet ballads, and Jack Corey's smoky voice enhanced each song. Like nearly every other girl, back then, Paige had all their cassettes and then CDs when the music industry changed everything. It wasn't the only band she adored, but one of the top ten. Back in college, she had seen them perform in a crowded auditorium in Toledo, Ohio. Even from her nosebleed seat, they were fantastic.

Laurel was on the board at the Marathon Performing Arts Center in their hometown, Findlay. She not only got front row seats but also a pass for Paige to join her at the meet and greet party afterward. The concert was a remarkable event. Their seats were unbelievable. And though the guys in the band had touches of gray and character lines on their faces, every man was still a dynamic performer. Like all the other members of the middle-aged audience, Paige couldn't help being a little star struck by Jack. When she looked back that's all she remembered. They made no eye contact, nothing significant. What happened subsequently was still a mystery.

***

The meet-and-greet was held in the theater's Pavilion, a big open room that housed wedding receptions and other parties. There was food set up on a table and a bar, a few chairs scattered about and a lot of open space. The wealthier patrons of the town were there, as were employees of the theater, the media and lucky extras such as

Paige. They waited for about 45 minutes before the band members wandered in from the downstairs dressing room. By this time Paige and Laurel each had two glasses of wine, and she was feeling relaxed. Paige had no intention of talking to anyone from the band, it was obvious by the dress and the excitement of the other local women that they still had that teen dream of hooking up with a rock star. As the musicians came in, several women clustered around them. Most were trying to get selfies with them, others looking even more aggressive. Laurel placed the refreshments on the table. Paige picked up her third glass of wine and decided that she would go sit down somewhere to watch the fun. At the right of the room was an open staircase that led to an encircling balcony. She climbed up to the 6th or 7th step and settled there, her boots resting on the step below. It was the perfect spot to get a look at all the interaction.

She didn't know how long she sat, and to be honest, she felt that third glass of wine. Her focus was on a parent of one of her students who was trying to seduce the bass player, practically forcing herself on him. Paige realized someone was standing in front of her. Turning her attention straight ahead, she saw it was Jack Corey. He was holding a wine glass and a bottle of the same Pinot Noir that she was drinking. With a smile, as devastating as the one she had seen for decades on CD covers and magazine spreads, he spoke, "Do you need a refill?" His voice was just as rough and deep as it was when he was belting out tunes.

For half of a heartbeat, Paige was silent, in shock, she recovered and said, "Thank you, yes." She honestly didn't need another drink but how could she refuse him? To her surprise, Jack sat down on the step next to her, filled her glass and his. He introduced himself as if she didn't know who he was, and she gave him her name, "Paige Baxter."

"What are you doing hiding up here?" he asked.

It pleased her that the wine had made her feel much more comfortable than she ever would have around someone of such celebrity, "I'm not hiding, I'm enjoying the people watching."

Jack observed the scene below and laughed, "It is quite a spectacle isn't it?"

"Is this how it always is?" she asked, taking a sip of wine.

Jack nodded his head, "Pretty much, sometimes worse."

"I can't imagine. It seemed a great opportunity to meet you guys, but I didn't want to be clamoring for your attention like everyone else." She threw in a swift afterthought, "The show was amazing, absolutely amazing. It was fantastic to get to hear you guys perform live again."

"Thank you," he was modest. She was almost embarrassed that she complimented him, something he must hear all the time. "So, you've heard us before?"

She caught herself before she gushed, but still said, "Oh yes. I saw you in concert when I was in college.

And that's how the next hour and a half went, the two of them sat and talked. Occasionally, they were in comfortable silence as they watched the activity below them. They'd emptied the bottle of wine. He was easy to talk to. She wasn't even certain when it went from conversation to flirting. Soon it wasn't just their knees touching, but it was their whole sides. The next move was a kiss. It had happened naturally. When they both stood, she knew exactly where they would go. She signaled Laurel across the room to let her know she was leaving. Her drive to his hotel had been both careless and lucky.

She recalled the time at the hotel too, very nice and surreal. Paige knew when she had fallen asleep, they'd been holding on to one another.

Now as she was climbing out of her car, the ends of her hair still damp. Her face was flushed from the heat of the memories.

***

Jack woke up in the hotel two-and-a-half hours later. He stretched in the strange bed, not at all an unusual situation for him. Noticing his surroundings, he looked next to him. The other side of the bed was empty. He lay there a moment, staring up at the ceiling and sighing. She'd left, and he hadn't even realized it. Most wouldn't believe last night was a rare occasion for Jack. He couldn't recall the last time he'd met a woman after his concert and slept with her. Jack knew the reason he'd done it was because she wasn't crowding around them, he'd glanced up and seen her sitting up on the steps by herself. She instantly attracted him. As they talked, he realized she was, in fact, something different from those women hanging onto them below.

He sat up and glanced at his phone. There was still an hour before they left. Was there any clue to who she was other than Paige? He thought she'd said her last name at some point when they met. Jack stepped into the bathroom and started the shower. Soon he climbed in and let the hot water pour down on him, thinking again about who she was and then he shook his sopping head. What did it matter anyway? What'd he think he would do, call her and make a date here in Ohio? They had two more weekends and cities in Ohio and then it was off to Chicago or Fort Wayne or wherever Tony had scheduled them next. As Jack squirted the hotel shampoo on his hair, he couldn't help smiling when he thought about her. They'd had a nice conversation and a great night.

Before he could contemplate any further, Tony was knocking on the door. He opened it wearing just jeans. His manager, and friend of 28 years, smacked him on the back, laughing out loud, "I haven't seen you behave like that in a long time!"

Jack had the decency to look embarrassed. He didn't respond about it and instead said, "I hope that's coffee you've got in there."

Tony handed him a tall Styrofoam cup, the mix inside just as he liked; two creams, no sugar. "Since when do you bring someone back to your room?"

After a few sips, Jack played along with Tony "I don't remember the last time I did it, but I have no regrets."

"Well, she wasn't some young thing," Tony teased.

Jack shook his head, "It wasn't like that, I can't explain it."

At that moment Trent walked in, "Yeah you're such a pussy, you would say it wasn't like that."

Jack looked at his bass player, a friend since they were teenagers. "Yeah I know, I'm not the man-whore you are." The teasing kept on as the three guys drank coffee. There was a brief talk about their plans for the day. They were moving on. They discussed the interviews that would occur once they got to Dayton. Later alone, he looked around for anything she may have left and found only one black and gray blended sock. No note on the pad of paper, no number in lipstick on the mirror, she hadn't left her number on his phone. Jack wished she had left a contact.

Chapter 2

Findlay, Ohio

Paige's half hour lunch break, which she spent in a fellow teacher's classroom with six other teachers, was up. Laurel didn't teach in this building and none of her coworkers knew of last night's events. All she had said was that the music was amazing. She said it was so cool to get to see the band members and yes, she'd even gotten to speak to Jack Corey. She received ribbing and directed the focus from her. Paige did this by telling the story of the mom and the bass player. She could only hope that Laurel, who taught in the elementary school, was keeping her secret. The bell rang.

Paige had just gotten to her desk when her phone buzzed. It was from David. David Blair was the man she had just started to see. They'd had only two actual dates. Paige thought she liked him. David was the finance manager at a local brewing manufacture. She was officially introduced to him by Laurel's husband, Pete, though she'd seen him before. His two children had graduated from the high school where Paige taught. He was present at some of the same sporting events, National Honor Society inductions and senior awards ceremonies. She was at a wedding reception with Laurel and Pete when David joined their table. He and Pete were golf partners. David was a good-looking man; tall with silver black hair, and a muscular shape he worked hard on maintaining. His mornings began at 6 a.m. at the Y. Paige and David got along well. Two days later he called her. Laurel had forewarned her, he'd asked for her number. She was fine with that. Divorced for several years, Paige had dated, but no real relationships. She felt she was ready for one.

They had gone to dinner for the first date, a nice steakhouse in town. Conversation came easily. At her door later, David had given her a light hug that showed his interest and yet his good manners. The next weekend, they had attended a local production of *Newsies* at the exact theater where Paige had seen the Jack Corey band perform. After the show; they'd gone for a drink. This time at the door, David had given her a kiss. It wasn't passionate, but Paige got the message; he liked her.

Now he was texting her, reminding her they were supposed to be headed to a movie tonight. "Ah shit," she almost said it out loud in front of her Art III students who were shaping clay into various forms. Her head was pounding, still the result of the excessive amount of wine she drank. That was only part, Paige hadn't even given herself any time to process what had happened; where her morning had begun. She could not fathom trying to be interested in a date with another man tonight. Paige wanted to go home and wallow in her thoughts about Jack Corey.

Hating to be inconsiderate but not wanting to talk, Paige sent David a text. She used a headache as an excuse to cancel the date. He sent a teasing response about the likelihood of her being hungover from the concert. Then he sent another about the possibility of doing something on Saturday. Paige apologized again and promised to contact him in the morning.

***

The school day ended. Paige climbed into her silver Honda CRV and rested her head back. At last! Her house was just three miles from the high school and soon she had her car in the garage. Paige had owned this 3-bedroom brick ranch for four years. It was the first home she'd ever lived in alone and she loved that she had decorated it to just her taste.

Hanging her purse on the hook by the door leading from the garage, she stepped out of her favorite leopard print flats. Paige had a tray for shoes there. Most times it collected all her footwear, they rarely made it into her closet. Padding to the fridge, barefoot, she already felt better. Retrieving a tall glass from the cupboard, she pulled the pitcher of strawberry lemonade from the fridge. She perched on a barstool. Elliott, the red tabby, who was technically her daughter's, came into the room. He meowed his delight at seeing her. Paige allowed him to jump on her lap for a brief scratch.

In front of her, on the granite gray and white bar that opened to her living area, was her laptop.

She took a long swallow of lemonade to cool her throat before she logged onto the screen. Her fingers typed the name Jack Corey on the *Google* search bar. Pages, videos, and images came up. Paige clicked on a photo. The screen opened to a large image of his face. It was recent. She could see the hint of gray at his temples and laugh lines around his eyes. "No way," she said to the screen. "I did not wake up in your bed this morning."

Paige got up from her chair and paced the house. This couldn't be real. She walked into her spare room and opened the closet. Reaching for a box on the top shelf, she pulled it down. Inside were CDs from years gone by. A quick search produced *Jack Corey-Road to Sorrow.* Paige looked at Jack's picture on the cover. "You and me? Impossible!"

She heard a car in the driveway and turned the Jack Corey music off her laptop. Paige had barely reached the front door when the knob turned. Laurel raced in. Paige laughed at her friend, "I was expecting a call, not a visit."

"A call? Are you kidding? I want to hear everything." Familiar with her friend's house, Laurel moved to the kitchen. "I'm thirsty."

Paige took this opportunity to shut off her laptop. "I have strawberry lemonade in the fridge."

"Hell no, this conversation needs cocktails!"

"No way, I'm still feeling last night's wine."

Laurel added more lemonade to Paige's glass and one for herself. "Girlfriend, that's not the kind of hangover you have." Now she pulled a bottle of vodka from the fridge and added a healthy splash to each glass. After a quick stir, she handed Paige her drink again. "I want details."

Paige decided that she needed it and sipped the cocktail, "A lady never tells."

"A lady doesn't go to a hotel with rock star. I about died when I spotted you on the steps sucking face with someone." Paige grimaced and drank more. "When the two of you finally came up for air, I realized it was Jack Corey. How the hell did it happen?"

Now Paige moved into the living room and settled onto her gray couch. "He materialized in front of me with a bottle of wine." She took on a distant look as she remembered that moment.

"And then just grabbed you and kissed you?"

"No, we talked forever." He had been so easy to talk to. They shouldn't have had anything in common, but it felt like they did.

"Then he grabbed you and kissed you?" Laurel looked hopeful.

Paige laughed, "At first, I realized our knees were touching. I'd had a lot to drink, at some point, I put my hand out in a gesture at what I was saying, and he grabbed it. The next thing I knew, we were kissing."

"That's what I wanted to hear," her friend nodded in satisfaction. "And then you went to his hotel room."

Paige remembered after about the third kiss, Jack had whispered, "I'm ready to leave. Would you go with me?" She hadn't even considered saying no.

"And at the hotel?" Laurel raised her eyebrows. The vodka lemonade was having its effect on both.

Paige grinned, "It's been a long time since sex was that much fun."

"Was he aggressive? Or kinky?"

"No," Paige was once again somewhere else. "Just tender and passionate."

Laurel collapsed back into the chair she was on, "You had sex with a rock star, a real rock star! Jack Corey!"

"I did," there was wonder in Paige's own voice.

Now Laurel sat up, "What about David? Don't you have a date tonight?"

"No, I canceled."

"Why? Did you and Jack exchange numbers?"

Paige laughed as she placed her glass on the whitewashed wooden tray that sat in the middle of her gray leather ottoman in front of the couch. "No. But Laurel, if I so eagerly jumped in bed with him last night, I must not have any real feelings for David."

"Oh, that's ridiculous. You're not exclusive. You don't think if Sheryl Crow did a show in town and wanted to sleep with David that he wouldn't?"

"But then I wouldn't think we were a serious couple."

Laurel finished her drink and clanged her glass next to Paige's. "You're not a serious couple yet. This was a freebie."

Paige sighed, Jack Corey would never come knocking on her door, that was true. Going out with David would remind her of what real-life relationships were like. She'd call in the morning to reschedule.

Chapter 3

Akron, Ohio

Annabeth Muldoon had spent sixteen years holding the coveted position as a celebrity interviewer and feature writer for *Rolling Stone Magazine*. Her wit and ability to snuff out trends kept her on top. That same ability helped her to realize that the publishing world was in a permanent struggle. Annabeth retired early and took on biography and memoir writing. Her first published book was on Genevieve Sterling. Genevieve had begun a solo career in the late 60s-early 70s. She was performing rock alongside a nearly completely male-dominated lineup. She had survived drug addiction. sexual harassment and three husbands. Annabeth spent six months with her; traveling for show appearances and hanging out on her ranch in Wyoming. The result was a 435-page biography that sat on the *New York Times Bestseller List* for 23 weeks.

Her next work was a book on identical twin brothers. They were child stars in the 70s who shared a role as a sitcom toddler. Later they chose different paths. One chose the stage in New York. The other spent twelve years as a lawyer on an award-winning television drama. Their final screen appearance together had been at 61, playing evil twins on a well-received horror movie. The book was a success because, at different points in their lives, they had each married the same woman.

Annabeth enjoyed the money and publicity from that book, but she missed the world of musicians. As she saw more memoirs popping up from the likes of Bruce Springsteen and Billy Joel, Annabeth wanted to write another rocker book.

Jack Corey had the All-American hometown boy-makes-good-story. He grew up in Middle America; Junction City, Kansas. His father worked for the Coca-Cola Bottling Company and drove a Harley Davidson. When not doing those two things, he played electric guitar with a *Deep Purple* cover band. His mom stayed home with their only child, Jack. She gave piano lessons from the house and played the organ at the Methodist Church on Sunday morning.

Jack played football and baseball from middle school on up. He also learned the guitar from his dad. He was a sophomore when his dad was on the Harley and hit a road sign, nearly decapitating him. His life insurance paid off their split-level home, but his mother's piano lesson income wasn't enough to pay the rest of the bills. She took on a job at the bottling company working second shift.

Now Jack came home to an empty house every day. His mother didn't arrive until 11:30 p.m. Feeling abandoned, Jack lost himself in music. Soon football and baseball dropped away. He had possession of his father's music equipment. Before he was old enough to buy beer in a bar, he played with local bands. He managed just passable grades and graduated. Jack Corey was ready to head out into the world of music.

The progress she was making on Jack's story, pleased Annabeth. She had spent a week in Kansas; doing interviews, unearthing photos, even discovering some VHS Cassettes of little Jack Corey playing in bars. Now she had joined the band on tour in Detroit.

Jack had been reluctant to do the book. His ego was not the same as a lot of celebrities. He didn't feel his story was interesting to anyone. Tony had convinced him to do it. Jack was a sucker for the phrase, "It's good for the whole band."

Annabeth was already enjoying talking to Jack. Today, as they headed to Akron, she was in the back of the bus with the rest of the band. It wasn't easy; they were too involved in a video game battle to converse.

Joe Casto, the Jack Corey drummer since 1982, was chatty. In Annabeth's experience, this was common for drummers. They were an animated member of the band on and off stage. He was, at this moment, regaling her with tales of conquests. "Back in the day, when our hair was longer and our legs stronger, we all indulged pretty regularly in pleasures of the flesh." He winked, "You know what I mean."

"Some of us still do," barked Trent, his focus on the screen and the controller in his hand.

"Even Jack?" Annabeth asked as she jotted notes.

"Absolutely. I mean as the band got famous, he ran to more champagne tastes." Annabeth assumed that was a reference to Jack's ex-wife, supermodel Mavis Corey-Steiner. "But now we've all slowed down, pretty much. A lot of the guys are married or have girlfriends."

"But Jack doesn't?"

Joe shrugged, "Not for a couple of years. He's single but never fan bangs."

Annabeth paused her pen, "But the other night..." Before she could finish, Jack appeared.

"Tony and I are done, if you want to continue," he motioned toward the front of the bus.

Annabeth thanked Joe and followed Jack. "He was telling me about the old days and the many women."

"He's proud of his conquests." Jack didn't turn around as he spoke.

"He meant all of you."

Now Jack sat on the makeshift loveseat and looked at her, "I stopped that as soon as I started it."

Annabeth sat across from him, nodding, "But the other night?"

Jack was quiet for a moment, Annabeth could see he was smiling, "That was very unusual and different from what Joe is talking about."

Annabeth raised an eyebrow, "More than a one-night thing?"

He sighed, "Well considering I don't know how to reach her, I guess not."

She pointed her pen at him, "If you want me to find her, I can."

Jack broke into the grin that had graced dozens of magazine and album covers, "I'll let you know."

***

Jack Corey had destroyed her love life. Paige stood with her back to the front door as the car in the drive backed out and moved down the street. Paige marched into her room and looked at the CD cover that now sat front and center on her dresser. "Damn you, Jack!"

She had kept her promise to Laurel and called David on Saturday morning. He seemed very pleased to hear from her. They made plans to grab a quick meal at a favorite BBQ place then catch a movie.

As Paige put on makeup, then a final spritz of hairspray she kept up her inner pep talk. David seemed interesting, very nice, and they had a lot in common. She was humming along with John Mellencamp's *Small Town*, as she put on her earrings. Just as she fastened the last back, the song switched to *Swept Away* by the Jack Corey Band. Paige strode across the room and shut the music off her phone.

"Oh no you don't, I will enjoy tonight with a man right here in town. You're probably warming up your guitar and flirting with the ladies before you go on stage somewhere." Paige knew where he was. She had looked up his schedule online. Tonight, he was in Akron. So close!

***

The date had gone well. David was charming and looking very appealing in his blue jeans and dark green polo. Through dinner and as they headed to the theater, he was giving off signals he wanted to touch her. His hand hovered at the small of her back when he let her go into the row of seats first. Later, he lightly touched her upper arm when asking if she wanted more popcorn. At her front door, he finally reached for her hand. It was obvious that he intended on pulling her close for a goodnight kiss. Just three days ago, she would have welcomed this. Not tonight, he wasn't the right man. Those weren't the right lips trying to head in her direction.

Paige had taken her other hand and patted the top of his, thanking him for a lovely evening and making a hasty retreat into the house.

And now, she was scolding a photograph for ruining her life; making her wish for someone she couldn't have.

***

The Akron concert was not followed by a party. The guys seemed glad for this. They had rooms at a local hotel, and most were happy to head up. Jack was the first one to disappear in the elevator.

Annabeth wasn't ready to go to her room. If she did, she'd feel obligated to type up notes. The hotel offered a lounge, and she made her way in. She sat at the bar and ordered a Jack and Coke. A voice behind her said, "Make that two."

It was Trent. Annabeth liked watching him play the bass. He stood almost 6'2" and was thin to the point of wiry. He had a mostly gray mustache and beard. They matched his thinning hair he kept long enough to pull into a small ponytail. "Want company?" His voice was rough from years of cigarettes.

"Absolutely, I promise I'm off the clock, no interview questions."

After a long drink, he grinned, "How about some stories that won't make the book?"

She knew Trent's reputation. He'd been married long enough to have kids in high school. That didn't stop him from still sleeping around. Annabeth had never married. She'd lived with a fellow journalism major from the start of their senior year at Columbia and over the next four years. Both were hard-working writers. He got the bug to do overseas correspondence. Annabeth loved her work at *Rolling Stone*. They parted ways.

Being around celebrities, but not being one, was not conducive to good relationships. She'd never felt the need to have children, so Annabeth was happy to remain single. She got what she needed when she needed it. As they switched to shots of Crown, Annabeth was sure she'd get what she needed. When Trent asked for a smoke and she said they were in her room, he'd said, "Well, let's go get them." They were kissing before the elevator doors closed.

***

The band headed to Pittsburgh on this zigzag of a tour. Annabeth was feeling quite hungover as she sat in the front of the bus trying to type. Tony was across from her on his laptop and phone. It annoyed her that Trent was in the back, Face-timing his family.

Jack came into the space and sprawled out on the loveseat. He had his guitar with him. He absentmindedly plucked the strings. Annabeth glanced over at him. Why couldn't she have hooked up with the single guy? She gave a mental shake. She had a hard and fast rule about sleeping with her subjects. Besides, she wasn't quite Jack's type, she thought as she attempted to pull her faded purple Lakers t-shirt over her stomach. Below the shirt, her faded jeans cut into her soft, pudgy waist.

One glance at his hair the color of honeyed oak was all she needed to know this was true. It was shorter than days gone by but still layered long enough on top to fall on his face when he was looking at his guitar. She self-consciously patted her own hair, frizzy with last night's hairspray. Her dark roots were showing two inches from the fading bleach blonde. He wasn't her type, too good looking and too nice.

Annabeth realized that he was staring out the window, playing and humming to James Blunt's *You're Beautiful.* He turned in surprised when she said, "You know Jack, I really can find her."

Jack looked sheepish, "No that's okay."

Annabeth shrugged, "You never know, she may be sitting at home waiting to hear from you." She thought, who wouldn't hope to hear from Jack Corey after a night of sex with him?

***

Paige had put David off when he called, ignoring his questions about her interest in him. She offered instead, a casual conversation focused on what he was doing. She avoided next weekend date plans by using a visit to her daughter as an excuse. The truth was, her daughter lived less than an hour away and a visit would only be a day trip.

Hannah, 23, lived in Toledo. She had graduated from college a year ago and was a surgical RN at one of the bigger hospitals in the city. Kyle was her boyfriend, they'd met sophomore year. Now they were both graduates, and he worked at one of the corporate bank offices. They lived in a townhouse in a younger suburb of Toledo.

***

On Sunday afternoon, the entire crew was sitting on the deck of The Redfin in Pittsburgh, overlooking the Allegheny River. They watched boats on the water as they enjoyed food and drinks. Last night's concert had gone well and now they had a few days off before a two-night stint in Cleveland. Annabeth sat at a table with Tony and Jack.

After another round with Trent, she had asked him about his days off. He informed her that he was headed back to New York to see his family. His wife, Gina, would come to Cleveland with him. "So cool it around me," he said firmly. He offended Annabeth. She hadn't chased him, they were equal in their sexual exploits.

Tony was dominating the conversation about his plans in Chicago this week. It involved a new woman. He looked at Jack, "How about you?"

"Going home to New York to be alone for a few days." Annabeth nodded, her plans as well.

"Jack, you're alone too much," Tony observed.

Before he could respond, Annabeth said, "You know Jack, we're headed back to Ohio next weekend."

It surprised her at how quickly Jack smiled. He then took a deep breath and nodded, "Okay, find her."

***

Annabeth was happy for the assignment and the distraction from Trent. Besides, what if this turned out well? It would be a good chapter in her book. On Monday morning, she called the director of the Marathon Arts Center in Findlay, Ohio. Introducing herself as the publicist with the Jack Corey band got the other woman's full attention. Annabeth would not reveal why she needed to find the mysterious "Paige".

Cat Greenwalt couldn't recall anyone by that name. When Annabeth said she was at the meet and greet, Cat said that narrowed it down. Her curiosity was getting the best of her. "Is there a problem?" Annabeth said no. "If anyone has done something wrong, I need to know." Annabeth assured her it was all good. She was on her computer while they talked because she said, "Here's the list of local attendees."

Annabeth waited patiently. "Okay, Paige Baxter is who you're looking for. She's on the list with Laurel Hensel, one of our volunteers. I think they both teach at the school."

"Do you have her phone number?" She used her most gracious voice.

"No, but hold on, I'll text Laurel and ask for it."

"Please don't mention it's for the Jack Corey band."

Cat hesitated, "Is this a surprise? Did she win something?"

Annabeth grabbed onto the suggestion, "If this works out, I'll be certain that the theater and you, receive recognition."

"That would be wonderful for the theater! Oh, Laurel sent the number!"

***

Paige was pushing her cart through the produce aisle. She was forcing herself to buy groceries right after work. May was becoming a long month, and she knew once she got home, she'd want to relax. A text buzzed in her phone. It was Laurel, *Cat Greenwalt asked for your number.*

Who? Paige responded before picking up two tomatoes.

The director of the Marathon Arts Center. She'll probably ask you to be a volunteer. Before Paige could reply, she sent more. *You did so well handling some of the band members.*

Paige sent her an emoji with the tongue sticking out and continued her shopping.

At home, she unloaded the food and set out a turkey burger to cook for dinner. As she was reaching into the cupboard to get a pan, she received a text. It was an unfamiliar number, and the message was several lines. Paige stopped what she was doing and read it.

Hi Paige. This is Jack Corey. With some help, I was able to find your number.

Paige read it three times, then said aloud, "No way! This isn't real!" She considered not responding. It must be a prank. Who had Laurel set up to do this? She decided to play along.

Oh? This is Jack Corey?

Yes, I know it sounds crazy. I wanted to get in touch.

Paige was feeling a myriad of emotions; anger at Laurel for breaking her confidence, humor at the prank but also disappointment because she wished it was him. *Okay, the joke's over. Who is this?*

I promise it's me. I have your sock. Paige remembered the sock she'd been unable to find in his hotel room. Had she told Laurel about it? Before she could respond, another message came in. This was a picture of Jack holding her sock. She thought she might hyperventilate. Her memory didn't do justice to that sweet smile.

That is my sock. She frowned at her own lame comment.

How are you? He included a smiling emoji.

I'm good. How are you?

Glad I found you.

She replied coyly, *I'm glad you were looking.* She was shocked that he was. *How'd you find me?*

Is it okay that I did?

Absolutely.

I have a biographer traveling with the band. She contacted the theater. They found you through your friend.

Now Paige understood Cat's call. *Are you traveling?*

No, I'm home in New York. We have a couple of days off.

As she was wondering if they would just make small talk, he changed the topic. *I enjoyed our evening together.*

Me too.

Can I call you?

Paige's heart pounded, *Yes.*

The phone rang. The deep voice that rang through the line shot straight to her middle. To add to his charm, he said, "Hello, Paige." Her name coming out of his mouth melted her. "Texting is too hard. I over think everything I say."

She gave a slight laugh, "Me too."

"What have you been up to?"

"Just teaching every day."

"That's right, did you say you're an art teacher?"

"Yes, at the high school. There are only a few more weeks of school and they're losing interest fast."

"I remember school. I felt the same way."

"So how long is your tour?" Paige asked, though she already knew it ended mid-August then resumed mid-September for another two months. It was on their band webpage. He repeated this information then added, "The best night was in Findlay." She recognized his quiet tone was flirting and played along.

"Did the band play exceptionally well that night?"

Jack chuckled, "They always do. It was the best after party."

"The best this year?" Paige wondered how many women had been in her place.

Now his voice was serious, "The best in many years." Her breath caught. "Paige, I don't do that ever." His flirty tone was back, "Almost never."

Her smile showed in her voice, "Me either."

"Damn, Tony, my manager is here. I forgot we have a business dinner. Can we keep in touch?"

After they agreed and said their goodbyes, Paige sat back on the couch. She let herself revel in the moment. That had been Jack Corey. She grabbed her phone to call Laurel.

***

Jack called later that night, they talked for an hour. His life was so interesting to her, the places they traveled, the schedule of events. They had barely touched on his life in earlier years; years when he was a video star, interviewed on MTV, winning Grammy awards.

She was shocked when he brought up Cleveland. "I'm going to play at the Playhouse Square Theater on Friday night and Saturday night. I'd love it if you'd come."

Paige was speechless for a moment. What would she do if she saw him again? Her silence was too long, he said, "Paige?"

She loved when he said her name. "Yes, I'd like to."

He laughed, sounding relieved. "Great. We can get together first and then after the show we can hang out too. Is it a long drive for you?"

"No, less than an hour and a half." And just like that, Paige had made plans to see Jack Corey. The time of companionship over the phone must just be fun for him. It was fine. Paige would go see him in Cleveland, get a tiny glimpse into his world. Afterward, she would drive back into her world. The school year would end in six weeks. She had plans to keep her busy over the summer. This was okay. It was absurd to think beyond this weekend. A relationship with Jack Corey? Paige laughed aloud.

Chapter 4

Cleveland, Ohio

Jack stood up and removed the large headphones. Across the table, SIRIUSXM Classic Rewind DJ, Kristine Stone, stood as well. His best seller from 1986, *Find Me,* was playing. She shook his hand, "Thanks again for coming in, Jack. That was a great interview."

He smiled at her though his eyes glanced at the clock above her head. Paige would be here in about half an hour. "My pleasure. I can't thank you guys enough for not only promoting my show this weekend but also for playing our music." Tony rose from a chair against the wall and the two men left the studio.

They headed down 9th Street toward their hotel. It was only a twenty-minute walk back to the Crowne Plaza. Jack appreciated the exercise. Keeping in shape was vital at his age if he was to perform well on stage. The Jack Corey band wasn't much on choreography, but movement across the stage was necessary to put on a good show. It was a warm April afternoon in Cleveland, Ohio, the wind off Lake Erie didn't blow them away. Tony touched Jack's arm when his pace quickened. "Slow down, this old man can't keep up."

Tony Rialto was only four years Jack's senior at 54. He'd been his manager for 28 years. The men had traveled the world together on business. Though they didn't see eye to eye on everything, it had been a good run. Jack watched Tony fail at three marriages. He had only failed at one. While Tony's children and now grandchildren were a combined total of eleven, Jack had one son. Jack Jr., which was regretfully what his ex had named him, went by J.J. He was a thirty-year-old entrepreneur making his own millions in a line of athletic wear. They didn't cross paths too often but kept in touch by phone. Tony was pursuing wife-prospect number four, a singer he met in a blues club in Chicago. Jack glanced up at the hotel as it came into view and smiled despite himself. He was pursuing someone too, for a change.

Tony caught his expression, "What's with the shit-eating grin?"

Jack shrugged, "I've got company arriving soon."

His manager stopped in the middle of the sidewalk and grabbed his arm, "You have what?"

Jack tugged his arm out of Tony's grip, "That's what I said. Come on, I don't want to be late."

"The blonde?" When Jack nodded, he whistled, "She's coming back for another round with the rock star?"

It was a point of irritation for Jack that a couple of his bandmates were open about their sexual activity, equally open about their infidelity to their wives. Even in the younger days when the stardom had girls throwing themselves at him, Jack quickly learned that screwing the desperate fans was a bad idea. This was not that at all, he felt the need to defend himself and her. "Her name is Paige and don't you fucking dare insinuate that in front of her or the guys. You know I don't play that game."

Tony held up his hands in mock surrender, "I'm sorry, man. I know you don't. I was teasing. This is great, you haven't had a girlfriend in ages." Having made the peace and accepting Jack's smile, the two men continued down the city street.

Jack wore sunglasses and a ball cap. He would have had both on no matter what the weather. Being out in the city when his show was so highly publicized was always risky. He didn't want fans flocking around him when Paige arrived. As if on cue, he saw her stepping out of a small silver SUV at the valet stand. Though he'd only met her that one night, he recognized her; she was tall and thin. Her skinny jeans accentuated her long legs. On her feet were light brown suede ankle boots. Her blonde hair that sat just below her shoulders, blew slightly in the wind. Paige lifted a purse over the shoulder of her tan, loose blazer styled jacket. She was wearing sunglasses, but he could tell when her eyes spotted him. Her lips curved into a small, possibly nervous smile.

Jack Corey didn't have a sense of doubt, he was used to his arrival anywhere being well received. He broke into a grin and sprinted the few steps toward her. After a moment's hesitation, ignoring that she was mostly a stranger to him, Jack pulled Paige into a light hug. He felt her arms responding in kind, her perfume, that was sweet yet mingled with a spice, tickled his nose. When she pulled back slightly, he kissed her lightly on the lips. Though her expression was one of surprise, Paige kissed back, then looked down, momentarily embarrassed. Jack knew his life in front of the world gave him more confidence. "I've been so eager for you to get here," his deep voice was close to her ear, the words were spoken only for her to hear.

The valet had waited but now approached. Paige handed her keys to him. The other young man in uniform had the hatchback open, loading her small duffle onto a cart. Jack pulled a bill from his pocket and with a wink whispered, “My suite.” Tony had discreetly headed on into the hotel.

“Do you need to go in for any reason?” Jack asked Paige, “Or are you hungry? I was recording for Sirius and missed lunch.”

“I don’t need to go in, and I could eat something,” her smile was easy. These daylight discoveries only compounded what he had felt that first evening after the concert. Paige Baxter was very interesting.

***

She was walking down the streets of Cleveland, Ohio with Jack Corey as if it was something that happened all the time. Paige forced her heart to calm. His kiss at her car nearly caused it to catapult right out of her chest. Now this man, a legend, was walking with her down the street. They would get some food together, a late lunch. Her skin flushed hot, she may die right here on the sidewalk.

They had discussed the decision of her overnight accommodations on the phone. The band had arrived in Cleveland late last night. Jack and his bandmates had checked into the hotel that evening. After working out in the exercise room, swimming a few laps in the pool, he had called her. Paige had learned through their nightly calls and numerous daily texts that Jack took his exercise seriously. It made sense, a man of 50 needed to be in good physical form to spend his evenings with a guitar on his back, singing, playing and moving across the stage.

On Tuesday, he had invited her to come to Cleveland for the weekend. If she left right after school, it would take her less than two hours to get there. This would leave them a bit of time before he began the long night schedule. Staying longer would give them all morning and the early afternoon together before the pre-performance cycle repeated. Sunday was a free day.

She didn't agree to come until Wednesday morning. Sleep had evaded her most of the night before as she volleyed back and forth with what she wanted to do and the madness of doing it. Finally, Paige realized she was a 48-year-old divorced woman, and it was perfectly fine for her to do what she wanted. Of course, she wanted to go. However, once she had sent him the quick, "I will come to Cleveland," Paige panicked. What would they do? What would be her place during the concert? Did she need to find a room?

Jack didn't even give her a chance to ask all those questions. In fact, it was disconcerting how quickly he sent her a thorough itinerary of her visit there. By lunchtime on Wednesday, she was having serious second thoughts. The list so efficiently answered her unasked questions, she thought this was a common practice for him.

***

While she was spooning lemon yogurt into her mouth, at lunch on Thursday, her phone vibrated. Paige surreptitiously looked at it, not wanting any of her fellow teachers sitting nearby to see who she was talking to. At this point, the entire meeting and subsequent connection with Jack was a secret. She nearly laughed aloud in relief when she read his message. *Gina, Trent Crosby's wife, has been helping me with the details. She said these are things you would want to know before you got here.*

Gina Crosby, the wife of the legendary bass player from Jack Corey's band, knew about her upcoming visit and was helping.

Paige continued to feel that she would wake up soon. Before she could respond, a new question, came in, *Were you planning on staying with me or did you want me to get you your own room?*

This time the yogurt got caught in her throat. This was the perfect excuse to leave the suddenly crowded classroom. Somehow, she couldn't respond to this in front of her unaware friends. Paige opened the door that led to the teachers' parking lot and let the cool spring air blow across her. She'd already slept with him, but that was after a lot of alcohol. How could she possibly spend the weekend in his room? That would involve getting ready for bed together, waking up in the morning together. Now Paige stepped outside, she'd broken out in a sweat.

Their conversations were flirty. The night they had spent together was not a taboo topic. Both had acknowledged it, even whispered things they remembered. Certainly, after a concert and a couple of drinks, she would end up in his bed. Apparently, her answer was taking too long, in her hand, she heard the ding of another text. *I'm sorry, did I offend you?*

Paige smiled as his words answered her own questions. *No, you didn't. I will stay with you.* She included the nervous face emoji. His response was one of agreement and three of the same emojis. The bell rang, and Paige let him know she was headed to class. He promised to call later.

Now it was late Friday afternoon. Paige was walking through the door of the *Yours Truly* cafe with Jack. They ordered omelets and coffee, hers with mushrooms and tomatoes, his with peppers and onions. Together they split an order of bacon and some wheat toast. The entire ordeal was intimate, and she couldn't believe how natural it felt. Jack was regaling her with tales of this midwestern tour. The event was a far cry from any of the arena shows they had done in the past and he said that he absolutely loved it.

Her eyes were watching his; a unique gray-blue with fine lines that had formed at the corners. She saw that silver had sprinkled in with the golden brown of his eyebrows. That same silver was present along the side of his face. Jack Corey, the beautiful boy of rock who adorned her wall in college, had grown into a gorgeous man. As this thought crossed her mind, her cheeks turned pink. He didn't miss this, instead, he stopped talking, sat back and flashed her with that grin. "What?" the word was slow and teasing.

She shook her head, "Nothing." Her lips curled in a grin and she playfully responded, "I will not voice the fangirl thoughts."

Now he reached across the table and clasped her hand, "I'm so glad you came to see me."

She squeezed in return, "Me too, thanks for asking." Someone had cleared the table, and they stood to leave. Jack put on his hat and sunglasses before turning around. The cafe was reasonably full, Paige understood his purpose. They moved out onto the street. This time he took her hand as they walked along.

Back at the hotel, Tony met them in the lobby. After a brief introduction, he gave Jack a scolding look, "You were ignoring my calls." Without waiting for an answer, he continued, "Jed doesn't like the speaker setup, insisting that the bass is overpowering, Trent says the drums sound like they're underwater."

Jack nodded, "I'll show Paige to my room and be right there." As they turned to the elevator, both could see that the lobby was crowded, and eyes were on him. He turned to Tony, who hadn't yet moved. "Send someone up to get me."

They snagged an empty elevator. He turned to Paige, "Tony will send up a roadie who can get me out the side and over to the theater. This isn't the time for fans." She nodded. The bell dinged, and the door slid open, Jack led her down the left hall. He stopped at a door and swiped a card.

They stepped into a suite and it impressed her. The expansive window across the room showed a magnificent cityscape. She could even see the sun twinkling off Lake Erie. Jack came up beside her, "I'm sorry that I have to rush off like this."

"I understand." She glanced around and saw that her bag was sitting in a corner.

He looked at his phone, "It's already 4:30. I won't be back here before the show." Now his eyes were on her, and he was close by. "I'm sorry, but after the show, we can be together."

"I'm so excited to see you perform again," Paige hoped she wasn't gushing.

Jack leaned in and kissed her softly. "Me too. Thanks for being here."

***

Paige hadn't moved from the window, watching the traffic of Cleveland and beyond it the waves of Lake Erie. The scenes, so small in the distance from her perch high in the hotel, calmed her. Their lunch together proved that they were just as compatible in person as on the phone. Now, though, was the rest of the evening. What should she do until that time? Where would she go?

There was a knock on the door. Paige didn't know who to expect but opened it. In front of her stood Trent Crosby's wife. Gina Crosby was a beautiful woman. She was tell and her hair was long, colored a copper red. Though she had on expensive clothing; black slacks with a designer tag, a silk cream blouse, and black strappy high sandals, she had no airs about her. Her smile was friendly when she introduced herself as Trent's wife. She asked where Paige was from, what Paige did and then she gave her a rundown of the schedule. She explained that the men wouldn't be back up here. She asked if Paige had questions.

She did, she wondered where she would be during the concert. Were there things going on after the concert? Gina told her that tonight would be a good night to attend the after party. She made a face, there was more to say on the subject. Paige looked curious. Gina said not every after party is a good idea, but tonight's would be fine. She didn't ask how Paige met Jack. Paige got the idea that she already knew. She admitted that she hadn't been on any of this tour until tonight. She and Trent had children still in high school, and she stayed at home in New York.

***

Beside the dusty velvet curtain, Paige stood. From this angle she could see Jack, his face toward the audience, animated as he belted out "Go Away" one of his number one hits from 1987. The crowd was singing along with the chorus:

I had fun with you

Now I'm done with you

You make my world cold and gray

Go away, go away, go away!

Jack had his guitar strapped over his shoulder, leaning out toward the audience. His smile was brighter than the spotlights overhead. He rocked on the balls of his heels with the beat of the drum. The women who weren't singing along were screaming. They raised cell phones, trying to get photos or footage of the superstar on stage. Jack moved along the front and hands attempted to reach out and grab at his boot. Men and women wearing black SECURITY t-shirts held them at bay. Paige could see that he was comfortable with all of this. His pace across the stage was something between a strut and a dance. She was having difficulty recognizing this man as the same one who sat across from her at the cafe today. Was this really the guy who had sipped coffee with her several hours ago, discussing their favorite foods?

She pulled the hem of her top down; it wanted to ride up over the waist of her black skinny pants. Gina had approved of her slim leg pants, sleeveless black top with a spattering of silver splashed across it and heeled ankle boots. Paige was a slender woman but wasn't accustomed to showing her bare midriff, which happened each time she raised her arms to cheer.

They finished the final notes of the big hit; the crowd went wild. The band members set down their instruments and stepped forward, bowing on the stage. Paige held her breath as they moved toward her. Was she in the way? Should she be somewhere else? Trent and the drummer, Joe, moved on by. Jack appeared to be moving directly to her. His smile had taken over his face. As he reached her, he swung her off her feet, then his hands slid down to her waist, and he gave her a long kiss. She could feel his heated body against her, a drop of sweat dripped from his brow to hers, it didn't matter. His eyes were shining eagerly as he looked at her, expectantly. "Jack, you were incredible! Fantastic! They loved you!" Though she felt her words were typical, they must have been what he wanted to hear, he kissed her again.

The crowd was still going wild and Paige realized they had an encore to do. Jack looked over her head to the rest of the band and nodded. Joe went in first and beat the rhythm of their number one hit in 1990. The response was intense as the audience recognized it. Trent and the second guitarist, Jed, headed back in.

Jack was still grinning, "I'll be back in a few minutes." A roadie approached, helping Jack strap on a different guitar. He walked onto the stage and the crowd roared. The song began and Paige glanced behind her. Gina stood with another woman a few yards back. She joined them, not wanting to be in the way as the band made their final exit.

Gina smiled, "Having fun?" The other woman was much younger than them, perhaps in her twenties. She was wearing a tiny leather dress and stacked black stilettos.

Paige nodded enthusiastically, "I loved seeing it all from this angle." Behind them, a bar was being set up, and a cloth being spread on a large table. She looked questioning.

"The after party is right here on stage," Gina responded. "These are the best parties, only a few big shots of the city and the theater people. They eat, drink, take pictures and we're done early."

"Not tomorrow," the younger woman said with a pout.

Gina nodded, "Paige, this is Keely. She's here with Joe." Paige wondered if she was Joe's girlfriend or daughter.

Keely gave her a once over, "You're Jack's girlfriend?" before Paige could confirm or deny, she added, "I always thought he was gay."

Gina snorted, "Keely, just because he doesn't have a woman around, doesn't mean he's gay."

Keely eyed Paige again, "I guess not." She remembered what they were discussing, and looked at Paige, "Tomorrow's party will blow."

"Take it from me, you won't want to attend the party tomorrow night," Gina looked seriously at Paige.

"I won't?"

Keely jumped in, her anger clear, "All the wives and rich bitches of the town come. They want pictures with the guys; on their laps or kissing them. Tony thinks it's important to make the money people happy."

Paige raised an eyebrow. This was shocking. She looked toward Gina for confirmation. "The city thinks they're doing a big favor for the band. Some band members appreciate it." A shadow crossed her face. Then she looked at Paige and shook her head, "I doubt Jack does anything, but you don't want to be there."

Before they could continue, Jack struck the final chord on his guitar and the crowd went wild. The show was over. Paige was just turning toward the curtain when the band members exited off, cheering, slapping hands and grabbing the water bottles offered from an assistant. Jack appeared last, a ready roadie took his guitar. In two long strides, he reached Paige and grabbed her up. His mood was catching, and she laughed as he swung her. When her feet were again securely on the ground, she spoke, "Jack, you were astonishing tonight!"

His eyes were those of an eager child, "Did you really love it? Was it different from back here?"

Surprised by his need for reassurance, Paige continued to gush, "I loved the way you moved, your voice was flawless. What you do with a guitar is beautiful." It had the desired effect. Jack used both hands to pull her face to his and kiss her.

Chapter 5

Cleveland, Ohio

Annabeth watched the three women talking. She was irritated, mostly at herself. Seeing Paige should've been satisfying. After all, Annabeth was the one who had encouraged Jack to get in touch with her. She'd even tracked the woman down. It was good to see Jack excited about her. However, when he wanted to get details for Paige about the weekend, he hadn't asked for Annabeth's help. Jack had gone to Gina; Trent's wife. Now the women were a tight circle with Keely. Keely was the stereotypical twenty-something groupie who went after anyone in the band, just to be a part of it all. Joe was at least twenty-five years older than she, but he went for her low class, trashy style. So now, there stood Keely, Gina, and Paige as the women of the rock stars. Annabeth felt left out. She was afraid to join them, what if Trent told Gina about her? Would there be trouble?

***

Jack had disappeared downstairs just long enough to throw a clean shirt on and freshen his hair, sweaty from the show. Paige was now resting her elbows on a makeshift high-top table a few feet from the portable bar. Jack came up behind her and lightly touched her back. She turned to face him, "Would you like a drink?"

"Yes," he answered and turned to go to the bar, she followed him. The bartender was a local woman who stared at Jack with obvious admiration. After offering her his star smile, Jack motioned with his head toward a bottle of wine. "The Cabernet's for me." The woman removed the cork and handed it over. "Two glasses, please."

Paige took these and noticed the shaking hands of the other woman. She wanted to lean toward her and whisper, "I totally get it." In most ways, she hardly knew Jack more than this woman. How was she acting so calm?

Back at the table, he poured the wine. "This is my favorite, it's what I like to drink over anything." He took an appreciative swallow.

Paige tasted it and nodded, "It is nice." She enjoyed the dark fruity flavor. Just then a couple of media people approached. She felt someone behind her and turned. A rather short, stocky woman wearing well-worn jean capris and a brown shirt so faded that the logo on it was indistinguishable, spoke, "Move back if they're taking any photos. You probably shouldn't be in them."

Paige stepped away from the table, "Definitely not, thank you."

"I'm Annabeth Muldoon, the biographer."

Paige's face lit up, "Oh, you're the one who found me. Thanks!"

The other woman seemed pleased with her response. She took a swig of her mixed drink that was in a plastic cup. "Jack needed some company. Everyone else seems to have someone." Her eyes scanned the room, a frown on her face.

"So how are you enjoying your travels with the band?"

"It's so interesting. Though I've written many stories on musicians, the daily aspect of the tour is a new experience. I really am getting a unique perspective."

"Have you written other books?" In response, Annabeth eagerly launched into the details of her career. This fascinated Paige. She could tell that Annabeth must be a good writer, her anecdotes were entertaining.

At one point, Jack had moved to their table to refill Paige's glass. He clinked his own against hers, and said, "At last." They'd not even drank on his words when he was absconded by more people.

Paige wasn't aware of how much time passed. They had emptied the wine bottle, a new one was also half empty. Jack had appeared for short minutes. She watched him talk to the people of Cleveland; media, a pitcher for the Cleveland Indians, theater patrons and others. He was always very gracious, polite but not too revealing. After the fifth group had his attention for several minutes, Jack held up his hand. Paige was close enough to hear him. "I thank you again for your support, but now someone I've met here in Ohio has come to see me. I'd like to spend time with her." Paige turned her back to the group, embarrassed, but thrilled.

Music had been playing on the sound system. Some people were dancing. As Jack turned to her, Annabeth moved away. He stood close, "Hi."

Paige smiled, "Hello."

"I'm all yours now," his voice was soft. Paige was speechless. Chris Isaak's *Wicked Game* began playing. He clasped her hand, "Would you like to dance?"

Dance with a man who makes his living moving to music on stage? Nervously, Paige allowed him to take her by the hand and lead her to the space where others were dancing. The music had a slow, enticing rhythm and this part of the backstage was shadowed. When Jack put his hands on her waist and pulled her close, she let him. They soon were moving together. "I thought I would never get to talk to you."

"Me either," she hoped her words didn't sound annoyed, so she lifted her hand to wave off the meaning. Her hand landed softly on his chest, through the cotton of his shirt she could feel the beat of his heart. She left it there. "You seem comfortable talking to everyone."

"I'm used to it. The questions are usually the same. It's just part of the game." The song ended, it rolled into Journey's *Anyway You Want It*. People moved apart and began fast dancing. Jack let go of her and pulled his collar away from his skin. "It's roasting in here. Want to find some fresh air?"

Paige nodded in agreement and they headed toward a flashing red EXIT sign. Someone had propped the ancient door open with a brick. They stepped out into the cool darkness. Stretched along the brick wall were five or six shadows, recognizable only by the orange glow of the cigarettes in their hands or mouth. A few mumbled "Hey, Jack's" were issued as the couple stepped out. Jack gave a quick wave and said, "Hey, fellas," then grabbed Paige's hand.

They moved away from the group. Around the corner in a darker, secluded area was a loading dock. Jack jumped up on the concrete corner and helped Paige climb the embankment to join him. Behind them, the backstage music was a dull thump of bass. The street noise of Cleveland was minimal at this time of night.

He ran his fingers through his hair as the breeze picked it up, "This feels great."

Paige pulled the heavy sequined top away from her skin, allowing cool air to blow in. It felt good. Jack skimmed his fingers along her bare torso. "You look great, tonight."

His fingers sent shivers up her spine. "Thank you," she responded, huskily.

"You're even prettier than I remembered."

Instead of being coy, Paige laughed, "You probably didn't remember what I looked like."

"Yes, I did!" Jack protested, then grinned, "Mostly." In the dark, his teeth glowed. "Did you remember what I looked like?" His hands rested on her hips as they sat facing each other.

"I can look at you anytime I like; online or on CD covers I have." She blushed thinking about her conversations with his photo.

"Have you looked at me?" he was shamelessly flirting.

Paige held up her hands in protest and he clasped them both, entwining their fingers, "That's between me and the cover of *The Jack Corey Band's Greatest Hits 2002*!"

They both laughed and he pulled their hands toward him until their faces met. He tipped his head slightly and kissed her mouth. Though the kiss was soft, it lasted a moment. When it ended, he pressed his forehead to hers, "Have I said how glad I am that you're here?"

"You may have," she whispered and boldly kissed him again. Now her hands were around his neck, his hands were back on her bare waist, below her top.

“Are you going to stay with me tonight?”

Paige shrugged, “It’s pretty late and I’ve had a bit of wine.”

Jack pulled her to a standing position, and they locked lips again. “Let’s go back to my suite.”

***

In the room, Jack didn’t give her time to feel self-conscious, after pulling off his own shirt and showing her a chest and set of abs that made her salivate, he carefully removed her top and pants. When had a man last undressed her? By the time he was reaching for the clasp of her bra, she was unbuttoning his jeans, freeing his desire.

Soon, they were both naked under the covers. Kissing, their hands roamed over one another. When he entered her, they were both ready for satisfaction.

Afterwards, they lay side by side, catching their breath. He finally spoke, “Damn, I forgot the music and romantic lighting.”

Paige turned her head to face him, “Not necessary, I’d say.”

Jack caressed her cheek, “Next time, then.” They both fell asleep with that promise between them.

***

Paige woke up in the morning, amazed at how soundly she’d slept. As she shyly climbed out of bed, nude, Jack continued to sleep. She grabbed her overnight bag and headed to the bathroom. With any luck, she’d get her hair and makeup done before he saw her.

She needn’t have worried. The hair dryer didn’t even pull him out of his slumber. Now she was fully dressed, and Jack was still out. Her phone buzzed. It was Gina, they’d exchanged numbers last night. *I’m guessing you stayed.*

Yes.

Dressed?

Yes.

They usually sleep until at least noon. Want to meet me downstairs for breakfast?

***

Paige discovered that she really liked Gina. Their lives were very different in some ways, but their ages and roles as a mother drew them together. Paige's divorce and Trent's occupation also gave them the shared experience of solo parenting.

Paige was finishing her second cup of coffee; they'd cleared away the food half an hour ago. Her phone buzzed. It was 11:30 and Jack was texting. *Hi.* Before she could respond, he added, *I thought you left me until I saw your bag.*

Just breakfast with Gina. How could he think she'd leave?

Good.

Would you like me to get you anything?

Coffee and wheat toast with strawberry jam.

How do you take your coffee?

Two creams, no sugar.

I'll be right up.

Good. Paige beamed. Across the table, Gina chuckled, "Was that Jack?"

"Yes, he wants breakfast."

"I can't believe he's awake." She stood, "Have fun with him today. I'll see you backstage later."

***

Paige's hands were full, she couldn't use the key card so instead knocked on the door with her foot. As she heard footsteps heading toward her on the other side of the door, her heart did a flutter. She would be face to face with Jack in a moment. The door swung open; he looked equally pleased. "Let me get those." As Jack reached for the coffee, he leaned in for a light kiss.

"What do you want to do this morning?" he asked as he buttered toast.

She sat down on the other chair at the table, "What do you usually do?"

Swallowing a bite, he answered, "If there's not a gym in the hotel, I take a run."

"Sorry, I'm not a runner. My time at the gym comprises of spinning class."

Jack smiled, "How about a bike ride? Can we rent bikes in Cleveland?"

Equally pleased with the suggestion, Paige pulled her phone from her jeans pocket and searched, "Yes, there's a place on East 4th."

Within the hour, they were ready to go. Paige had retrieved her workout bag from the car and changed into her lycra black knee-length pants with a cherry red band at the knee. She wore a coordinating T-back tank and a black pullover. Jack was in black workout pants, a fitted gray shirt and a black pullover with a half zipper.

As they headed down the block, he held her hand. Soon they were pedaling through Cleveland, side by side when they could, or single file on narrow spots. Paige had looked up a few destinations.

They found the giant FREE stamp on the lawn of city hall. She asked Jack to take her picture in front of it. She felt a secret thrill when he did so on both her phone and his. Paige had no idea if a photo of them would happen and didn't suggest it.

Jack loved the Fountain of Eternal Life. Once again, she posed for both phones. He then surprised her, taking her spot and posing his arms like the statue; one bent at the elbow and one straight up in the air. He urged her to take the photo with both phones. They rode through East 4th street again; the road closed to cars. This time they stopped at Flannery's Pub and got fish and chips for lunch. Jack looked at the House of Blues, disappointed that it didn't open until evening.

The afternoon was moving quickly. They headed to 5th Avenue, near the Rock-and-Roll Hall of Fame. Together, they leaned over the pier and watched the water. Jack reached to her and pushed a curl behind her ear, "This was so much fun."

She turned, while his hand was still on her hair, they kissed. "It was." Their pullovers had been removed hours ago when the afternoon sun and exertion of the bikes and warmed them. Jack's hands rested on her bare shoulders. "Finding you again was the smartest thing I've ever done."

"I think Annabeth was the smart one," she teased him.

They stood for a moment, watching the waves. "So, you're an only child?"

Jack turned to her, "Yep, how about you?"

"I'm actually the middle child of three. My brother, Doug, died two years ago of a heart attack. He was 52 and in great shape, it was a complete surprise."

They were moving away from the pier. Jack stopped and clasped her hand, "I'm sorry, Paige."

She gave a small smile. "Thank you. I also have a younger sister, Krista. She and her husband work for an international company and live in Germany. They have seven-year-old twin boys. In fact, my parents are with them. Last October, they flew to Germany to stay with them for a year."

"A year?"

"It's been hard on them since they lost Doug. Krista encouraged them, claiming that she needed help with the boys. I think she thought the change of scenery would do them good."

They had reached the front of the hall of fame where a giant statue in red spelled out, "Long Live Rock." Jack parked his bike, Paige followed. He climbed inside the letter *C*. "That's perfect," she said, pulling out her phone.

"Wait." Jack saw a jogger nearing them, "Hey!" The man stopped. "Could you take our photo?" Paige was delighted as she handed the man her phone and climbed up next to Jack. He had his arm on her shoulders and she rested her hand on his knee. With their heads touching, they smiled at the camera. The man took three shots.

Paige jumped down and retrieved her phone, "Thank you, so much." She moved back and leaned against Jack's leg. Together, they looked at the photos.

"Send me this one," Jack reached around her and pointed. Paige did, then tucked her phone into the side pocket of her pants. *Jack has a picture of us together and so do I!*

***

Back at the hotel, Jack picked up his guitar and strummed. In a matter of minutes, he seemed to forget where he was, his focus entirely on the music. Paige guessed this was his routine before a concert. She climbed up on the bed and looked at social media on her phone. Seeing he was still engrossed in his guitar, she opened the Kindle app and began reading a novel.

After more than a half an hour of playing, he took a shower. When he emerged from the bathroom, he was just in jeans. He went straight to the guitar and picked it up again. After a few moments, he pulled on a T-shirt and his boots. Jack grabbed his guitar. It seemed then he finally noticed Paige sitting on the bed, barefoot, still in her lycra pants and tank. Jack gave her his best smile. Laying the guitar at the foot of the bed, he sat next to her and pulled her close. "Sorry, just getting my mind ready for the show." He kissed her and stood up. "You'll be backstage?"

"Of course, can't wait," she thought he sounded mildly insecure.

"We can have fun at the after-party." He gave her one more kiss and left the room.

Paige had yet to tell him what the other women had said about not attending tonight's party. Perhaps they would feel differently today.

***

Soon, she was showered and wearing her favorite skinny ankle jeans. She added an ivory flowing tank that gave the appearance of delicate crochet. On her feet were gladiator strappy sandals with a small heel. There was a knock on the door as she put on lipstick.

It was Gina. She too was more casual this evening in white jeans and a black halter. "Keely's got a table for us across the street at the pub."

The women were enjoying bottles of Summer Shandy and eating burgers. Paige looked at these women who were a part of a successful rock band. She had seen clips and photos of Gina through the years at awards shows and other things. Now here they were together.

Gina said that she and Trent spent the day shopping. Their youngest, a girl, was turning sixteen next week. Keely shared that she and Joe went to the theater to see a new horror film. They lived pretty normal lives away from the music.

She broached the subject of Jack and his guitar after their own outing. "Ah yes, Jack and his true love. I should have warned you," Gina responded, "that he would have to spend some time playing."

Keely nodded, "Before you, Joe used to suspect that he slept with a guitar in his bed."

"There's a reason it's called The Jack Corey band." Gina took a swallow of her beer. "Don't let my husband, Joe or any of the others say they work equally on the music. Jack's the magic behind it all because he's devoted to it."

"It's true, when the rest of them are playing video games or watching movies in the back of the bus, Jack's always up front with his guitar."

Paige considered, "I figured it was like an athlete before a big game."

"Exactly. I hope he noticed you enough to say goodbye when he left."

"Yes, he said we'd be together afterward." Now Keely scowled. "I said nothing to him about the party." She looked at her companions, "Do you still think I shouldn't go to the party?"

Keely grabbed at the fresh beer bottle the server had just placed in front of her, "Will it bug the hell out of you to see women on his lap, kissing him?" Paige decided that it would. "Joe will empty his pockets after a party like this and it will be full of phone numbers and room keys."

Gina's expression was serious, "I have my own reasons for not wanting to witness women throwing themselves at Trent. Whatever you've started with Jack is new. What you'd see tonight would make you very jealous. I wouldn't recommend going."

Paige hadn't a clue what would happen between her and Jack after tomorrow, but she trusted these women. She'd rather be happy with Jack later than have fans ruin it.

***

The concert was another triumph. Paige enjoyed her view from off stage again, maybe even more so. Her familiarity with Jack and growing feelings made her appreciate him further. His fingers raced along the guitar strings with grace. His voice, which she was now accustomed to speaking her name, sang lyrics with such emotion. The day they shared only increased her feeling of being star struck.

Just like the night before, he came to her between the encores. She lavishly praised him, and he ran his fingers on the skin of her back possessively. As the band exited the stage for the final time, he handed his guitar to an assistant and made his way directly to her.

"I'm going to freshen up and then we can head to the party together." Tonight's event was in a banquet room.

Paige took a deep breath and spoke, "Jack, I'm not going to the party."

His look was one of near anguish, "You're leaving?"

"No, no," she patted his arms, "Gina and Keely said it would be better if I didn't go with you."

"What? Why?" he seemed angry. "Is Gina going?"

She shook her head, and he seemed to think about it. "No, I guess it's mostly women from here."

Jack's face registered understanding, he clasped her hands, "Honey, I won't do anything."

"That's not why they said I shouldn't go. I know it's something you guys have to do and ..." Paige lost her words trying to explain.

Jack reached up and stroked her cheek, "Thank you for understanding. I absolutely despise these parties. I promise to be as quick as I can." Now he gave her a long kiss, his tongue tasting her lips.

As he walked away, Paige felt someone move beside her, "Want to catch the elevator with me?" It was Annabeth.

"I'm not going."

"You're not? Are you leaving?"

"No." She explained to the other woman about the event.

"Sounds like good advice. I'm going, it's all part of my research. If anyone gets too aggressive with Jack, I'll kick her."

Paige laughed, "Thank you, Annabeth." From behind her, she could hear her name being called, it was Keely.

"Come on, let's get a drink in the hotel bar."

When Paige joined them, Gina said, "If I go back to the room, I'll be asleep before Trent gets in. That would defeat the purpose of being here."

"That's what I was afraid of," Paige said as she climbed up on a barstool.

***

Annabeth nursed a scotch and water while watching from the bar. Gina had given Paige sound advice, even she was feeling territorial of the guys. These women were sharks and the Jack Corey band was chum. The people here were from the wealthy Cleveland suburbs. The clothes were designer, the jewelry blinding, and the boobs paid for. They launched at Jack as if he was Santa and they were six years old. He was seated in the center of the room, the other guys milling behind him. The women were taking turns on his lap or leaning in from behind with cleavage in his face; taking selfies. Annabeth now knew him well enough to recognize fake and almost pained graciousness. When one woman reached inside of his collar or another let her long nails move up his thigh, Jack was a professional and removed them with a flirty response.

Trent, true to his nature, was more accommodating. He was unphased by the touching and was willing to pose for photos with his hands in scandalous places. The insanity of this behavior was that the men present appeared to be the husbands or boyfriends of these women. They were guzzling drinks and taking their own selfies with the band. Apparently, their wives' behavior was all fun to them.

Annabeth had finished her drink and was considering a second when she felt a hand on her shoulder. From the cloud of perfume that accompanied it, she assumed it was one of the women. To her surprise, Jack spoke close to her ear, "Get me out of here."

As Annabeth turned to him, she could see two more women making their way to Jack. She spoke in her former reporter voice, "Jack Corey, I'm Annabeth Muldoon, a reporter for *Rolling Stones Magazine*. We had an interview scheduled?"

The dazzling smile was for her, but Jack kept it on as he faced the women, "I forgot all about it. I'm sorry, ladies."

In the hallway, he gave her a side hug, "Thanks Annabeth, I felt like I was drowning."

"You were, in their perfume. If you're planning on meeting Paige, I would suggest you wash the smell off you."

"Ah shit, is there a bathroom close?"

Annabeth pointed to the MENS sign, without a word. Before he entered, Jack reached into his jean's pocket and pulled out a variety of business cards. "Destroy these."

She entertained herself by reading the messages from the women. One was a lawyer. Was her lewd suggestion scrawled on her business card even legal? Another a surgeon. Two women had the audacity to leave him names and numbers on their husbands' business cards.

Jack pushed out of the men's room, giving off an air of hand soap. "So much better." Annabeth patted down a wet piece of hair.

"Your girl is in the bar with the other wives."

Jack grinned at her, "My girl?" On impulse, he gave her a real hug, "Thank you for finding her."

As he walked away, Annabeth felt lonely for the first time in a long time.

Chapter 6

Findlay, Ohio

Paige traveled down the interstate in silence. Her mind was too full of images, words and the sound of the concerts to need any background music. It was 2:32 on Sunday afternoon. She'd said goodbye to Jack just forty-one minutes ago. They had been standing at the valet spot in front of the hotel. He had his arms around her waist; hers were around his neck. They kissed like teenagers in a parked car.

She had already agreed, over room service breakfast, to meet him in Dayton next Saturday for their show. Just before he closed her car door, Jack had said, "Looking for you was the best thing I've ever done."

Now Paige squeezed the steering wheel and said aloud, "He said that to me!"

At that moment, her car's Bluetooth belted out her ringtone, it was Laurel. "Hello?" Paige attempted to sound casual.

"Where are you?" Laurel whispered as if anyone near Paige could hear her.

"In my car, alone."

"Thank God. How was your weekend?"

"My weekend was not real, it couldn't have been."

Laurel squealed, "Start at the beginning." Paige conceded and began with the omelets. She took Laurel through both concerts, and her time with Keely and Gina. She gave the details of the bike ride. Her conclusion was the morning brunch.

"This is a fantasy come true," Laurel sounded exhausted just from listening. "How did it end today?"

"I agreed to go to Dayton on Saturday for their show."

"You're dating Jack Corey. Holy shit!"

"I don't think dating is the right word. Spending time with him in Ohio, maybe."

"Sleeping with him in Ohio."

'That still doesn't qualify as dating."

"How is the sex?"

"Laurel," Paige protested, "We usually save that talk for wine time."

"Good try, answer me."

Paige focused on her exit off the interstate. When she was safely onto the next road, she said, "It's amazing."

"Of course, it is, you bitch!" Both women laughed. "Seriously, Paige, this is so great. You are seeing a rock star."

Paige just laughed again, but in her mind, she had to agree even if just for now; she was.

***

That night, she forced herself to iron a pair of blue slacks and a pale-yellow blouse for Monday. She was dragging and wanted to crawl under the covers. If she didn't get things ready for the work week, it would be worse in the morning. Paige had been up until near morning both nights of the weekend. This was highly unusual for her.

Just as she hung the top in the closet, her phone buzzed. It was Hannah.

"Hi, Mom."

"Hey, Sweetie."

"You made it home?"

Paige switched her phone to the speaker so she could get her pajamas on while she talked. "Yes, this afternoon. How was your weekend? Did you go to the lake?"

"Yep. How was your weekend? Did you stay in Cleveland until today?"

"I did. The shows were amazing, I got to stay backstage and watch from the side."

"You did?" her daughter's voice registered surprise and Paige wondered if she'd really doubted her mother's story. "What did you do the rest of the time?"

"Yesterday, Jack and I rented bikes and rode around the city."

Hannah laughed, "Mr. Rocker went biking with you?"

"Yes Hannah, he has to keep in shape. He suggested a run, I said I preferred bikes."

"Who are you?"

"What does that mean? I go to spin class." Paige wasn't enjoying this conversation anymore. "Tell me about your weekend, did you stay on the island?"

Hannah wouldn't be deterred, "So that's it? You spent a weekend together and now it's back to your normal life?"

Paige sighed audibly, "No. I'm meeting him in Dayton on Saturday."

"I thought you were dating David."

"Well, I'm not."

"Mom, you don't think this will last, do you?"

"Hannah quit acting as if I'm a naïve teenager. I'm enjoying myself. Let it be. I'll be fine."

"Did you stay in his hotel room?"

"That's enough. We're not discussing my private life. This conversation is over."

"Have you thought about how many other women he's probably slept with?" Hannah's voice was very condescending.

"I repeat, it's over. It was lovely talking to you, darling. Have a good work week. Love you and good night." Paige barely stayed on the phone long enough to hear her daughter's murmured good night.

***

On Monday night, she received an unwelcome call, this was from her ex-husband, Kurt. As soon as she saw his name, she knew Hannah had told on her. Paige answered with mild irritation in her voice, "Hello, Kurt."

"Good evening. How are you?"

They weren't friends, nor were they enemies. The end of their marriage was probably the best decision they'd ever made together. Paige met Kurt while at her first job. She was teaching art at Perrysburg Middle School outside of Toledo. Kurt was the father of one of her sixth-grade students. Ashton Baxter possessed a real gift. Her ability at painting was remarkable. She was the dream child that every new teacher hoped to discover.

When Ashton won a poster contest at City Hall, Paige attended along with Ashton and her newly divorced father. After the mayor awarded Ashton a blue ribbon and together, they posed for a photo that would be in the local newspaper, her father invited Paige to join them for lunch. Paige declined, not appropriate.

In late fall, she was asked to paint a holiday mural in the lobby of the high school. Paige invited Ashton to join her in the project. By the time they finished, which was through three after-school sessions and one long Saturday, Mr. Baxter had asked for her phone number.

She hadn't yet met a single friend in Perrysburg. Though he was twelve years her senior, Kurt was handsome with chocolate brown eyes and hair. At 6'2" he made her feel petite despite her 5'6" height. Kurt had his own business as a home inspector. He made a nice income assessing the value of homes before they were bought and sold. Their second date was at his company's annual holiday party. At 23, she knew she looked fabulous in a tiny sparkly black dress. On the day after Christmas, he and Ashton came over and they exchanged gifts. Ashton had picked out a beautiful set of Goldstar brushes to the delight of Paige who had bought the same set for Ashton.

The romance wasn't heart-stopping or passionate, but Paige told herself that was just what young love felt like. This relationship was an adult relationship, just what she needed. He was a good companion, and she loved his daughter. They married the next Christmas. Within two years they were expecting Hannah. Ashton was headed into her freshman year and started high school in Philadelphia where her mom and stepdad had moved. They were both crushed, but the birth of Hannah helped.

When Hannah was five, Paige got a call from a friend who taught art in Findlay, Ohio. The two women had met at a conference. She was retiring and felt that Paige would be perfect in her position. The high school appreciated art and several students had gone on to prestigious art institutes. It was what Paige had always wanted to do.

She accepted the position. Both she and Kurt were impressed with the Findlay schools. Together, they decided to sell the house in Perrysburg and move to Findlay. He commuted for a year and a half, then opened a local office.

Their life as a family flowed along with few waves. They were involved parents. When Ashton visited, they all got along. Each summer, they vacationed at Hilton Head, South Carolina with Kurt's family. They didn't fight, any disagreement was mild. But they also weren't friends. Paige didn't even realize it until Hanna was in high school and busy with her own life.

Paige and Kurt found themselves alone on weekends and discovered that they really didn't want to spend time together. For the next few years, they built separate lives. She began creating commission art; painting and pencil drawing for clients. He took up motorcycling, bought himself a bike and rode most weekends and often weeknights too. There were a few local businessmen who traveled on their bikes, Kurt eagerly joined in.

Finally, it was the summer before Hannah's senior year and the time for the annual Hilton Head trip with Kurt's family. "I don't want to go," Paige told him as they sat in bed one evening. He was on his laptop, she had her sketchbook and pencil. She couldn't recall the last time they'd been intimate. This was not the romance she thought she'd have at 42.

"Will Hannah be upset?" She noted his concern was about their daughter, not his own desire to have her there.

"I don't think so, she'll have her cousins and you."

After that it was easy. They spent Hannah's senior year separately with no real discussion about it. Kurt slept in the guest room when Paige got the flu, then never moved back into the master suite.

They announced their decision to divorce when Hannah returned home for her first Thanksgiving from college. It was not a big surprise to her either. They put their house for sale, split their finances and moved on. Kurt was married by the next summer, revealing he must have moved on sooner.

Now, this all flashed through her mind. She was certain he was calling about her weekend. It was none of his business. "I'm just fine, Kurt. What's up?" She would not engage in small talk.

"Hannah called me. She's worried about you."

"No, she's miffed because I told her to mind her own business."

He laughed nervously, "So you're really seeing Jack Corey?"

"Yes," she hated to even answer.

"Wow, that's crazy." With that, she could agree. "Hannah's just worried that you'll get hurt."

"Kurt," she took a deep breath to keep her voice even, "I'm 48 years old not 18 or 68. I can engage in a casual affair without getting my heart broken."

"So, you know it's just a casual affair?"

"Did you or Hannah think I was running away with the band?"

He seemed contrite, "I'm sorry. I should've guessed you know what you're doing. You're entitled to one wild weekend."

His words weren't helping. She should've just agreed and thanked him for his concern. He, however, was her ex-husband, and he didn't have the right to ask her about her plans or make judgment calls. "Kurt, my wild weekend isn't over yet. I'm headed back to see him this week. But this isn't your concern. Please tell our daughter that mom's a big girl. When she's done playing with the rock star, she'll return to her normal boring life." She quickly ended the call.

Chapter 7

Findlay, Ohio

Tuesday morning, Paige walked out of the teacher's lounge with a fresh cup of coffee. She took advantage of the three minutes between classes to slip down for a refill. Maneuvering her way around students; some stopped in groups, others racing in both directions, her left hand sheltered the mug in her right from an oversized book bag swiping it from her hand. From the pocket of her black cotton slacks, she felt her cell phone buzz.

Once in her room, she set down the mug and pulled out her phone.

I miss you

It was Jack. The words shot a thrill through her. She had just left him on Sunday. They talked last night and now he missed her.

Thank you! I miss you.

The final bell rang, and she slid the phone into a desk drawer. In front of her, twenty-one students were getting situated. "Get a laptop from the cart, we're researching today." The moans and groans as a response made her smile. For the next forty-five minutes, it was nonstop interaction with her students. She barely had time to drink her coffee while it was warm much less check her phone.

When the bell signaled the end of class, Paige checked her phone. A surprising six messages showed on the screen from Jack.

Just thinking about you.

I loved having you with me this weekend.

Everyone is considering catching a plane home for 3 days.

You must be very busy.

Can't wait to see you again.

Hello?

Paige made a slight frown as she first responded. It was difficult to match these rather needy texts with the confident man who held thousands in his hand while performing on stage. However, she knew that on the road he was alone quite a bit. It was incredibly flattering that she was the person he wanted to communicate with.

I'm sorry, Jack. Class time is busy. I'll send you more on my conference break.

While she text, a new set of students filed in. Her morning continued.

***

At lunch, she sat out on the picnic bench and talked to Jack. Though he was pleased that she called, he seemed distracted. Paige had never been the one to initiate a call and regretted it. Her hello was received with a rushed, "Paige?"

"I'm sorry, did I call at a bad time?" her voice was embarrassed.

Jack recovered quickly, "No, no. Free moment?"

"Yes, lunch," she felt better. "What are you up to?"

He hesitated, not a good sign. "Not much. I have errands."

"Are you headed back to New York?"

"I, uh, don't know. Haven't quite got all my plans finalized. So, what's the teacher teaching today?" She could hear a smile in his voice and her own tone was lighter.

"I am being wicked and making them create their own interpretation of Starry Night."

"Ah, a Van Gogh project."

"You get an A, Jack Corey. That is correct." They exchanged a few more pleasantries.

"Sweetheart," Jack spoke, and Paige thought she may melt right on the school picnic table, "I hate to cut this short, but I've got to go. I'll get hold of you later, okay?"

Now, she felt the swoon turn to mortification. She would never be the one to call again, he was most definitely dismissing her. "That's fine. Have a good day, Jack."

His voice was soft, smoothing things over a bit, "Thanks for calling. I really miss you."

As she walked back into the building, Paige realized the entire communication with Jack today had been confusing. First, he had been peppering her with texts all morning, then when she called, he seemed not to have the time or desire to have a conversation. She shook her head as if to scold herself, what did she expect? This "thing" was just a temporary distraction for Jack. Enjoy it for what it was.

***

The bell had rung fifteen minutes ago, and the students made their typical dash to the parking lot. Some climbed onto yellow buses. Most of the older teens jumped into vehicles and tore out of the lot. Paige was hanging up her paint apron, deciding she could wear it another day before she swapped it out for a clean one. She pulled her purse and lunch bag from her closet. Calling a "See you tomorrow" to the Algebra teacher across the hall, she walked out the door. As she stepped out into the lovely sunny afternoon, the first thing she saw was a man leaning against the back of a black convertible, a Mercedes to be exact. A coworker just behind her, saw him too, "Who's that hottie?" Paige's heart stopped, she knew exactly who it was. Incapable of even responding, when he flashed that million-dollar grin at her, Paige headed straight at him.

Others, slowly heading to their cars, were watching. Paige was unaware. She moved to Jack. He spoke slowly, "Hey teach, can you help me with my homework?" She was now right in front of him and he opened his arms to pull her into a tight hug.

"What are you doing here?" she smiled at him, incredulous that Jack Corey was standing in her school parking lot.

"Everyone was headed home, and I thought, 'Where would I want to spend my days off?' With you, of course!"

This confused Paige, "But when I talked to you this afternoon, you seemed so distracted."

"I was at the car rental agency, I didn't want you to hear me making plans. I wanted to surprise you."

She rested her hand on his upper arm, his skin below the sleeve of his shirt was warm, "You did that." Now she glanced at the small group who had gathered, watching the meeting. "Okay, how about if I lead the way to my house?"

"Perfect," with that Jack leaned in and gave her a soft kiss. Paige thought she might have to find a new job.

***

In the car, she called Laurel even though she knew the elementary school was still in session. Her friend answered after the fourth ring. "Hey, is everything okay?"

"No, it's definitely not!"

Laurel yelled out, apparently to another teacher to watch her kids, her voice was serious, "What's wrong?"

"Jack Corey just showed up at school."

"What?"

"I'm serious, he has a few days off, rented a car, a Mercedes convertible, and was in the parking lot when I walked out. Now he's following me to my house. Is my house even clean? I have no food in the fridge. What am I going to do?"

Laurel let out one of her famous whoops, then laughed, "Paige, this is awesome. After your time in hotel rooms with the man, I don't think I need to tell you what to do. He's here? He came here to spend time with you! What exactly is going on? I think you're in a relationship."

"That's impossible," but even as she protested, Paige smiled to herself. Was she?

***

In just a few minutes, they were pulling into her driveway. Paige tried to imagine what her brick ranch looked like to him. From the front, it was a very typical one-story home. They both drove up the cement drive. She opened the garage from her car. As was her habit, she pulled into the spot on the left. To her surprise, Jack pulled into the spot on the right. Paige closed the door behind her and got out of the car. She was reaching for her lunch bag and purse and noticed he had opened the trunk to pull out a duffle and his guitar.

Jack noticed her grin as he tossed the instrument onto his shoulder, "What?"

"I've never had a guest bring a guitar."

He laughed and followed her into the kitchen. "This is like another arm, I must have one with me. I couldn't take a risk you wouldn't have one. You don't do you?" As Jack spoke, he glanced from the kitchen out to the living space.

She tossed her bag on the counter, "Nope, just a piano."

"You play the piano?"

"Not really. Like most kids, I took lessons and so did my daughter. I play around on it occasionally. Do you?"

Jack was setting his guitar in a corner near the television, "It's the best way to write music." Now he picked up his bag and winked at her, "Do you have a spare room for me?"

Paige smiled coyly, "Yes, if you would like."

Jack was in front of her in two quick steps. He placed a hand on her waist and pulled her in for a kiss. "I would not."

Paige watched Jack Corey move toward her bedroom. Her heart was pounding up into her ears, she thought she might pass out. How was she going to get through the night? It felt better when he came back into the room; she remembered this was the man she'd had such a great time with in Cleveland. But that was all fun like a vacation, this was her tedious life. This was the life where she had to get up and go to work in the morning. What would they do tonight? What did he expect them to do tonight?

If she were alone, she'd probably throw a load of laundry in and watch some TV and eat a light dinner. Dinner? What was she going to feed the man standing in her living room? Jack seemed to see the emotions cross her face. He walked to her, "Is this a bad idea?" *Had he seen her house and her small-town life and realized the mistake?* He continued, "Did I spring myself on you and it's not good? Did you not want me to be part of this life?"

He was being so considerate. Paige couldn't believe he thought she didn't want him around. She just didn't know what to do with him now that he was here. Not knowing what else to say, she said, "What about dinner?"

Jack laughed, "If that's the biggest problem, then I think we'll be okay."

They ordered in Chinese. She had a bottle of wine and they sat at the barstools in her kitchen and ate. Jack talked to her about how he had decided to go back on tour. He told her about the eight years since his last tour. About how he spent the first year just relaxing; traveling where he wanted to go, dropping in on friends and other musicians, spending a couple of months with his mom. He even got to be with JJ just as JJ graduated from college and was starting his business. Jack was proud of his son, it was clear. It was also clear that he'd been integral in his son meeting the right people to kick-start his business in the world of athletic wear.

Tony had been pushing them for the last four years to go back on the road. Jack hadn't been interested in releasing a collection of their songs again. There was no new material, and he'd seen other bands of his era try to release new collections with a new single or two. It didn't work. There were those few classics like Aerosmith and the Eagles who produced new music that still became hits, but he didn't want to take the chance. They didn't need the money and frankly, he was busy enough. Eventually, though, the tour appealed to him. He missed that feeling on the stage with fans.

When he and Paige met in Findlay that was their sixth show of the tour and he hadn't regretted a minute of it. Now he smiled at her over his wineglass and spoke, "One of the things I was already missing was any privacy and relaxation and apparently intimacy. Meeting you came at exactly the right moment. I spent the last couple of weeks remembering how nice our time was together. But I kept telling myself to get over it. I changed my mind and I can't tell you how lucky I feel that when I found you, you wanted to be around me too."

Paige smiled and looked down at her plate. She couldn't believe he was saying these things to her. Suddenly she felt comfortable with Jack at her home. As she was throwing away the containers of food, Jack placed the wineglasses in the sink. He caught her yawning. "You must be exhausted after a whole day of work and then I show up and you're entertaining me."

"Well," she said, "school starts early. I go to sleep usually before 10."

Jack looked at the clock it was 9:52. He smiled at her, "I'm not opposed to turning in early."

***

Page was walking into the kitchen after school, she could hear Jack's guitar. He would play a few chords and then stop. Then a few more and some additional minutes of silence. He must be songwriting. She'd seen his legal pad of notes and lyrics. The sound was coming from her backyard. He sat on the wicker cushioned sofa. His guitar was on his lap, the paper and pen on the glass table. Elliott, the cat, was stretched out on the opposite chair. She opened the sliding screen door and said hello. He gave her only a cursory glance and turned back to what he was doing. Paige stepped out onto the patio as he plucked out a few more chords. When he stopped to write the notes, she spoke, "Can I get you some iced tea?"

"No, I'll be done soon." It was a definite dismissal. Trying not to feel scolded, Paige headed back into the house. She changed into khaki shorts and a pink V-neck tee. After checking her social media on her laptop, she perused the kitchen for dinner. Jack's guitar was still busy.

Two loads of laundry, roasted chicken breasts with red potatoes in the oven, and painted toenails later, Jack strolled into the kitchen. He rubbed his palms together, "That food smells delicious."

Paige had spent the last two-and-a-half hours unnoticed and was feeling irritated. She did not respond. He seemed unaware of her mood and came up behind her. His arms snaked around her waist and he kissed her neck. "You can cook too? You are a marvel."

The feel of his lips on her skin softened her mood. "Don't be too impressed, it's only chicken." She turned into his arms and they kissed. "Did you finish your work?"

Jack stepped back and nodded his head excitedly. "Yes, I woke up with this melody in my head. It's coming together."

Was she really going to hold a grudge because this man was writing a song on her back deck? She remembered when Gina had warned her, he could "get in the zone" about his music.

They took dinner out onto the deck. Now the birds provided the music. Jack was in a grand mood. Paige took a breath before she spoke, “Do you need to work on your song tomorrow?”

He started to answer in the affirmative, but then looked at her, “Why?”

Paige smiled, “Well, I took the day off.”

His expression was one of delight. “You did? Fantastic! What shall we do?”

“I thought maybe we could go up to Lake Erie, take the ferry over to the islands.”

Chapter 8

Put in Bay, Ohio

They set their plans. As they cruised on the highway in his rented convertible, Paige once again had the feeling of living in a fantasy. This would be so much fun taking him to the restaurants and shops on Put in Bay Island or Kelley's Island, or both. They hadn't yet decided. Jack was navigating with his phone, when he made a different turn than the ferry dock, Paige questioned him.

"I've got another plan," was all he said. Soon they pulled up to yacht dealership.

She laughed, "Are we buying a boat?"

Jack grabbed her hand as they walked toward the sales office, "No, but we're borrowing one for the day." An eager salesman was heading toward them.

As she boarded the 35-foot yacht, Paige was reminded of how different Jack's world was. Her normal trip to Put-n-Bay or Kelley's Island on Lake Erie was by boarding a ferry filled with other tourists, cars and work trucks. This was perfectly fine with her. On two occasions, she had gone with friends who had a boat that was large enough to navigate the great lake's waters from Port Clinton. Jack's form of boating was entirely different.

He climbed up to the steering wheel; she followed. The many gages were like a high-end car. Jack scanned them with the eye of a familiar captain. Someone from the shop jumped on to discuss it with him. Meanwhile, Paige stepped below deck. There was a small bar, a half circle white leather couch, a kitchen, a tiny bathroom, and bedroom. Was this necessary for a quick trip across the water? She felt underdressed in her blue cotton shorts and a striped pullover.

As she turned to the steps, another employee of the marina was heading down the three steps with a cardboard box in his hand. With a polite, "Excuse me," he stepped past her and placed food items and wine bottles in the mini fridge. He also added other food and dishes to the cupboard. Next, he stepped into the bathroom, she noted he was putting away toiletries. Finally, he returned to the table in front of the white couch and placed a vase with two roses in it on the small table. With a nod, he disappeared back upstairs.

The yacht roared to life. Over the purr of the engine, she could hear the employees offering Jack farewell. Dazed at this monstrous plan that was apparently made while she was getting showered this morning, Paige dropped her bag on the couch and headed back upstairs. They were slowly moving out of the marina; the water sparkling blue in front. Jack stood at the wheel. When she moved up next to him, he put an arm around her waist. "Surprise! I thought we would take this trip a little differently." He placed a soft kiss on her cheek, and she got caught up in the excitement.

"This is incredible. I've never been on something so beautiful." The yacht seemed to roll seamlessly over the waves. Paige went down to the galley and discovered that Jack's favorite Cabernet was there. She poured them each a glass and returned to the top. The breeze flew over the windshield and blew Jack's hair down onto his forehead. Paige reached into her shorts pocket and pulled out a hair tie. With a quick maneuver, she pulled her hair into a short ponytail. Jack grinned at her, "I like that," he tipped the edge of the glass and they toasted this adventure.

After a tour of a portion of Lake Erie; cruising around Johnson's Island, past the cliffside homes in Marblehead, they pulled into the pier at Put in Bay. It was slow for a weekday, still early May. They were lucky for the unseasonable warmth. He moved the yacht away from the main marina and headed toward a smaller one.

"Where are you going?" Paige watched as a young man stepped out on a pier and eyed their approach. "I think this is a private place." The sign came into view *Put in Bay Yacht Club.*

"This is where he told me to dock," Jack responded, referring to the yacht dealer.

She was about to ask how they would have permission, when the youth reached for the side, "I was expecting you. Welcome to the island."

Paige looked at Jack quizzically, he laughed, "This is the dealer's yacht."

"You rented his boat?"

Amused, Jack spoke, "No, he let me borrow it." He shut off the engine and pocketed the keys. The young man pointed across the street at the restaurant, a quaint building with umbrella-covered tables and chairs scattered across a fence-enclosed lawn. "There is a table reserved for you." He reached into his pocket, "Oh, and this is for your golf cart." He pointed to a row of them parked along the boating office. “It’s the red one.” The red one was customized with thick tires and plush seats.

Handing him some cash, Jack lightly smiled as if this was normal treatment. He stepped off the yacht and held his hand out to Paige. “Are you hungry, my dear?”

She thought of her own parents when they once had box seats for a Cleveland Indians game. Paige was just a young teen; the family had all gone to the game. As they settled themselves into the luxury spot, her dad had taken in the view of the diamond and said, “So this is how the other half lives.” Paige was feeling the same way as they were ushered into the private lawn where she had never eaten before. Her eyes could see the yacht and nearby the luxury golf cart all loaned to Jack. Normally, she would pay forty-five dollars for one of the basic carts that were rolling past them as they munched on crab salad. The yacht dealer had loaned them the cart they would soon climb into. Celebrity opened doors that was for certain.

The other tables were eyeing them. Jack’s confidence and charisma were clear even when clad in slim khaki jeans and a navy half-zip pullover, not his on-stage looks of tight blue jeans and black shirts. As was normal, he had a cap on his head, and sunglasses. If they recognized him, no one approached at lunch.

Afterward, they cruised up to the busy main street. People were milling about, going into restaurants, bars, and shops. A few places had live music. The Roundhouse was one of Put in Bay’s most famous spots. The stage for bands was a round platform above the bar. Jack and Paige went in, a guitarist playing Tom Petty piqued their interest. The crowd was light for a weekday. They nabbed two bar stools and watched the band above them. Soon, they each sipped a Corona. Like everyone else in the place, they swayed and sang to, *Last Dance with Mary Jane.* When the band launched into *Start Me Up*, they simultaneously stood up and joined the others on the makeshift dance floor.

Though he had his hands entwined with hers, and his movement in sync with hers, Paige saw that Jack's eyes were watching the guitar player. His first love mesmerized him. The song ended, and he gave an enthusiastic fist raising that knocked his hat off his head. As he scooped it off the floor and placed it back on, the guitarist moved to the microphone. "Thank you. Our next song is a favorite. We'll be playing *Swept Away.*" The crowd cheered for one of Jack's number one hits. "Unless," the guitarist looked directly at the two, "Jack Corey would like to come up here and play it himself."

Paige laughed, "Busted!"

The crowd went wild, seeking the rock star out. They chanted, "Jack."

Jack took his hat off, placing it on Paige's head, then offered the crowd his devastating grin. He placed both his hands on her waist, pulling her close, "Sorry." Then with a kiss on her cheek, he headed up to the stage.

On the round stage, Jack Corey swung the guitar strap over his shoulder. The transformation was instantaneous. The legend was in the house and the lucky visitors of Put in Bay were in for a treat. To their credit, the band played well. When Jack's smoky voice ushered the first line, the audience went wild. Bodies poured into the little tavern. Paige was pushed toward the bar. A burly man with a gray beard and a T-shirt that read "It's five o'clock somewhere", saw her being shoved. He pushed back his stool and picked her up by the waist. Now she was sitting on the bar, legs hanging over the bartender side.

Jack was doing what he did best, making the crowd of strangers love him. When the song ended, he was handing the guitar back to its owner, and graciously spoke into the mike, "Thank you for letting me play." This brought a fresh onslaught of cheers. "These guys are great! You give my band a run for its money." Someone yelled out for more, but Jack shook his head. He searched the crowd for Paige. When he spotted her, he added, "Today's about my sweetheart. Thank you, Put in Bay." He made his way off the stage and planted a big kiss on Paige's lips before helping her off the bar. The crowd parted as they made their way to the door, hand in hand. The sea of cell phones was its own kind of paparazzi.

Jack and Paige climbed into the golf cart. As he maneuvered around people crossing the street, she asked, "Did you enjoy that?"

"Absolutely. I could jam like that on a little stage with a small crowd for hours." He then laid his hand on the top of her leg, "However, I think taking you back to the yacht sounds even better." His grin was wicked.

***

The next morning, she headed back to school; he left for another leg of his tour. When they kissed goodbye, it surprised her how forlorn he seemed. Jack stroked her cheek, "You will definitely be in Dayton after work today?"

She nodded, "I'm packed, and I'll go straight there."

***

Annabeth was happy to be back in her studio apartment in Queens. She needed to do laundry and check her mail. An appointment to the hair salon had also occurred. It surprised her longtime stylist when she asked for a new cut and color closer to her own natural auburn. Afterward, she was pleased with the way her hair now framed her face, adding depth to her cheekbones. Her only concern was that Trent might misread her efforts.

Repacking for the return to the tour, she dug through her closet for decent attire. It was time to update the stained jeans and faded out T-shirts. Two new dark pairs of jeans and some tops were packed in the suitcase. The shirts were still casual; one a vintage Led Zeppelin. This improvement of her appearance was for her. Paige had been the catalyst. A small-town schoolteacher had caught the eye of Jack Corey, not by being flashy or trashy, but just a classy and kind woman. Annabeth nearly laughed at herself for the optimism this gave her.

***

Jack was optimistic too. One weekend with Paige and he wanted her around more. He was cruising down I 75 in Ohio from Findlay to Dayton. He'd put the top down on the Mercedes and was enjoying the fresh smells of cornfields and wildflowers. Driving was something he had always loved, and he didn't do it nearly enough. When he first made money, he had bought a little black Ferrari that he wished he still owned. Life in New York and on the road didn't lend itself to driving time. This was a treat.

Paige would be back with him tonight. He was going to back out of after-party obligations. He'd rather be with her. Jack frowned at himself in the rear-view mirror. He believed in the process, it was what had taken him from dive bars in Kansas City to Madison Square Garden.

When he and Tony had cooked up this tour, he knew what it would entail. It had been eight years since the Jack Corey band had been on stage. If these cities welcomed them back, then he would return the favor with media interviews and meet and greets. He would devote Sunday to Paige.

He reflected on the week he had just spent with her at her home. The day at Put in Bay turned out to be as filled with fun as any he had spent on a Caribbean beach. Jack had second-guessed himself on the yacht when they first set out on Lake Erie. Paige had sent mixed messages about it. The luxury was what Jack was accustomed to. The dealer's generosity of his boat, golf cart, and country club were common. Jack posed for a photo at the business which they would display, it was an ordinary trade for him.

Once they were gliding over the waves, Paige had seemed to enjoy herself. Driving around those beach cottages and shops with her was ridiculously enjoyable. The Round House held such a great vibe. Jack would have been happy to have danced and drank with Paige for a couple of hours. It wasn't unusual for him to get recognized. Now that he was older, it was a low-key thing. The chaos caused twenty years ago, rarely if never happened anymore. He was happy to oblige the band and stand in for a number. If he'd been alone, he might have jammed for hours. Stepping on the old stage above the bar was like coming home. But it was fine for a song, and the adrenaline was still pumping when they were back on the boat.

Jack grinned to himself when he remembered the nice time they'd had below deck. The other guys in the band were convinced they needed to sleep with twenty-year-olds to feel young. Paige was just a few years shy of his fifty years. Their sex life was exciting and made him feel like the guy he used to be. Sometimes she would smile at him in a way which was as arousing as those women of long ago who purposely brushed up against him, sometimes touched him. Every night he'd slept in her bed, they'd made love. He could add satisfied to the list of positive feelings inside him.

Was it too soon to ask her to join the tour? She would be free for the summer. Jack thought the idea was perfect. Paige had indicated that she hadn't traveled to too many places. The tour was covering at least six states this summer. Remembering how charming they had made Cleveland, he knew together during his free time they could explore more. A sense of rightness filled him, Paige had to come with him. This could be his best summer yet.

A phrase, "the perfect summer" struck something in his mind. Jack was familiar with this moment. He reached over to his phone and let Siri find his talk to text app. After repeating, "the perfect summer", he tried out phrases that would become lyrics.

***

If Annabeth had hoped for compliments from the members of The Jack Corey band, then those hopes were dashed. No one mentioned her hair which she felt was a major transformation. Only Trent had given her a once over and then a half nod. She flushed with what she felt was his approval. The pleasure was quickly replaced with annoyance at herself. Her appearance wasn't the only thing that Annabeth had wanted to change. She'd continuously coached herself in New York; no more fooling around with Trent. It was disrespectful to Gina. She seemed like a decent person. It was also an insult to herself.

She noticed that Jack was also transformed. He was friendly to everyone, even funny. Annabeth also saw him with his guitar and notebook, hard at work. This would be a love ballad.

Taking advantage of his good mood, she managed over an hour conversation sitting in the seats of the Nutter Center Theater. Above them, on stage, the roadies were hard at work laying cords and setting up microphones. Jack shared much about his childhood. He was reverential about his father. Losing him as a boy had been painful. He gave him credit for the gift of his guitar skills.

Jack also had great affection and respect for his mother. Now as an adult he didn't fault her for leaving him alone in the evenings while at work. "I make a lot of money doing what is second nature. I love being on stage. Mom had to leave her love of teaching piano to work a second shift job on a factory line. She was forced to sacrifice time with me." Jack paused, emotion cracking his voice. "We didn't have many hours together and had to do our grieving alone."

"How are things between you now?" Annabeth asked.

Jack smiled brightly, "My success changed everything. The first things I did was pay off all her bills and buy her a nice car. When JJ was younger, Mom traveled on vacation with us. Now, she lives in a condo in Naples, Florida that she insists is mine, not hers."

After that, they called Jack on stage. Annabeth headed to the hotel to get changed. As she sat in the cab, she thought about this book. Her two previous works were successful largely because there were conflict and scandal. What she had gathered for this one was information on a man who was gifted, hardworking and kind. Would the Jack Corey story be interesting enough to sell?

***

Paige stood in the doorway of her principal's office, "I'm sorry, Pam, I can't meet after school. I'm heading out of town for the weekend." A frown flickered across Pam's face. "Can we have a discussion now?"

Her boss sighed and motioned for her to close the door. Paige sat in a chair across from the desk. Her principal nervously shuffled papers and asked, "Are you going to another concert?"

So, she knew about Jack. Still, why should that matter? "Yes, in Dayton."

"Mr. Dickerson wanted to speak to you. I'll tell him I handled it." *Why would the superintendent want to speak to her?* Pam continued, "So you're dating a musician."

Paige considered; their time together this week could be called dating. "Yes, Jack Corey."

It was quiet for a moment as the name sunk in. Her principal looked up, "Jack Corey the Grammy winner?" now her eyes were big. Paige just nodded. "Do you have an Instagram account?" This was a strange question.

"No."

Her boss, a woman in her late fifties, nodded, "Me either. I only got on Twitter for the school." Another pause. "Apparently one of our parents' sisters was at Put in Bay on Thursday and posted a picture of you with Jack." She sounded out his name carefully as if wrapping the reality of him around her brain.

Paige reflected on their day. She could not recall any scandalous moments. She was in a bar, but she was an adult. Instead of responding, she looked up waiting for Pam to continue, which she did. "You were sitting on a bar and um, Jack was kissing you." She attempted a look of disapproval, but reverence won out.

Paige had the decency to look embarrassed. "I was sitting on the bar because the crowd pushed me up to it. The guitarist recognized

Jack, and he invited him up to sing. When people heard him, the place became mobbed. He kissed me after the song." Why was she having to explain this to her boss?

"You weren't dancing on the bar?"

"No, I didn't even have a drink in my hand," she despised having to defend herself. "Pam, I am 48 years old, not married. I had a legitimate day off and was not in a compromising position."

The other woman looked embarrassed, "You're right, Paige. Social media is tricky. Parents hold teachers to a higher standard. I'll talk to Mr. Dickerson."

Paige rose, "I'm sorry, not for my own personal life but because you had to deal with the complaint."

"Don't worry about it, have a safe trip," Pam turned toward her computer as she added, "with Jack Corey." Paige could see a smile playing at her lips.

Chapter 9

Dayton, Ohio

Two hours later, Paige was walking away from the hotel desk when Keely came across the lobby. Today she was wearing tiny jean cutoffs and an equally small tank top. “The guys are already at warm-ups.” Paige nodded. Jack had texted her as she was on the road with the same message. Keely looked like she had something to discuss. “Want to grab a drink in the bar?” Paige wasn’t really in the mood for a drink yet but followed the young woman to a table. Keely ordered a Cosmo, Paige an iced tea.

After a sip of her drink, Keely spoke, “Gina’s not here this weekend.”

Paige responded, “She said she stays in New York a lot, with the kids.”

Keely toyed with the drink stir, “You guys seemed to be best buds in Cleveland.”

“She was just helping my first time coming to a show.”

After the second swallow of Cosmo, Keely continued, “It’s a rule we don’t tell Gina what Trent does when she’s not here.”

Paige felt her stomach tighten, “What do you mean?”

“There’s an after-party at a bar tonight. The sort of party where girls come in from local dance clubs. Trent likes to enjoy himself. We don’t tell Gina.”

“He’s with other women?”

Keely shrugged, “Some guys do it occasionally. Trent always does it.”

“Why don’t you tell Gina?”

Finishing her drink then signaling the bartender for another, Keely smacked her lips, “Because Gina doesn’t want us to.”

Shaking her head in disbelief, Paige responded, “She knows?”

“They’ve been married like forever. How do you think that works? He’s a rocker.”

“So, you don’t care if Joe fools around with other women?”

Keely was now drinking out of the second glass, “That’s how we got together, at a club in Philly two years ago, after a show.”

“Was he married?”

“Yes. He’s divorced now. But he will not fool around, I travel with him everywhere.” Paige thought that was rather pathetic and the distaste must have shown on her face. “Come on Paige, the rules are different for them. I know Jack acts like you guys are a love thing, and I really thought he was gay before, but I’m sure he’s had his share of women.”

Standing up, Paige signed her bill. “Thanks for the warning, Keely. I’ll see you backstage later.” She examined her own irritation as she headed to the elevator. It wasn’t about Jack. It had only been a few weeks. She wasn’t naïve enough to put any titles on their relationship. Her frustrations were about Trent, Gina, and the entire idea that it was okay with everyone.

Her thoughts were gloomy as she took out her outfit and hung it in the closet. Reapplying her makeup and touching up her hair, she wished that she hadn't come. Just then the door clicked open. Jack raced in wearing jeans faded nearly to white and an old Fender t-shirt. He looked so glad to see her, she forgot everything else.

"Hello lovely," he headed straight for her. Their kiss was long and the embrace that followed tight.

"Everything ready?"

Jack groaned, "It didn't go smoothly. They had to have an electrician come in, problems with the wiring. Joe had a drum skin tear. Nightmare." As he talked, he walked over and stretched out on the bed. He patted the mattress at his side, "How was your day?"

"Well," she settled down beside him, "I got called to the principal's office."

He laughed and turned to his side to look at her, "You naughty school girl! What did you do?"

Paige faced him, her hand on his chest, "We made Instagram; kissing on the bar. Someone sent the photo to the superintendent."

"Who the hell cares?"

"Apparently the superintendent thought he'd make something of it, but my principal promised to smooth it over."

"That's horseshit, you're an adult."

"I agree, but they have told us to be careful about being seen on social media."

Jack played with a lock of her hair, "Well darling, I've got bad news. You're with the wrong man to stay off Instagram."

She warmed at his words. "It's okay, I think my boss is a fan. When I mentioned your name, she had to say it in the conversation several times."

"Maybe we should get a copy of the photo and I can sign it for her," he laughed.

Paige pushed him lightly, "Stop. But maybe I will have you sign something for her."

Jack laid down on his back. Now he reached out his arms, "Come here, Paige. I have to be back downstairs soon."

***

The bar was a historic brick building. Inside everything was dark wood and dim lights. The media people had hired vans to transport them, not wanting people to see the tour bus or limos parked there. It was a closed party. Jack had insisted that the two of them go in her car. She was glad. The conversation with Keely hadn't been brought up, but she was dreading the night. After the troubles before, the show had been perfect. Jack was his normal post-performance self; high on adrenaline.

Once inside the bar, he was surrounded by the local VIPs and media staff. Paige allowed them to press her back. She made her way to the bar ordered them both a drink. This was an establishment known for its brewery. She ordered a dark beer for Jack and decided on pale ale for herself. Now she tried to get near Jack to give him his drink. No one was budging, and they ignored her polite "excuse me"s. Finally, Jack spotted her and motioned for the people to let her in. He took the beer and placed his other arm around her shoulders. "Guys, I really am ready to sit for a moment and have a drink with my girl."

The others, all men, seemed to notice her for the first time. One of them frowned, "Is that why the girls were cancelled?"

Jack paused, then forced a smile. "I appreciate the effort. Years ago, we were eager young men and loved the adoration. Now, it's just a good time to hang with you guys. Thanks for the offer." His words seem to placate the crowd. It did wonders for Paige. He clasped her hand and pulled her to the bar.

They sat with their back to the crowd. "Keely told me about tonight. Thanks for canceling it."

Jack took a sip of his drink, "I know these events are part of the process, but that's unnecessary. Most the guys have someone with them, anyway." Now he looked at her, "Like me."

Music pulsated through the place, a dance beat. Paige could see in the mirror behind the bar. Some couples with the band were dancing. Paige noticed Trent in the reflection, glad that there weren't young women for him to mess with. As she thought that, she watched him approach a female. The woman had her back turned; he put his arms around her and at first; she pushed him away. He then put his lips to the side of her face, when she turned away laughing, Paige recognized Annabeth. Trent must have won her over because they moved to the dance floor and he was so close that his own hips were grinding against hers

"Unbelievable," Paige said aloud.

Jack glanced into the mirror to see what she was talking about, "Yeah, I thought this was going on."

"What's that supposed to mean?" her voice was sharp.

He shrugged, "It's how he is."

"But you're friends with Gina."

"Sure, we've known each other forever."

"And you say nothing?"

He sighed, “Paige, you don’t get it. It’s Gina’s choice to accept it. Many people in the industry are like this. This lifestyle doesn’t lend itself to fidelity.” He saw her stiffen, “You have to make a choice to be loyal, every night you’re offered sex from an adoring fan or someone with the tour.” He leaned close, so that the side of his head was next to hers, “I made the choice long ago not to play that game.”

“But the night we met, you did.”

Now he faced her, “That’s not fair. It was and still is entirely different from that.”

Paige gave him a weak smile, “I know it is. It makes me sick to see Trent like that,” as she spoke, she glanced up, he was now tongue deep into a kiss with Annabeth, his hands up the hem of her top.

“Are you ready to go?” He placed his empty beer bottle on the bar.

“Can we?”

***

Back in the hotel, Jack stripped off his clothes and climbed into the bed. Paige took more time; removing her makeup and jewelry. With his arms crossed behind his head, Jack watched her. “You’re quiet,” he observed. “Weren’t you ready to leave?”

She was pulling off her pants, now down to bra and panties. “You know I was. Thank you for leaving.” Walking to her suitcase, she pulled out a short nightgown.

“You don’t need that,” his voice was low and coaxing. She frowned slightly but dropped her nightgown back into the suitcase. He saw her expression, “Come on baby, I know Trent upset you.”

Jack turned toward the nightstand and picked up his phone. Soon Billy Paul was softly singing, "Me and Mrs. Jones." She flipped off the overhead light and now naked, climbed into the bed with him.

"It's difficult for me to accept. I know you're used to it."

He stroked her arms, softly crooning, "Me and Mrs., Mrs. Baxter, Mrs. Baxter, Mrs. Baxter." She faced him, running her fingers over his cheekbones and jawline.

"Why are you still Mrs. Baxter?" he asked as his hands moved to her collarbone, gently stroking her skin.

Paige ran her fingers through the hair over his ears, "Because by the time I got divorced, I'd been teaching at the school for several years. It felt like an uncomfortable announcement."

They kissed slowly, tongues tasting one another. "We've got a thing going on," Jack sang quietly. Her hand wandered down his chest. They continued kissing. Jack rolled, so he was looming above her, "I love the thing we've got going on." Those were the last words he spoke for a while.

***

It was nearly noon the next day when Jack got out of bed. Paige had showered three hours before and then gone down to breakfast. She had seen no one from the band while she was eating. The bar party must have been something. As she was returning to their room, a busboy wheeled a cart to the room three doors down. Paige didn't mean to glance into the open door. When she looked, she wished she hadn't. Annabeth stood next to Trent in his shirt. He had on only his jeans. He was greeting the young man bringing breakfast, sounding perfectly jovial. Paige felt her coffee rebel in her stomach.

Back in her own silent room, she couldn't help herself. She sat on the couch; her legs on the coffee table and picked up her phone.

Missed you this weekend, was Paige's text.

Gina responded instantly, *Reed had a baseball game. How'd it go?*

Paige hesitated, *Fine.*

At breakfast alone?

I was. Back in the room now.

Bar party last night?

Yes.

Gina took longer to respond. When she did, her words shocked Paige, *I know why you texted me. We've been married for almost twenty years. Reed was born a month later. We traveled with the band until Callie was born. I couldn't live that way with two kids. But it's the only way Trent knows how to live.*

Paige regretted texting, *I'm sorry.*

Don't be. When you come to NY with Jack, I'll let you see how good my life is.

Deal.

Thanks for worrying about me. I think we'll be good friends.

Paige laid her phone next to her. She wouldn't tell Jack about the conversation. Though she was pleased to have a friend in this, she was sad about Gina's marriage. She looked across the room at the beautiful man in the bed. He was on his side, sheet pulled down to his waist. His arms were holding the pillow. Paige had the urge to spoon behind him but didn't.

Would she still be a part of this long enough to go to New York? To Jack's home? She knew this relationship was fleeting. She thought back to the day on the yacht. His world was so different from hers. Paige couldn't imagine the places he'd been. She'd never even left the country. Oh, but this was fun. The time with Jack Corey was precious. She'd never have imagined that in her late 40s she could have such a love affair. She would enjoy it while it lasted.

***

Annabeth lay in her hotel bed nursing the worst hangover she could remember, it may top her college years at Columbia. After Trent approached her at the club, they'd ended up in his room. This morning, Gina had called just as room service finished delivering breakfast. He'd looked at the phone and ordered her out. She grabbed a bagel and coffee and left, humiliated. She was angriest at herself. Of course, he would screw around with her when he felt like it and kick her out when he wanted to. She had promised herself that it would not happen again. Why had she let it last night? This damn book about Jack was getting to her. His own new relationship was making Annabeth want things for herself. Whatever she wanted, it would not be with Trent Crosby. But it was lonely on the road. She'd try to be stronger, but she may have to wait until she finished her research and was back home.

***

They sat on the couch together, her leg over his. His hand behind her head, playing with her hair. "So, if you had a day to spend with a man at home, what would you do?"

"Hmmm, let me see. An all-day date? It's been awhile."

Jack pulled her face close to his and kissed her, "I don't believe that." As they both settled back against the couch, he added, "Before we met, were you seeing anyone?"

Paige chuckled. "Not really."

"What's so funny about that?"

"I kind of was when we met. I went out with him the night after the concert but couldn't enjoy myself. It was your fault."

Jack laughed triumphantly, "How was that my fault?"

She put both of her legs over his so that her feet were on the couch beside him, "He wasn't you." They kissed again. "So how about you, Jack, are you seeing anyone?"

"I wasn't." Now he took her hand, stroking her fingers. "I think this is a good time to discuss what's on my mind."

Paige was apprehensive, it was all good talk, but he seemed nervous. Was this a goodbye? She hadn't expected it yet.

"School gets out soon, right?" his voice was softer, almost vulnerable.

"Yes."

Now he looked her in the eyes, "Will you spend the summer on tour with me?"

She nearly coughed as her breath choked, "What do you mean?"

"When school is out, will you pack up and spend the summer with me? Travel on the bus with me, spend the free days with me. I mean, we can go to your house on breaks, and to my place."

One night and two weekends together, and Jack was asking her to spend the summer with him. This shocked Paige into silence, her head spinning with thoughts. "So, you mean that we would be together every day?"

"I'd rather do that, then you popping in and out like you have to now."

"Can I think about it?" she hated watching his face fall. She continued quickly, "I can't even remember if I have a vacation or anything planned with anyone. You caught me off guard."

"Do you want to spend time with me?" Jack was looking at her so earnestly and hopefully.

"Oh yes, I do."

That seemed to mollify him, "Okay, you check your schedules and think about it. I mean it, I would love to have you with me on tour this summer."

The band had a concert in Indianapolis that night. It thrilled Paige that she and Jack were driving her car to the venue. Alone in the car, they sang and talked. It was the most natural thing in the world to be with this man. Jack told her about a night when his jeans split on stage, the two of them laughed. For some reason that shared mirth did it, Paige looked at Jack, her eyes shining, "I want to spend the summer with you."

***

From the king-sized bed, their view of the buildings across the street was not the most picturesque view they'd had in a hotel. Jack took her hand and placed it on his chest, entwining her fingers in his. "So next weekend we'll be in Portland and Salt Lake City. That will be the last time you come for only the weekend. It's too far to drive, I'll get you a plane ticket."

Paige held up her hand, ready to interrupt, but he continued, "Then we will be together every day. Thank you for agreeing to come."

She absent-mindedly watched a pair of pigeons vie for a windowsill on the building, then turned in his direction, "Jack, I can't leave town this weekend. It's graduation and I'm required to attend. Plus, several of my students have parties and I always go."

A deep shadow passed his face. "You can't come at all?"

"No, it's an entire weekend of activity."

He rolled to his back and stared at the ceiling.

"I have finals all week and a teacher's end-of-year thing on Thursday evening. I won't have any time to hang out with you." Jack was still and silent. Paige was shocked at his reaction. She'd just agreed to spend the summer with him, how could one weekend be a problem?

"I see," he finally said and climbed out of bed. Without another word, he headed into the shower.

Paige got up, pulled on a robe and walked to the window. Was she reading his reaction correctly? She hoped that she'd made the right decision about the summer. To distract herself, she pulled on a pair of jeans and a t-shirt. With her hair in a ponytail, she placed one of Jack's hats on her head. At the mirror, she wiped away stray mascara, then picked up the room card and headed to the elevator. She was back in less than ten minutes with a tray of coffees and bagels from the restaurant downstairs. Just as she set them on the table, Jack stepped out of the bathroom.

He noticed she was dressed, key card in her hand. His voice was hurt, "Are you leaving?"

She attempted to hide her surprise at his tone, "No, I went down to get us coffee." Taking off his cap, Paige used this as an excuse to turn her back on him. *What was going on? He sounded like a deserted child!* Instead of reaching for the coffee, she grabbed the robe she had earlier laid across the bed and headed into the bathroom.

As the water splashed down on her hair, Paige considered the situation. Jack was a famous musician, he was used to getting his way. He wanted her with him every weekend. On the one hand, it was unbelievably flattering. But this response was dramatic.

She was standing at the bathroom mirror in her underwear, bra, and tank when Jack knocked on the door. She murmured for him to come in, her focus on her eyeliner. He was holding one of the mugs, "Your coffee is getting cold, love."

Paige sat down the wand and reached for it, "Thank you."

He caught her eye in the mirror, "I'm sorry that I acted like a spoiled ass. I just can't imagine not having you with me for the weekend." He put his hands on her hips. "Do you know how I feel about you? I can't believe it's only been this short of time and already you're a major part of my life."

She turned to face him, "It is insane, and I feel the same way."

Now he stroked her cheek, "Do you? Because I'm falling for you." He kissed her forehead.

She placed her hand on his chest. "Me too," she whispered.

"I understand that you have work things." As he spoke, she moved out of the bathroom and retrieved her clothes. "I get selfish and think only about my schedule."

Paige was buttoning a pair of skinny, khaki cotton slacks, "No, it's okay. This is only one weekend apart."

Jack brought her mug out of the bathroom and placed it on the table beside the bed. "I know, I'll just be so lonely."

Now she pulled on a loose white tee, rolling the sleeves and knotting it at the waist, "I only have to go to work on Monday after graduation and then I'm done." Across the chest of her shirt was the insignia of KISS.

Paige was pulling the back of her hair out of the collar when Jack nearly shouted, "What the fuck is that?" he was pointing at her shirt.

She shrugged, "It's my shirt."

"KISS? Why not Jack Corey?" he truly looked offended.

"It's vintage." She gave him a teasing look, "Besides, I don't have a Jack Corey shirt."

He strode across the room and grabbed his cell, "Well I can take care of that." Before she could protest, Jack was barking orders to someone. When he quit the call, he returned to her. "Take that one off," he reached for the hem of her shirt.

Paige playfully batted his hands away, "Stop it. I don't need another shirt."

There was a knock on the door, a roadie stood on the other side, holding out a T-shirt. Jack grabbed it making a gesture toward Paige, "My girl thinks she can strut around in my hotel room in a KISS shirt." His voice was unusually arrogant. The roadie laughed as he shut the door. Jack tossed the t-shirt to Paige.

She picked up the shirt. Standing still and taking a deep breath, Paige gathered her words. "Jack, what's going on today? At first, you're upset with me because I can't be with you next weekend. The next moment you profess that you're falling for me. Then, you have an outright tantrum about my t-shirt. I spend my days with teenager, I don't need you acting like one." Paige crossed her arms.

Jack was speechless . Just when she thought he would leave the room, he broke into a grin. "Sweetheart, this is exactly why I need you around. You keep me in my place." He came to her and lightly placed his hand on her jawline, "I sincerely apologize for my spoiled behavior." He kissed her, "You can damn well wear whatever you want; your choices and obligations are just as important as mine."

Chapter 10

Findlay, Ohio

Monday afternoon, she was back in her classroom. Her Art I students were drawing their hands as their final exam. Three junior boys were taking the class to get a fine arts credit. They were tracing their hands and using colored pencils to create elementary school hand-turkeys. Across the room, one sophomore boy was using charcoal to draw a hand that looked so real it appeared to be reaching off the page. Two freshman girls were having a lively discussion on what color of nail polish to add to their own hand drawings.

Paige was sketching hands too, she had begun this drawing on Sunday morning. After they had made up from their quarrel, Jack had picked up his guitar. He explained that he was working on a new song, and an idea for a bridge had hit him. For forty minutes he played, unaware of his surroundings. She had dug out her sketch pad.

The hands she drew were a pair of strong, narrow hands plucking on guitar strings. One of the turkey artists got up and walked behind her, checking the supply shelf for feathers. He glanced over her shoulder at her picture, “Sweet, Mrs. B.”

One for the girls squealed, “Let me see!”

Reluctantly, Paige lifted her drawing to show the class. The girl’s friend said, “Is that your boyfriend?” When the other girl questioned her, she announced to the room, “My aunt saw Mrs. B with some old singer at a bar last week.” As the entire class swung their heads in her direction, Paige thought now she knew who had complained to Mr. Dickerson.

Gluing feathers to his paper, the junior boy asked, “What old singer?”

Paige opened her mouth to end the discussion when the girl spit out, “Jack somebody, Gary or Carey.”

“Corey?” the talented charcoal artist looked at his teacher, impressed, “Jack Corey is my dad’s favorite. We listen to his music all the time.”

Mr. Turkey feathers whipped out his phone, “Jack Corey.”

“No phones in class,” Paige intoned, preparing to rise from her high stool perched in front of her desk.

“Here he is,” the boy said and pleaded, “Just for a minute.” In an instant, the class circled around the tiny screen as YouTube showed the video of *Swept Away* by the Jack Corey band.

As the second verse began, Paige stood in front of the group, “That’s enough. Put it away. You have ten minutes to finish your exam.”

“He’s cute!” said the girl now coloring her drawn nails with a fuchsia marker. Paige glanced at the calendar; only four more days of classes.

Yesterday afternoon, they'd done a little shopping. Both had bought a few items of clothing at a mall. It embarrassed Paige when he insisted on buying her things.

They'd gone back to the room. Paige needed to head home, it was a three-hour drive. They took a nap and then packed their clothes. The next show was in Portland on Wednesday. The buses had left. Jack would fly home to New York. As they kissed at the parking lot, he said in a serious tone, "You're really coming with me?"

Paige decided his insecurity might be the thing that would take the most getting used to.

***

After school, she texted Laurel. *Help, I've lost my mind!*

Over a sexy rock star?

Paige laughed out loud, *Yes.*

The women met at Riverside Park. Paige had too much nervous energy to sit and talk. Together they followed the path along the Blanchard River. Tulips and daffodils surrounded the base of trees adorned in new green leaves. Ducks swam at the shore, eager for handouts. They'd not gone over twenty feet when Paige blurted out, "He asked me to go on the tour with him this summer."

Laurel stopped in her tracks, "He what?"

Paige kept walking and her friend scurried to catch her, then grabbed her elbow, "You mean for the entire summer?"

"Yes, he said it would be better than what I'm doing now, heading out every weekend."

"You'll see him again this weekend?"

"No, it's graduation," Paige waved her hand dismissively.

They walked in silence for a moment. “So, when school is out, you would join him somewhere, then what?”

“Jack said we would ride the tour bus with the rest of the group to the concert venues. We would explore the different cities we visit. During breaks, we could come here or to his place in New York.”

“You’d go hang out at Jack Corey’s New York apartment? And, you’d travel on the Jack Corey band’s tour bus.”

Paige squeezed her temples and groaned, “I know it’s insane. If I was 21, it would be a dream come true. I’m far from that, it’s absurd to consider.”

They headed past the playground. Children on swings and climbing jungle gyms squealed. Mothers clustered on nearby benches. “Paige, do you want to go with him?”

She took a deep breath, “I would love to.” Her smile radiated her face. “We have the best time together. We never run out of things to talk about.” Now she frowned, “What if it’s a disaster? He feels cramped or I feel like an intruder. Or we just don’t get along?”

Laurel draped her arm around her friend’s shoulders, “Then you come home. So, what?”

Paige rested her head on Laurel’s shoulder, “Have I lost my mind?”

“Sweetie, if you could see your face when you talk about him, you’d know. He obviously feels the same about you. You two deserve to try it.”

Paige hugged her, “Thank you. I really want to do this. As you said, if it doesn’t work out, I can always come home.”

***

Jack tossed his bag on the floor at the front door. His apartment had the scent of a place rarely used. He didn't know when the cleaning service had last been here. He could handle dust. Now here he was for just a few days.

Striding into the kitchen and pulling out a bottle of water, Jack slammed the steel door with irritation. He didn't even want to head to the weekend event. Paige wasn't coming. It would be dull without her. He twisted the cap off the bottle and took a long drink. When had he needed someone around to make touring fun?

Back in the living room, he sat on the couch and picked up the remote. Before a show even came on screen, he turned it back off. Next, he walked to his baby grand, his long fingers glided along the keys. He had no desire to sit and play. What was wrong with him?

The sun shone through the glass doors in the back. Jack went into his bedroom, intentionally avoiding the bed he would climb in alone tonight. Instead, he went to the room-sized closet and found swim trunks. He pulled off his jeans and changed.

Out on the patio, he found cold IPA in the fridge behind the bar. After twisting off the cap and taking a first long draw, Jack turned on the sound system. He turned to 70s classic rock and moved toward the pool. A dip of his toe showed it was properly heated. Jack stepped gingerly in, making certain that his beer didn't spill. Soon, he leaned against the side, his beer on the ledge. The surrounding outdoor speakers filled his space with the sound of Eric Clapton's voice.

This was perfect. He let the warm water relax his muscles. This morning he'd checked out of the hotel before hitting the workout room. Sitting for a few hours in cabs and the plane, he felt stiff. The water helped, but as the warmth spread across his lower half, Jack considered the other muscle workouts he'd been enjoying lately. Damn.

Frequent sex was not something he'd allowed himself to take part in for the last few years. He hadn't been in a relationship and the options of partners came with consequences. Even though his last hit record was 18 years ago, Jack was still Jack Corey. If he was seen in public with a woman, someone on social media would notice, or he'd make the pages of tabloid magazines. Returning to the tour life offered lots of opportunities for sex, but Jack avoided it. When this tour kicked off, they were all so excited after those first few shows. He would have loved to take a woman back to the hotel and work off some of that adrenaline. Prospects were readily available; the band still had groupies that showed up at shows, and there were also local women there who would be thrilled to go to bed with him.

After the second show, in Detroit, he nearly went home with a news anchor. Jack was glad he didn't when he flipped on the news in the hotel and there she was. He was no longer interested in anything that resembled a conquest. Meeting Paige that night in Ohio was entirely something else. Jack had spotted her on the steps with a glass of wine in her hand, long booted legs stretched out in front of her; watching the party like a movie. She drew him to her like a magnet. When he sat down beside her, Jack knew it would be something different. Paige hadn't even attempted to flirt with him, at least not until he first flirted with her.

Now the song switched to Bad Company singing *Feel Like Makin' Love*. Jack groaned aloud this was not helping. He lifted himself out of the pool and forwarded to the next song. *Freebird* was a much better choice, but his mood was darker. Why did he do this?

The beer was empty, so Jack got out of the water to get another. The air had cooled down; he decided he was done at the pool. On the shelf next to the bar were stacks of plush white towels. Jack dried off, then wrapped one around his torso. As he stepped back into the apartment, he heard his phone ding.

He had to dry his damp fingers again to swipe the phone open. It was from Paige.

Jack considered what day it was, Tuesday. She should be home tonight. *Hi, Jack.*

Hey, he wanted to hold on to his irritation.

Is this a bad time?

Jack wanted to say, how could it be, I'm all alone. He really was a selfish bastard. *Nope.*

Good. Are you home? How was your flight?

Yep, it was fine. What are you doing?

Laurel just left. She wants to have a double date.

So, she wasn't walking away. Jack shook his head. When had she said she was? He smiled at the thought of a double date in Ohio. It sounded irrationally charming. *And where do you guys go on a double date?*

Usually out for drinks and dinner.

Have you double-dated with Laurel often?

Well, when I was married, we did. But we all eventually disliked Kurt. Then she fixed me up with some disastrous blind dates.

Jack ignored the annoyance of her ex-husband's name. *And why were they a disaster?*

I'm pretty picky.

How did I make the cut?

Jack, please. The question is, how did I?

He smiled, she was saying exactly what he needed to hear. *Can I call you and tell you?*

Please.

Chapter 11

Portland, Oregon

Annabeth watched Jack, it was unusual for him to be in the back of the bus, gaming with the guys. This was obvious because they were all soundly destroying him, and the ribbing was obnoxious. She had only gone back there hoping to get time with him. They were just beginning a conversation about the band's first album. She knew there had been a scandal with a previous roadie. Because Paige was gone this weekend, Annabeth was hoping to monopolize Jack's free time. Soon the couple would be together full time, how was she going to get her book written?

She stood at the door and waited for an opening to speak to him. From behind, she felt a hand reach under her shirt and gently stroke her back. The warm fingers sent shivers throughout her body. Dammit, Trent! Annabeth arched her back as she turned away from him. The move put them face to face in the narrow opening. Trent grinned, "Are my fingers cold?"

"Don't!" Annabeth hissed.

As she attempted to move past him, he leaned down so that his lips were against her cheek. “Ah come on darling, we’ve got a long weekend ahead of us.”

She wanted to make a snide remark. She knew she should shut this down. At the same time, she felt his rough cheek against hers and his fingers had found their way back into her shirt. Annabeth sighed, “You bastard,” then followed him to his bunk.

***

The Jack Corey band milled around the green room of the Roseland Theater. Tonight’s spread resembled the band’s normal requested selection; fresh fruit and vegetables, cold sliced turkey and chicken, whole grain bread, protein and granola bars. The youngest member was 42 and the oldest 54, it was vital they nourish their bodies before a performance. These were the foods that would energize their performance, not sugar and heavy carbs. The majority drank water or sports drinks. They reserved alcohol for after the show. Even weed could enhance sleepiness, not good for a concert. Jack was popping large grapes into his mouth, looking at his phone. Annabeth saw the frown on his face. She picked up a water bottle and placed it on the table in front of him, “Is Paige busy?”

After a nod of thanks for the drink, Jack opened the bottle, “She’s texting me.”

“Oh, from the scowl on your face, I figured she was ignoring you.”

He sat the bottle down, “She’s at some teacher party for the end of the year.”

Before Annabeth could respond, Tony headed over, “Some VIPs want to take us out after the show.”

Jack powered down his phone, and stuck it in his jeans pocket, "Why not."

***

Three hours later, the band was making its way out of the theater. The roadies were still hard at work loading all the equipment into the semis that traveled with the tour bus. Annabeth watched as Tony and Jack were ushered into the backseat of a white BMW. She'd wanted an invitation, more story fodder. Trent walked up to her. "Joe, Jed and I are going down the street. There's a dive bar with billiards. You play pool?"

Annabeth didn't even attempt to fight her conscience. "I'll beat you, Trent. I guarantee it."

He guffawed, "Let's see how good you are after a few shots."

***

When his phone lit up on the table in front of him, he saw it was 11:15. Jack stifled a yawn. He was tired and a bit drunk. There were two men and a woman with him, executives of the local bank that had sponsored the show. They'd brought them down to show off the bar in the city's new luxury hotel. It was nice, lots of blue light raced around the bar. A sexy atmosphere.

This thought irritated Jack. If Paige was here, they'd be wishing these people a good night and headed up to their room. Her text had just said, *Miss you.* His angry thought was, "Really, then be here." He didn't respond.

The man on his right, a beefy guy with a shaved head handed Jack a drink. "This is the best bourbon in town." Jack had had enough, more than usual. Still, he smiled and took the glass. It burnt going down, but he swallowed most of it. The man slapped him on the back, "I knew drinking with Jack Corey would be awesome."

The woman next to him looked to be about ten years younger than Jack. She'd obviously put a lot into her appearance tonight, in her black sleek pants, and black top underneath a jean jacket meant to look vintage. Now with a nervous expression, she faced him, "Would you take a selfie with me? My sister will just die."

"Sure," he agreed. She leaped from her chair and stood next to him. He leaned his face near hers, she snapped the photo.

"One more?" This time she got up enough courage to press her head next to his. Jack rewarded her with his killer grin. She was so pleased that she stumbled walking back to her seat.

The last drink had pushed the limits. Jack felt his eyelids drooping. He gave Tony a look that years of partnership gave his manager the signal; it was time to go. Tony got his phone out, a car was on the way. They said their goodbyes. The woman's phone snapped pictures until they were out of sight.

***

The ceiling was too close to his bunk; it spun. Jack was trying to fall asleep. The bus was moving, and though that was usually sleep-inducing, not tonight. Tomorrow's headache would be a killer. He pressed Paige's number. Her voice, when she answered, was thick with sleep. "You're still up?"

"I just got back, now we're on the road. You're in bed?"

"Jack, it's after midnight and I have to work tomorrow." Paige seemed to wake up. Now her voice was kinder, "How was the show?"

"Fine, good, boring," he was sulking.

"Your shows are never boring. What was the best song?" This was a game they played when she attended a show. He'd tell her which song they'd performed best.

"I don't know." As inebriated as he was, Jack knew he sounded childish, but he didn't care. "Probably *Go Away.*" He said this pointedly.

Paige sighed, "You sound like you've been drinking."

"Yeah, I went out," he responded like a defensive teenager.

"Why don't you call me tomorrow? If you're up before seven thirty call, otherwise we can text. Get some sleep, Jack and drink lots of water."

"This whole night sucked. I like you here with me."

The paper-thin walls offered no privacy. Trent pounded on it, "Quit whining, you pussy."

On the other side of Trent's wall came another knock, "You stop screwing Annabeth on the bus. And Jack, get the hell off the phone, I'm trying to sleep!" this was Jed.

Paige heard the exchange, "Jack, good night. Go to sleep." She didn't wait for his response. He tossed his phone across the small space. It banged against the TV.

Chapter 12

Findlay, Ohio

Paige was up before her alarm, this was surprising considering the party had lasted until eleven and then Jack's call at midnight. After a quick shower, she pulled on shorts and a T-shirt. Today with students gone, she would spend her hours scrubbing the art room. It was a long and arduous job. With that thought, she pulled her largest travel mug from the cupboard. This would be a heavy coffee day.

Bread popped from the toaster. As she sat at the counter, her focus was on social media. A new habit was to check out Jack Corey mentions on Twitter and Instagram. After the Put in Bay incident, she'd gotten her own account. There he was, a selfie with some woman. He was giving his best smile, but his eyes looked intoxicated. So, he'd practically accused her of abandoning him, but not sat alone on the tour bus. Nice, Jack. Her thoughts of him apparently brought him to her. Her phone buzzed in a call.

"Hello," Paige's tone was neutral.

"Hi, Paige," she loved to hear him say her name.

"How are you this morning?"

Jack groaned, "Miserable, and I deserve to be." Though his voice was rough from too much to drink, she found it sexy. "Did I act like an idiot last night?"

Her smile showed in her voice, "No, I liked you saying you missed me."

"I did, I do."

"Twitter and Instagram disagree," Paige stated dryly.

"The banking woman already posted her selfie? Tony and I went out with three sponsors."

"There's also a shot of you walking away."

"Shit."

"Can't blame her for staring at one of your finer points."

Now Jack groaned again, "When will I see you again?"

Paige was grabbing her purse and coffee, then reaching up to a hook by the door for her keys. "Don't start, I've got to get to work. Can we have a long talk this afternoon? I have a ton of questions about packing."

"That makes me feel better, packing to be with me. I'll call you this afternoon."

"Good. Go back to sleep, Jack."

***

Hannah had the day off and agreed to meet her mom at a shopping center midway between their cities. Levis Common was in Perrysburg. The mother and daughter hugged in the parking lot. "Should we eat or shop first?"

Hannah glanced at her smartwatch, "It's early. Do you have shopping to do?"

"Yes, I need clothes." They walked toward *White House/Black Market.*

"Big event?"

"Maybe a few." As they spoke, the women walked in the shop each looking at clothes. They moved around, near each other.

"Are you going on vacation?" Hanna watched her mother pull out a dress and seemed to notice her for the first time. She scrutinized Paige's outfit; slim white ankle jeans and a royal blue off the shoulder peasant top. "Mom, that's gorgeous. Since when do you wear anything off the shoulder?"

Paige straightened her top and smiled, "Thank you, I got it last weekend"

Her daughter raised an eyebrow, "With Jack?" She put an emphasis on his name.

Paige sighed and turned back to the dresses, "Yes, we shopped."

"Did he buy you that outfit?"

"Uh-huh, he got things for himself and insisted on paying for me too."

Hannah watched as her mother picked up a slim black cold shoulder dress, cut above the knee and held it against herself. "Where exactly is this vacation?" To her continued surprise, Paige added a short white beaded dress and a black halter jumpsuit. "Are you still seeing him?" Her voice was accusatory.

A saleswoman appeared, "Can I put those in a dressing room?"

Paige gladly handed the items over, "Thank you." Now she was looking at a sequined knit tank.

Hannah grabbed her mom's arm, forcing Paige to look at her. "Mom, for real, are you going to travel with the band?"

"Yes, some," Paige laid a wine colored sleeveless floral blouse on top of the tank. Skirting around her daughter, she chose a couple pairs of skinny jeans. The saleswoman was back once again relieving her of the apparel. "I'm ready to try it all on." She followed the woman to the dressing room. Hannah hadn't spoken again but trailed close behind. "Come in and help me pick."

Her daughter sat on the stool in the dressing room. "You're 48 years old and you're going to follow a rock band around the country?"

"Keep your voice down," Paige's own voice was harsh. As she pulled the black dress over her head, she continued, "Jack is fifty, I'm not some cougar. And, I'm not following him around, I'll be with him."

Hannah was busy on her phone, she turned the screen toward her mother, "This man?" She'd Googled his name and an album cover came up. "This man wants you to spend the summer with him?"

This offended Paige. She grabbed her own phone from her purse. Opening the photos, she found the one on the letters in front of The Rock-and-Roll Hall of Fame. Now she stuck it in her daughter's face, "This man."

Hannah took the phone and looked at the photo. She slid to see the others taken on that day and more from last weekend. "Mom, I'm sorry." when she looked up her eyes were shiny. "This is, I mean, you guys are a couple."

Paige turned toward the mirror, her own eyes bright. She focused on the black dress, smoothing it down.

"Damn Mama, you look hot in that!"

Paige burst out laughing, "Oh, stop!

"I mean it!"

She bought the black dress, the jumpsuit, both tops and a few pairs of jeans. They went to Basil Pizza and Wine bar where they shared a veggie pizza and a bottle of wine. Paige could finally tell her daughter about Jack. Hannah really listened. She reassured her that if the tour and their time together didn't work out, she could always come home.

At their cars, they hugged. "I love you, baby girl. Thanks for understanding."

"I love you too, Mom. I'm sorry that I've been so nasty." As Hannah unlocked her car, she spoke again, "Maybe Kyle and I can come to a show."

"I would love it! Yes!" She was about to get in her car, when she called out to her daughter. "I forgot, I have one problem."

Hannah paused, waiting to hear.

"Elliott."

Her daughter nodded, "Its time I took my cat back. He shouldn't be alone at your house." She considered a moment, "I can come and get him Wednesday."

"I'll be gone, but I'll make sure he's fine alone for a day."

Chapter 13

Baltimore, Maryland

Jack was bouncing around the bus. His usually mellow self on show mornings was absent. He was humming and chopping up vegetables when Tony appeared in the kitchenette. “Must you drink that crap every morning? It smells.” When they were on the bus, Jack made himself smoothies and avoided carbs and caffeine.

His lead guitarist and vocalist slapped him on the back and laughed, “You’d be smart to follow suit, old man. If you’re going to try merry matrimony again with your singer in Chicago, you may need something that gives energy.”

“Well, maybe next time I see her, I’ll have you make me one,” Tony pulled a box of cereal off the shelf.

Jack was whistling again.

“Okay, what’s up?” Tony stopped what he was doing and looked at him.

“I’m just glad to be in Baltimore. Big day.”

“Really this show? I’m surprised.”

“No, Paige arrives today.”

Tony frowned slightly, "She's coming back again. Another round with the star?"

The smile slid off Jack's face, "Don't be crude. Paige is coming to travel with us for the summer."

The slight frown turned into a scowl. "The whole summer? That will be a lot of distraction."

"I need the distraction. I know my music, what else am I going to do in my free time?"

***

Climbing out of the SUV, Paige saw Jack on stage. This was an outdoor venue. The stage opened out onto a concrete pit, followed by a platform of VIP tables that then led to tiers of open lawn. The driver who picked her up at the airport pulled in near the left side of the stage. The crew was completing the maze of cords. Jack had his guitar strapped on his shoulder, helping with the soundcheck.

Her driver said he had instructions to take her to this spot then drop her things off at the tour bus. Brooklyn, Jack's assistant, would put things where they belonged. He'd requested that she come right to the stage. Carla, one of the stage managers who traveled with the band, approached. "Hey Paige, welcome to the tour." Her familiar face and happy greeting did a world of good for Paige. This was the first time she'd gone directly to the show. She was feeling awkward about "moving in" to the bus. Carla had a lanyard with several laminated cards attached. "These are your identity. Protect them. We will add a new one at each show. This is your permanent ID as part of the band and a resident of the bus." She held up another one, "This one identifies you at hotels as

Jack's," here she stumbled, then laughed, "partner, roommate, whatever."

The physical proof of each of these caused Paige to shake a bit as she took the lanyard and placed it around her neck. "Thank you, Carla."

"You can go right up to the steps. You'll be near the stage."

Paige needed the support of the banister as she moved up. Her nerves were still jangled. A few roadies said hello. Tony was working with the sound engineer at the boards. His nod was curt. Did he not approve of her presence? Looking toward the stage, she made eye contact with Jack.

He broke into a smile and removed his guitar. A nearby crew member took it. In a few quick steps, he was in front of Paige. Jack put his arms around her waist, "You're here."

The stress melted away. He was all that mattered. She'd learn to adjust to the rest. "I am." They kissed.

"We'll have the best time," Jack kissed her again.

Tony spoke into the system, "Let's get this setup done. It's time to be offstage."

Jack looked torn for a moment. Paige patted his chest, "Get done what you need."

"Is your stuff on the bus?"

"The driver took it. I didn't see where."

"Brooklyn will get you settled in." At the shake of her head in protest, he added, "It's her job."

Just then Keely walked up, "I'll take Paige to the bus."

Jack gave her a hard squeeze and jogged back to the stage. Keely led Paige to the back of the private lot. "I'm so glad you're here."

***

The VIP section was a collection of outdoor high-top tables. The venue offered Paige and Keely a seat at the one which was front and center. They sat with a morning DJ at the local rock station, the entertainment reporter of the local news affiliate and two adult sisters who won the seats on a radio contest. Keely had forewarned Paige to not be specific what her relationship to the band was.

She had worn her new jeans and beaded tank tonight. The weather was comfortable, in the low 70s. Keely wore her typical black spandex dress and stacked stilettos. The section had a server. Paige was drinking lemonade and blueberry vodka, a delight that the prize winners told her was the best drink ever. Keely stuck with Corona.

***

With the first lick of his Gibson electric, Jack brought fire to the stage. His chord was recognizable as the opening to *Find Me*, one of his most popular hits. Paige watched, enthralled. Not only was she able to see the expanse of the band on stage from this angle, but she could see Jack displayed on the jumbo screen over the stage.

She saw his smile as he faced the audience. They roared at his expression, loving him as much as he loved playing his music for them. Trent thumped the bass and their bodies swayed to the deep rhythm. It was a treat watching those crowded into the pit in front of the stage, immediately raise their arms in motion.

When Jack put his mouth up to the mike and belted out the first lyrics, "*The night I left, disappeared in the dark. I swore I'd never come back*," the fans screamed and applauded. Paige clapped too.

From the screen, she could see Jack's eyes light up. He still relished the moment when he remembered that millions of people loved his music. After the first chorus, he launched into his guitar solo. The guitar angled higher than his elbow, his fingers sliding across the strings, his other hand picking out each perfectly matched chord. Jed stepped to him, they stood together, a harmony of spirited guitar sound. Then, he was back in front of the mike, "If you want me, find me." The audience chanted *Find Me* with the rest of the band as back up. Then Jack was in front of the audience making magic with his guitar. After the final words "Find me!" left his lips, he tossed his pick into the pit. There was a scramble to get it.

Jack's guitar man crossed the stage, holding his acoustic. They traded guitars. Jack pulled a fresh pick out of his jeans pocket. Joe started a rhythm on the drum, signaling to the audience they were slowing things down. The next song would be *Indigo Sky*, it had been the theme song for a smash hit romance movie in the late 80s. Jack yelled to the audience as he lightly strummed his acoustic, "Hello Baltimore." The audience yelled a greeting back as if it were a conversation. "Thanks for the beautiful weather tonight." His fingers played the introduction and Jack began to sing.

From her vantage point, and on the big screen, Paige watched him. Her insides tingled as his mouth formed the first words of the love ballad. She knew she'd listened to, sang along with, watched the video and even other live performance of the Jack Corey band performing this song. Tonight, was special, this beautiful man and music genius was on stage, his face projected in giant proportions to thousands of people spread out on the lawn behind her, and when he finished the show, they would begin a summer together. When he climbed into his bunk on that luxury tour bus to head to another show, Paige would climb into his bed with him. She wanted to pinch herself, how had this happened? They were now into the chorus; the audience did a slow sway; they raised cell phones in the air like candles. Paige put her hand to her heart, she was the luckiest woman alive.

Later, as the band moved off, preparing for their encore, Carla appeared to escort Paige and Keely backstage. The sisters' eyes widened, "Are you with the band?"

Paige offered a mysterious smile and thanked the table for allowing them to sit there.

***

Jack bowed to the audience, feeling the satisfaction he always did at the conclusion of a show. The venue allowed him to shake hands and lean down for a selfie or two. Now as he turned to head off the stage, his heart swelled. There on the side stood Paige. She looked hot in tight jeans and a black tank that had shiny bits picked up by the spotlight. She was here with him. He ran off the stage and she flew into his arms. "This is the beginning of a great summer."

"I agree."

The crew was already hard at work; they were packing up tonight and heading straight for Philadelphia. They would make the less than two-hour trip then park and sleep at the venue there.

Someone set the green room up for the after-show meal. The guys were hungry and ready for some carbs now that the performance was complete. Pizzas, sandwiches and pasta dishes were spread on the table next to chicken wings. They replaced the healthy drinks with alcohol bottles, soda, and the ever-present water. Jack fixed himself a large plate of Alfredo penne topped with chicken and a glass of his favorite Cabernet. Though Paige had had two vodka drinks during the concert, she also had a glass of wine. She went for a slice of veggie pizza. Tonight's show had satisfied everyone. Tony was the only one still in work mode. He bustled into the room and headed straight for Jack. He was eager to discuss the ticket sales and plans for tomorrow.

Jack sipped his wine and held up a hand, "Tony buddy, we have the morning to discuss. We'll be in Philly early." He reached across the table and entwined his fingers with Paige's. "Tonight is all about us, she's here for the duration of the summer."

Tony closed his laptop and sat it on the table, none too gently. "Well, okay. I guess I'll get food." She noticed Jack was oblivious to Tony's mood or didn't care. They finished their food and headed to the bus.

By now the back lot was largely cleared out. The roadies were still packing the trucks. They parked their own bus behind the band bus. It was a single-story unit, not the double-decker luxury vehicle that Paige had stepped into this afternoon. She climbed aboard Jack's bus. Brooklyn had stowed her things into the junk bunk below his sleeping bunk. Keely told her that in some bands the lead would demand a full-sized bedroom at the back of the second story. Jack allowed that space to be the lounge area. Other than nights like this when they needed to get on the road for a long journey and a concert the next day, they would stay in hotels.

A few of the band members were already on the bus. Some were relaxing on the first floor, seated in the overstuffed seats, watching tv. Jack had taken a shower at the venue in the dressing room. Paige knew she wouldn't get one in the morning. Not the way she wanted the first morning to go, but Gina had warned her. She grabbed her bag of necessaries off the junk bunk and stepped into the tiny bathroom to brush her teeth and take off her makeup. When she got back into the bunk area, Jack had sprawled onto the bed.

The idea of anything happening between them tonight embarrassed Paige. What did he expect? She could see that beneath the sheet, he didn't have a shirt on. Was he naked? Jack seemed to read her expression and laughed. "It will kill me, but I'm not hoping to do what I want to do. Do you have something to sleep in?"

She flushed, but appreciated his candor, "Yes, let me grab it and change." A moment later she was once again back from the bathroom, this time in shorts and a tank.

He pulled the sheet back, and Paige appreciated the glimpse of his black boxer briefs. "Think we can squeeze in here together?"

"It will be like college," she climbed next to him and they lay side by side facing one another.

"So, you spent a lot of time sharing a dorm bunk?" He grinned.

"I won't ask you how many women have been in this spot with you, and you won't ask me about college." They laughed and faced one another.

"This will be fun." He kissed her softly, his hand running under her tank.

"I hope so, I'm a little nervous."

Jack removed his hand from her ribs and instead pushed her hair off her face gently, "It will all be fine. If I'm doing anything that's annoying; tell me. If you have questions, ask."

"Thank you." They could hear movement outside of the curtain they had pulled across their bunk for privacy. Others shuffled in, the sounds of shoes and clothing being removed, the movement as others climbed into their bunks. The small televisions in each bunk turned on, momentarily with sound then silenced as they attached headphones. Soon it was quiet. The lights went out, all was dark.

Paige was convinced that she'd never sleep. She was glad she'd had a few drinks to relax her. When the bus moved it lulled her to sleep.

***

Life on the bus was alien to anything Paige had done before. She'd lived alone in a house for four years. The only schedule was hers. Everything in the house was hers. Every decision, from what lights were on to furniture placement, was hers. Living quarters on the bus were reminiscent of college life except no one was nineteen. Not only were they older, but most were affluent and accustomed to a life of luxury. They crammed the tiny kitchen space with food and beverages. Each member demanded different bottled water. There was an espresso machine that looked like a high-tech robot squeezed in next to a standard coffee maker. The fridge held every kind of milk but cows. They labeled containers of food with people's names. Large amounts of fruits, vegetables and protein powders for smoothies filled the space along with three smoothie machines.

Paige had to laugh at the large boxes of children's sugar cereal squeezed between granola and steel-cut oats. Jack had explained those belonged to Keely and Joe. He was adding kale to the other ingredients in his blender. "Joe thinks he's a kid like her."

"She's twenty-six, Jack." The noise of the fruits and vegetables being reduced to green liquid halted their conversation. When it was complete, he poured it into a tall travel mug. "Do you want some?"

Paige eyed it skeptically, "I will stick to my coffee and breakfast bar."

After the first gulp, he smacked his lips, "I'll convert you yet." He pulled her close for a kiss, "Doesn't that taste delicious?"

She licked her own lips, "Strawberry flavored Jack?"

He raised his eyebrows, "Gives me a few ideas."

Paige laughed and filled a mug with coffee. Peering into the fridge, she asked, "Is it okay if I use some of this soy creamer?"

"Go ahead," it was Tony. "Is there coffee left for me?"

Paige reached for another mug, once it was full, she handed it to him with the creamer.

"Look at you two sharing a caffeine-induced heart rate."

"Neither of us wants to drink a liquid salad." Paige took a swallow of coffee.

Tony grinned, "Careful, I might like you yet."

By this time, Jack had moved to the leather couch. His smoothie finished, he picked up his guitar. Paige sat next to him, enjoying the personal performance. Tony sat across from them.

More than a half hour passed. Jack was in the zone. Paige returned to their bunk to retrieve her bag. Once again next to him, she pulled out a sketchbook and pencils. Next, she opened her phone to a photo. It was of a small boy and a Labrador pup. The puppy was lying on his feet, the boy's shoestring in its mouth. She began a rough sketch. As she worked on the curl falling across the boy's forehead, Jack leaned over and peeked at the paper. "What's that?"

Paige was in her own zone, "It's a commissioned piece, I'm doing."

He took her phone and looked from the photo to the page. "People hire you to do this?"

"Yes." This interested Tony. He got up next to Jack to see.

"You're good."

"Thanks."

"I mean, I knew you were an art teacher, but not an artist."

Paige looked up at him, humor in his eyes, "It's kind of the same thing."

"Is it?"

Jack laughed, "Isn't that like saying you play guitar but you're not a musician?" He turned back to Paige, "That's amazing. How long does it take you to complete one?"

She shrugged, "If I put a lot of time in, I'm usually done in a week."

"Do you make good money for this?" Tony was back on his side of the bus.

"A fair amount."

"Isn't there an app that will do that?"

"Nice, Tony," Jack chided him.

"No, it's okay," Paige closed her sketchbook. "There are some who do something similar with an app, but people like a personal touch."

Annabeth came from the back of the bus. "Is there more coffee?"

Paige hadn't seen her since that night in the hotel when she'd been in Trent's room. Without responding to the other woman, she got up and headed to the kitchen.

Unaware of her feelings, Annabeth followed, "You don't need to make more Paige. Thanks."

"I wanted some too," Paige kept her face on the task at hand.

Holding a mug, Annabeth turned to Jack, "If you have time today, I was hoping we could discuss your first arena shows." She sat down where Paige had been.

Paige saw and sat next to Tony. She put on her headphones, aware that Annabeth had retrieved her materials for recording and taking notes. Now she returned to her drawing. The two across the way were too distracting. She wanted to just listen to him discuss his past but felt she was invading. Finally, she packed up her things and moved to the top of the bus. She found Keely lounging in front of a giant television screen watching *Housewives of Beverly Hills.* Paige sat next to her. Keely looked over, "Bored with Jack already?"

"He's working with Annabeth. I didn't want to interrupt." Trent was sitting nearby, looking at his phone. "Will Gina be joining us soon?"

"She'll meet us in Denver and stay with us for all the west coast, she loves that area. Her mom stays at the house with the kids. They're teenagers now, but that can be even worse."

Paige chuckled, they shared a commonality, "I remember." She would be happy to have Gina with them. She liked her so much. They'd talked more than once since they'd met. Gina was a wealth of information about packing and life on the bus. Paige wanted her here not only as a friend, but to keep Trent from Annabeth.

***

After the interview, Annabeth moved to a table a few rows behind Jack. She tried not to contemplate her own foolish actions last night. Trent had decided that when the opportunity was there, they were a hookup item. A few drinks and the exhilaration of watching them on stage seemed to prevent her from having any resistance to his assumptions and crude advances. Paige was cold to her this morning. She knew when Paige and Gina had been together; they seemed to be friends. Was Paige aware? Probably. Perhaps Jack had complained. He said nothing to Annabeth about disapproving, but maybe he's said as much to Paige. The woman's approval wasn't necessarily important unless it had a direct effect on her relationship with Jack. As time passed, she felt this would be a decent piece of writing, she couldn't afford to have that halted because his girlfriend didn't want Annabeth around Trent. It was one more reason to stay away from him.

As Annabeth sipped the latest cup of coffee, she frowned, not because of the bitter liquid but because she knew her willpower was shamefully weak.

Chapter 14

Philadelphia, Pennsylvania

The next night was like the first. Paige had spent the rest of the morning watching a movie with Keely. They arrived in Philadelphia around lunch. The bus dropped the band off at the hotel and those staying in rooms had their bags and larger luggage from underneath the bus taken to their rooms. This gave the members a chance to sort through their clothes and repack the tote they kept with them. This also gave them time to have an assistant get the laundry done. The jobs of assistants proved to be a large adjustment for Paige. A single, independent woman who had always lived a middle-class lifestyle disliked ordering anyone around or expecting them to take care of her personal needs.

That day, she discovered Jack was very accustomed to this. It was someone else's job to get their luggage to the right room. Brooklyn or Katerina pressed his outfit for the show. The laundry was done and returned to their hotel room. Before they left the next day, it was packed for them and placed on the bus. If he needed anything, all he had to do was say it and it was purchased; food, toiletries, entertainment things.

***

Paige told him she'd never been to Philadelphia. He promised her that on Sunday, they would do some exploring. They had a few days afterward off. They had not yet decided where they would go each time there was a break in the tour. They would enjoy a normal day like two people in a new relationship who have the day to spend together. They weren't weary travelers or rockers headed to another venue.

Paige thought these things and smiled to herself as she rubbed her bath loofah over her neck and shoulders. The tropic scent of her body wash filled her nose. From the speaker on her phone, she could hear Corrine Bailey Rae telling her to "Just go ahead and let your hair down". She was in a decisively good mood.

The curtain opened, a naked Jack stepped into the shower with her. Paige had the momentary urge to cover herself, but when his body pressed against hers, she forgot about it. "Hello darling," he quipped. "Shall I wash your back for you?" He took the loofah out of her hand and began smooth circles down her spine. She arched like a cat. Once her skin was slick with soap, he pressed his chest against her, his arms around her, and glided close. His mouth was against her ear, "You feel delicious."

Paige turned, so they were facing, "You do too." The water dripped into his face, and she pushed the wet hair off his forehead. They kissed slowly. "Shall I wash you?"

"Yes, please," his voice was low and husky.

***

An hour later they stepped through the hotel revolving door into the Philadelphia sunshine. Today Jack was not a rocker but just another wealthy man exiting a posh hotel. He was wearing khaki shorts and a hunter green shirt. Holding hands with him was Paige in white shorts and an olive-colored flowing top. His sunglasses covered his eyes, he had on a hat. They hoped to blend even though tonight's concert was sold out.

The downtown street was bustling with people. Shops and cafes were in abundance. They snaked passed dog walkers, shoppers and many like themselves looking for a good lunch location. At a stoplight, they waited with a dozen or more people to move to the next block. Jack's phone buzzed, and he lifted his sunglasses up to look at it, then put it back in his pocket. A woman nearby was watching. Paige saw her whisper to her friend, who spoke to another.

The middle woman finally asked, "Are you Jack Corey?"

Paige saw Jack fight the urge to deny it and instead flashed the grin, "Good afternoon, ladies."

There was a stir among the crowd. The brave woman pulled out her phone, "Could we get a picture?"

"That would be fine." They moved near him, struggling to hold the phone out.

Paige intervened, "Let me." She moved a couple of feet away and took a few shots as the women surrounded her boyfriend.

By now the light had changed but a half a dozen more people had chosen not to cross the street. The photo process went on for three more groups. Finally, Jack held up his hand, "It's been great to meet you all, but we're starving. Thank you so much for listening to my music."

The crowd murmured goodbyes and praises for his music. Jack placed his hand on the small of Paige's back and they moved at a rapid pace down the street. For a while, it seemed others were following but only one called out for an autograph. He obliged and then they ducked into a hotel lobby. It wasn't their hotel, which was even better. Jack approached the concierge, pleased to discover that they had a rooftop restaurant. Together they hopped onto the elevator.

They got through the meal before the server finally asked for a picture. Tony called. A local radio station asked for a quick interview and would then play a Jack Corey band four-play to promote the night's show.

Paige went back to the room while he went to the station. She was already looking forward to four immobile walls and privacy. Stretched out on the large bed, she called Hannah.

***

The concert had ended. Jack was just giving Paige their routine hug and kiss when he looked over her shoulder and his eyes lit up. His hands dropped from her waist, and he exclaimed, "Hell no, Tim!"

Paige turned to see a man close to their age, his longish black and grey streaked hair barely covered a diamond stud in his ear. Despite the heat, he was wearing a well-worn leather coat, jeans, and boots. Though she wasn't sure from what band, Paige knew he was a rocker. The two men hugged. Soon they were immersed in guitar talk. Tim said he was admiring the Gibson Custom 59 Les Paul

Standard VOS that Jack had used. Jack took it from the assistant and they both examined it. Paige heard Jack ask if Tim would like to try it. The other man agreed eagerly. They called a roadie to return it and another to stage and leave a couple of amplifiers up.

They were nearly past Paige and headed to the stage when Jack stopped, "Hey babe, I'm just going to jam. I'll be out soon."

After he gave her a quick kiss, Paige responded," No problem. I'll just head back to the hotel."

Carla was walking toward the exit, a case of electronics in her arms. "Hey, I don't know if it's my place to say, but you're new here. Jack could be at this for hours."

"What?"

"Over the years, the equipment truck driver has had to wait for him half the night. Once guitarists like this get playing, they lose all track of time."

Paige started to say that wouldn't happen. It was only her first hotel night with him this time. He'd be done soon. However, she didn't know. Instead, she mustered a small laugh and said, "Thanks for the warning. Do you think I can get a cab from here?"

"Don't worry, I can take care of that. We always get a vehicle for a show to run errands. The buses and trucks stay parked. I'll have someone drive you back."

"No, I really can call a cab."

"Jack would have my ass if you did." With that Carla whistled and one of the younger guys dropped the equipment in his hand and stepped over. She gave him quick orders. Soon he and Paige were on their way to the hotel.

***

It was 2:42 am when Paige woke and looked at her phone. The TV was still on; she was in bed, in her PJs, pillows propped up. She had come back to the room, taken a shower then ordered room service. Apparently, during the *Friends* marathon, she had nodded off. Jack unlocking the door must have roused her because at that moment it swung open.

She had left the bathroom light and one table lamp on. Jack took in the scene and saw her sitting up. "Hey babe," his tone was pleasant. Paige didn't respond as he sat on the couch to remove his boots. Then, he pulled his shirt over his head and strolled into the bathroom. Soon Paige could hear the shower running.

Well, now what? Did she behave like an angry lover and complain about being forgotten? Did she let it go after all he was a star and she was lucky to be with him? Paige climbed out of bed, straightened her flyaway hair, mussed by sleeping. She removed the plate leftover from her snack, still at the end of the bed. In the bathroom, the shower shut off.

The door opened and out walked Jack in just a white hotel towel. Well, the angry lover would not work, her pulse quickened. "Did you miss me?" he grinned, seemingly unaware of how she might be feeling.

Paige turned and headed toward her phone on the nightstand. "Should I have?" She picked it up, scrolling through the screen. "It was nice to have a bit of peace and privacy after all the hours on the bus." As she lay the phone down, music came on. Now she turned to him.

He was moving toward her quickly, "Yes. I was gone for way too long. I'm sorry."

Paige reached down and pulled the towel loose, it fell to the floor. She leaned in and whispered in his ear, "Prove it."

***

Brooklyn and Katarina had come for the larger luggage, it was now late morning, Jack and Paige were checking out of the hotel. As she took the last swig of her coffee, Paige congratulated herself on handling the evening events well. Though she knew she had to come to terms with all that was part of living in Jack's world, she refused to do it as a pushover. What would happen next time the opportunity to "jam" arose or something similar? She didn't know, but she hoped he remembered last night.

Chapter 15

Boston, Massachusetts

Jack was chopping apples when Page appeared from the bunks and headed to the cupboard for a mug. He looked her up and down, "That outfit won't work."

Paige looked at her own jean shorts and printed cotton sleeveless top, "What's wrong with my outfit?"

"You look adorable, but it won't work for our plans." Jack tossed the fruit into his blender and hit the button.

Paige helped herself to coffee, frowning as he gave her a mysterious grin. She then noticed that he was wearing athletic shorts and a t-shirt with the sleeves cut off so far that it revealed a decent portion of his chest. When the machine quieted, she spoke, "I'm not running."

He poured his drink into a tall glass, "I know. Trust me, after breakfast put on something that gives you more movement."

***

A half an hour later, she was pulling on workout shorts and a spandex tank, placing her feet in trainers, when Jack called up to the bunk, "Meet me outside." Paige had kept herself in shape since she had started this relationship, she'd been going to the YMCA to work out as many nights as she could. However, she worried what he might have in mind. His nightly moves across the stage plus the biceps and abs revealed in this morning's shirt had her concerned that he way out of her league.

She heard him head outside and followed suit. He stood with his arms proudly displaying two shining Raleigh Merit bicycles. "I bought us a present."

Paige smiled in relief and circled the bikes, "These are beautiful."

"I asked the salesperson what was best for beginning cyclists, this is what he recommended." Now he pulled a helmet off each handlebar, "He said it's vital we wear these. Growing up as a kid I did crazy things on my bike like jumping over puddles and rolling down gravel roads hands-free and never cracked my skull." He placed the black helmet on his head and buckled the strap, "But at fifty, I guess I'll listen. I don't want to end up in a home because of a bike ride."

Paige was putting hers on too, "I agree, never worn one, but everyone I know who rides does. These are perfect. We had so much fun in Cleveland," She moved to him, once her helmet was fastened, and gave him a hug, "Thank you."

Jack pulled his phone out of his pocket, and pulled her close for a picture, "Let's mark this moment, a new adventure."

He'd picked the perfect city to use the bikes. Boston was crawling with bicyclists. Jack had gotten instructions to find Arnold Arboretum. It was a five-mile ride to the bike path. By the time they reached it, both were ready for a break. Jack had placed water bottles on the bikes, and they drank eagerly. Though she was winded, this exhilarated Paige, the activity was exactly what she needed after feeling lethargic on the road.

In front of them, a couple was kicking a soccer ball with their two young children. The smallest, a boy, would pull his leg back as far as it would go, then release it, only to miss the ball.

"Do you want more kids?" Jack asked.

Paige coughed as water caught in her throat, "Absolutely not! Do you?"

Laughing as she wiped dripping water off her chin, he spoke, "No." He continued to watch the kids. "I wouldn't mind a couple of grandkids."

"Me too, though Hannah's not ready for that. I just gave her cat back last week. I was only supposed to watch him for a weekend, and that was a year ago."

"I remember Elliot."

"How about you?" Paige looked at Jack as she snapped her bottle back onto her bike, "Have you had pets?"

"Oh yeah. When JJ was growing up, we had boxers."

"Those are good dogs. We had a German Shepherd. She was Hannah's very best friend." They both fastened their helmets.

"Maybe when I'm done with the tour, I'll get a dog," Jack mused as he climbed on his bike. As his feet moved the pedals, he added, "What kind do you want?"

Paige followed him down the path. *What kind did she want?* She smiled at his assumption.

***

They returned the bikes to the bus. By now their hotel room was ready. In no time, they were snuggled under the covers in a king-sized bed. Paige was on her stomach and Jack was doing amazing things with his fingertips on her bare back. She was certain he was playing guitar chords, and this was her new favorite song. "So, you have art projects you will work on, on the road?"

Her response was barely audible, her face buried into the pillow, "Mmhmm."

"Good, I can't wait to see more of your work."

In response, Paige jumped up. The sheet fell from her and she climbed out of bed naked, "I have something for you."

Jack grinned at her nude body, "I love it so far."

Paige still not used to their intimacy, grabbed her robe. Ignoring Jack's protests, she tied the sash and moved to where her bags were placed. Unzipping her large portfolio bag, she carefully drew out a canvas. It was wrapped in a protective layer of film. She peeled that off and looked at it once before she headed back to the bed, concealing the image from Jack by pressing it against her chest.

Jack sat up straight, his eyes bright, "Did you draw something for me?"

She moved down, next to him. "I started it in the hotel last week when you were working. I finished in class while my students were doing their final drawings." She handed him the canvas. It was her pencil drawing of just his hands on the guitar. The details of his fingertips on the struts were completely lifelike. Jack was quiet for a long moment as he examined it. Paige felt a but of trepidation.

Finally, he looked at her face, "Paige, you drew this?" She nodded. "You're an incredible artist, seriously the details look like a photograph. I can't believe you were watching me that close."

Now she touched his hair, "Of course I was watching you closely, you're awfully nice to look at."

"Thank you, so much." Jack reached over and pulled her face to his for a kiss. "I can't tell you what this means." A moment of silence followed and then he spoke again, "So we are set to head to New York tonight after the show?"

Paige took a deep breath and released it in a squeal, "This is huge, my first trip to New York City and going to your home." Jack laughed and pulled her close.

They were riding is a small jet with the other members of the band, this too a first for Paige. The crew managed the busses and trucks which would leave for New York for their days off. The vehicles would be serviced and cleaned to prepare for their next journey.

Chapter 16

New York, New York

New York City did not disappoint. Jack and Tony had a studio meeting that would take most of the day. Apparently, they were working on a project for a movie, Paige wasn't clear if the soundtrack included one of their songs or if it was some musical they were arranging it for. She explored like any other tourist. Though Jack had scoffed at her, riding a tour bus through New York City had been perfect. Paige enjoyed each tidbit the trained guide offered. She had seen everything from Central Park to Soho. The September 11th memorial touched her heart. The theater district and 5th Avenue shopping were a delight. On the bus with others who had never been to the city, Paige didn't feel alone.

Jack's return from the studio was still two hours after hers. She was happy to be tired and had time to shower. By Tuesday, he had yet to take a day off; she wasn't sure he would. On this day, she'd shopped. Jack insisted on hiring her a driver. It was a woman who took Paige to some of the best shopping spots.

That night, Jack ordered in Chinese. They sat side by side on his endlessly long white sofa that curved around a matching block of white and chrome where they both stretched out their long legs and bare feet. His day had been a big success, he enthusiastically discussed the sound they were creating. At one point, he nearly upended his General Tso's chicken to rush over to his white baby grand and played a part of the melody. After hurriedly placing the containers of food safely on the coffee table, Paige sat back and listened to his low sexy voice.

She took in her surroundings and the feelings for him and felt close to tears. Jack looked across the room and saw her reaction. He left the piano and moved back to her. Sitting beside her, he touched her cheek, "Everything is going so well because I know you're here with me." Now he ran his fingers through her hair by her shoulder, "I'm sorry you've been alone so far. Soon enough, we can enjoy New York together."

***

Sweet words, but after another day, Paige was considering heading back to Ohio. She had nothing to do alone in the city. More shopping was out of the question. Though Jack had given her his cards to use, Paige wouldn't unless she was with him. Sightseeing alone had lost its feeling of adventure. Pacing around the apartment, she had plucked at the keys of his phenomenal piano. Her own work didn't interest her. Next, she stretched out on the giant sofa and watched a romantic comedy on the largest television she'd ever seen. This was where Jack found her when he breezed into the apartment.

His mood was excellent, and at first, he launched himself next to her and covered her in kisses. "What's this about?" she asked, trying to climb out of her bored state and share his enthusiasm.

"We finished the song," he sat up, taking a sip from the glass of ice water on the table.

"Fantastic!"

"Tonight, there's a party to celebrate. Cain, the producer, is having it on his rooftop. You'll love it, a pool and bar on the roof overlooking the city."

***

Paige took one more look in the mirror and shook her head, "This is as good as it's going to get," she whispered to herself. She ran her hand down the front of the black dress she was wearing. The spaghetti straps and trumpet ruffle just above her knees were flattering. Paige sighed, "Here I go." Jack had been flippant about who might show up at the party. There would most likely be other musicians, film stars, tv stars, and Tony. She hoped she could pull off this evening. She gave herself an encouraging smile with her shiny, painted lips, if Jack was by her side, it would be fine.

***

Jack was not by her side. Once the elevator had taken them up to the roof, he was off with Tony. He had ridden up with a comforting arm at her waist and made casual conversation with the actor from a police drama on television and his wife who was starring in a comedy on an opposing network. Paige had smiled and nodded, but not said much.

Once they stepped onto the rooftop, she was in awe of the scene. The space was lit with lights strung along the black railing that did not block the view of the sparkling city; tops of building and glowing windows of taller skyscrapers. Tables and chairs were scattered about the space. At one end was a lit, aqua pool and at the other, a jazz trio played. Jack ushered her to the bar and got them both a glass of the signature cocktail designed just for the party. Paige had just taken hers from the bartender and turned toward Jack, he was gone. He had moved to a table where Tony and another man sat. He stood between their chairs in animated conversation. If she trailed him over there where would she stand? Paige felt a moment of panic and her eyes traveled the rooftop. She knew no one, Gina was not there, none of the women were. In fact, most of the band members were not. This party was about Jack's career in the industry that didn't involve the band.

Paige sipped at the citrus cocktail, it was strong. She waited a couple minutes more, expecting Jack to remember that he had left her. Instead, she saw him pull a chair from another table and sit down with the men. Once again, she searched the party, still no one familiar. To the right of her was a small table for two. It was up against the rail; the view would be spectacular. She reached for her glass, which was half empty. The bartender placed another glass beside it. "One for the road," he gave her a friendly smile. Paige took both drinks and headed to the table.

She chose the seat where she could see Jack and if he looked, he could make eye contact. So far it hadn't happened. Paige looked out at the city. Her first drink was empty. The alcohol seemed to fuel her irritation. Suddenly she felt someone at her elbow. Assuming it was Jack, she said, "Finally."

A server stood with a tray of appetizers. Paige mumbled an apology and took a small plate with what looked to be some sort of dumpling on it. The tasty bite was spicy and agreed with the fruity drink. She wished she had taken more than one. Across the roof, she could still see Jack engrossed in his conversation. He was very animated, hands moving about. The men had a bottle of liquor in front of them. Apparently, she was forgotten.

She glanced at the variety of people on the rooftop. There were familiar faces. Was that Ryan Reynolds and Blake Lively? Paige casually picked up her phone and held it as she would to read it, then snapped a picture of the Hollywood power couple. This she sent to Laurel, the response was to send more. Next, Paige found an NBA star and a hip-hop producer chatting with two cast members from *Chicago Fire*. Laurel appreciated her sly photography skills. Most of the other guests were unrecognizable or had their back to Paige.

By the time the second drink was empty, a server had appeared with a third one. She drank half of it and knew she'd had more than enough alcohol. The one dumpling was not keeping her from feeling the effects. For a moment, she considered marching to his table and demanding his attention. Paige looked around and shook her head. This was his world, not hers. She would get a cab and head back to his place. Perhaps it was time to do some serious thinking.

Paige walked past his table, intentionally. She remained unnoticed. Down the elevator and into the lobby, she was still on her own. The doorman hailed her a cab.

***

Paige returned to the luxurious apartment, feeling very sorry for herself. Having too much alcohol in her system, the first thing she did was head to the kitchen. Inside his mammoth stainless-steel fridge, she pulled out the chocolate cake they had brought home from the restaurant the other night and ate directly from the container with a fork. She nearly drowned herself with bottled water, hoping to counteract the alcohol. Paige soon released her feet from her high-heeled sandals. Leaving the cake on the counter, she padded barefoot back into the other room.

With a firm nod of her head, she marched into Jack's room and gathered her things. After four days this was quite an undertaking, by the time she dragged it all into one of the guest rooms she felt better. Back in the living room the pool just outside caught her eye, how inviting on this warm night. Standing in the middle of the living room, she undid her dress and pulled it off. Now down to black panties, she slid open the door and switched the pool lights on at water level, leaving the rest of the area dark. At the sound system, she carefully chose a playlist that would most definitely not have any of his songs on it. Paige slid into the warm pool and rested her head against the concrete, closing her eyes.

She wasn't certain how much time had passed when she heard movement at the door. Soon she heard Jack say in an icy tone, "Is this an invitation?"

Without opening her eyes, she spoke, "Not really, but it's your pool." She could hear him removing his clothes. Like a shark, he slid into the pool and soon she felt his shoulder a hair width away from hers.

"Why did you leave?" he asked with obvious irritation.

Paige finally opened her eyes but looked at the lights twinkling in the water. "That was hours ago. You just noticed?"

He sighed, an exasperated sound, "Look, Paige, I'm sorry. It was a work thing."

She gathered her words, "When we're on the tour it's all about the shows. I've respected that. I never supposed our time in New York to be like this." Jack opened his mouth as if to protest. She held up her hand. "Three endless days in the studio is one thing. Engrossed in business so much at a party you didn't notice I left is another. Both together is unacceptable. It's my time too, Jack. I'm going home tomorrow." Now she stood.

He reached for her, his hand lightly grasping her calf. "Come on Paige, I'm sorry."

She climbed out of the pool, scooping a towel from the shelf. "Neither of us is in the right condition to talk about this, Jack. I need to leave for the airport at eight tomorrow." With that, she returned to the house and locked the guest room door.

***

It was 7:30 when she opened the door, pulling her first large bag behind her. It would take more than one trip. "Let me get that for you," Jack's voice was soft as he stood in front of her. Damn him, he had the nerve to look handsome in gray chino shorts and a pale-yellow tee. As he held out his hand to take the luggage from her, he added, "Can we sit down for just a moment first, and talk?"

Paige acquiesced and followed him to the couch. Hoping for distance to give her strength, she sat near the arm. Jack sat next to her, not at the other end as she had hoped. Taking a deep breath, he spoke, "I'm very sorry for my behavior here in New York. You're right, I've been selfish." He momentarily clasped his hands in a nervous gesture, "I'm out of practice at relationships. My music and the work surrounding it has been my priority for a very long time. This, however, is no excuse." Now Jack looked at her, placed his hand on her knee, "But dammit Paige, meeting you this summer has changed my life. I can't remember ever feeling so comfortable with another person. I completely took you for granted this week."

Paige chose not to respond yet, he seemed to have more to say. Her resolve was quickly disappearing

"Today we will be back on the road together. This afternoon we're in Virginia and then it's on to Texas." Even he saw that this was not making things better, "Next break we go to your house."

"Jack, I don't want to force you into my dull world," Paige sighed. "What kind of relationship do we have if we can't both be happy here?"

"We'll figure that out, eventually. We're still getting to know one another." Jack was thinking, suddenly his eyes lit up, "After the shows in Texas, we have five days off again, let's go on vacation!"

Paige was silent, she knew this long conversation would probably make her miss her flight. Heading back out on the road and moving past this most disastrous week, didn't seem to be the answer. Then again, was she ready to toss it all? A vacation away from their own homes and everything involving the band seemed to be a solution. How would the relationship go if the band wasn't around? She had a feeling it would be good; their alone time was great. Was this worth the risk? Paige looked at the man next to her. He focused his hazel eyes on her with a hopeful expression. "Let's try it."

Jack smiled victoriously and pulled her to him. "Baby, I'm so sorry for being a jerk. Thank you for giving me another shot. I'll make it up to you."

"Where do you want to go?"

He shrugged, "It's your decision."

"Somewhere around water, but not too fancy."

"Have you ever been to Naples, Florida? The gulf coast is stunning."

"No, but that sounds nice."

"My mom lives there."

Paige delighted at the idea of meeting his mother. This was an entirely different direction for them. She would love to see the side of Jack that wasn't a star. "If she wouldn't mind company, I'd like to meet her."

He laughed, "She'll be thrilled to see me, meet you and she'll tell you I'm not company. She tells everyone it's my place, not hers."

Now Paige gave an admirable look, "Did you buy it for her?"

"Yes, no big deal."

"Maybe not in your world, but in the world the rest of us live in, it is."

As they spoke, Jack was rolling her luggage into his room. At Paige's words, he stopped and turned to her, "I grew up in a house where my parents and eventually just my mom struggled to pay every bill. It's my honor to spoil her now."

Paige moved quickly to him and wrapped her arms around his neck, "Let's go see her, I can't wait."

Chapter 17

Portsmouth, Virginia

Tony approached their seat, his frown at Paige was blatant. "Jack, I need to talk to you."

Jack motioned to the seat across from them. Tony's eyes clarified that he wished to talk alone. Paige knew Jack noticed, but he didn't respond. Her first inclination was to get up, but sensing that, Jack lightly laid a hand on her leg. "What's up?"

With a resigned look, Tony opened his laptop, "Sales are great, they already sold the next five shows out."

"Good," Jack seemed unsurprised.

"I was thinking maybe we pick up a few more small shows along the way. Hit smaller towns with historic theaters."

"How many nights in a row would we be playing?" Paige appreciated Jack's question. She wanted to groan at the thought of non-stop shows for the next several weeks. That part of this adventure was, if she was honest with herself, tedious. She still loved to see the band, especially Jack, on stage, but the hours before and the possible demands afterward were difficult.

"In a seven-day stretch, we would still have two days off." Now Tony looked at Paige, "Like average people do."

"No, I don't want to work that much."

Tony tried what Paige guessed had been a successful tactic in the past, "The increased profits could mean quite an extra payout to everyone on the payroll."

Jack hesitated for a millisecond, then shook his head. "No, Tony, everyone on this tour was made aware of how many shows and how much money they'd be paid for them. I don't want to do five shows a week."

Seeing he would not win this argument, Tony tried another suggestion, "Ken Watkins, at the label, has been looking at the numbers. He thinks a live greatest hit record from the tour could sell well."

"They'd record us on stage?" Jack seemed more interested in this.

"Well, you know how it goes, some on the road, some studio work. Time on publicity." He looked at his screen, then turned it for Jack to see. He made certain it wasn't in Paige's view, though she had no desire to look.

"It's a nice chunk of change, but seriously, we've made live albums and greatest hit collections. There's no new stuff to milk our fans for more money."

Tony was desperate, "You have that new song you're writing, that might merit a new single attached."

Now Jack's eyes lit up. Paige could tell this may be the winning note. Then, Jack sighed, "No, Tony, I don't want to go back to the studio and the album-release circuit. The purpose of this tour was to share our favorite songs with the people who love them. I want to do that," he grasped Paige's hand, "and enjoy this lady."

The look Tony gave her was as if she had been the one speaking the entire time. "Seems like a cop-out," he said as he got up and moved to the second floor.

Paige squeezed Jack's hand, "Do you really not want to do more shows or another album?"

Jack reached over and pushed a strand of her hair over her shoulder, "There's always more to do, but I don't want to recycle my music or squeeze in more shows just to make money. I'm fifty years old, I'm doing fine in that department. I went on tour to enjoy performing again, not to wear myself out." He pulled her chin to his with a finger and kissed her softly. "Discovering you is a treasure I never expected to find. I almost blew it, I'm not making the mistake again."

***

That evening, when the band was getting their final adjustments on stage, Paige wandered over to the sound deck nearby. She liked Cliff, the sound engineer, who handled it. They had just exchanged hellos when she felt someone next to her. At a glance, she saw it was Tony.

Before she could offer a pleasantry, he spoke, his voice a harsh whisper, "Jack's been in this business a long time. His music has outlasted any relationship he's ever gotten into. Keeping him from it will only end your relationship quicker."

Paige's immediate reaction was to be offended and respond in a protest, but what Tony didn't realize was that Paige spent her days dealing with teenagers. The cutthroat approach to get someone's ire up was a teen's favorite tactic. Instead, she used her professional skills; took a deep breath, even pasted on a smile and turned to Tony. "Tony, if Jack was threatening to walk away from the tour for me, I would agree with you. The magic of that music makes him. I'm not deciding for him, but I will support his choices."

Tony was unprepared for her calm but stern response. "You don't care if he adds dates to the tour?"

She knew a setup when she heard one, "Why don't you talk to Jack about the business side of things. My relationship with him is personal, not professional." Paige turned and headed away from Tony. It was disconcerting to think he may consider her a nemesis. She didn't want Jack to think at some point he'd have to choose between them.

As she moved back to where the regulars were milling about, Annabeth approached her. "Were you and Tony having words?"

"Nope, in fact, quite the opposite. I told him I'm not a part of any decisions that Jack makes." Now she gave Annabeth a meaningful look, "Jack and I don't see eye to eye on everything, but I respect his feelings even if they're different from mine."

Annabeth got the message, and her face flushed. "Paige, can we take a walk, maybe find a place to have a drink. I really want to talk."

Not sure if she wanted to talk, but aware that Annabeth would be here as long as she was, if not longer, Paige nodded. She couldn't keep letting the Trent and Gina situation eat her up.

***

It was a nice night in Portsmouth, Virginia. The two women sat in chairs that the smokers of the tour kept outside the busses. Annabeth had wanted to get them both a drink. She thought it would help. That was probably the exact reason that Paige had declined. "I want to talk to you about my involvement with," here Annabeth faltered.

"If this is about Trent Crosby, don't bother. They have told me that his life is none of my damn business."

Annabeth flinched at the other woman's venomous tone. "I keep saying I will not hang out with him, then I do."

Paige was silent, staring straight ahead. She'd decided not to make it easy.

"I hate it that you and Jack might think poorly of me."

"Don't worry, Jack is accustomed to Trent's behavior." That remark stung. "It doesn't bother him at all."

"And I would hate for this to be a reason for me to lose this opportunity. The book will be big. If Gina would try to get me kicked out of the tour."

Paige now looked at her, "Annabeth, you have nothing to worry about. Gina doesn't want to know what her husband is doing or who with. The rest of the group, including Jack, abides by this. If you're concerned about that, don't be."

Annabeth ran her fingers through her hair, this wasn't going as she had hoped. "You seem to despise me for this."

"I won't cause problems for you or Trent." Without another word, Paige got up and headed back to the stage. Annabeth sat alone, *what had she expected?*

***

The big news around the bus was that Theo was coming back. Theo was their rhythm guitar player. He'd been with the band from the beginning. Paige recalled his looks on the album covers; crazy blonde hair that stood up straight on the top of his head and hung below his shoulders at the back. He was more influenced by the 80s hair band groups and chose flamboyant colors of spandex pants to wear. He even sported eyeliner.

She'd known he was no longer with the band. When she'd been doing internet searches on her new potential love interest, his name had popped up in some headlines. Immersed in all things Jack Corey, she'd ignored most, though some stories mentioned, "drug use" and "overdose." It was easy to conclude that Theo wasn't with the band any longer because of this.

Jed Pearson was the second guitar now. He was a nice, quiet guy. His wife, Tammy, had visited for some shows. They were from Tennessee, he'd met the band in Nashville. He was low key, spending his days playing video games or watching movies. Jed was friendlier with some of the road crew than the band members.

What would happen to Jed if Theo was back? Paige had whispered this exact question to Jack this morning when they were still in the cocoon of their bunk. He had just had a text from Theo that said he'd meet them in Dallas. Now Jack placed his phone on the shelf by the TV and turned to face Paige. Sleeping in these close quarters wasn't ideal.

It was different in the morning, here they were in such a confined space that their knees and toes were touching. This, she liked.

"Jed knew this was a possibility. Theo has worked hard on his sobriety."

"So just like that, he goes home?"

"No, no, no. I'm sorry, but we can't trust Theo that much." He rolled onto his back, staring at the ceiling in memory. Paige remained on her side, her head resting on his chest, he cradled her under his arm. "Theo caused so many problems for us; not showing up for shows, showing up but being incapable of playing. We had at least three concerts where he was missing, and we had to hunt him down. Over the years, he also got in trouble for trashing hotel rooms."

"Whoa, are you concerned now?"

"Yes, he's sobered before and then fallen. But he's part of us. He's one piece of The Jack Corey band. An important part of the days when we created who we were, wrote our songs, recorded them, fought to get things done our way. He's like a brother. I want him to be clean and back in the family."

***

Just one night later, she headed downstairs. Grabbing a blanket left on one seat, Paige wrapped it around her and curled up on the small bus couch. The only light she could see were those of the buildings outside of the parked bus. She closed her eyes, hoping to block in the tears. What was she crying for, anyway? Angry at him? Angry at herself? Sad? Disappointed? Apparently, the words Jack had spoken in New York meant little to him.

It had all started as a nice evening. The show ended and there were no demands on the band. Jack had gone into the dressing room and showered. Paige had sat out on a picnic table on a breezy evening, watching the methodical way the crew packed each crate and rolled it into the truck. Were they going to find a hotel room? The next show was two days away not tomorrow. Jack hadn't mentioned it earlier, she hadn't asked either. He'd spent two hours with his guitar. Paige had sat across from him engrossed in her drawing and then on a new summer read she'd picked up at a bookstore. When he had finally set his instrument aside, he'd said he wanted a little nap before the show. At first, she thought he meant alone, but as he stood, he held out his hand to her.

They climbed the few stairs to the top deck of the bus. "Sleep only," she'd whispered, a smile on her face.

He grimaced, "I'm aware." His response caught her off guard. They had both agreed and kept the promise to not have sex on the bus. They'd both been very aware when others hadn't been as discreet. It was embarrassing and vulgar. Paige and Jack were adults who could control their urges until they were alone.

"We'll be in a room of our own soon enough," she'd offered. Even then, Jack had not suggested they reserve a room in town. Paige was still feeling as if that was not her decision. She never saw payment change hands; an assistant would give one of them a key. Was the band paying for the room? Was it Jack's own personal expense? Either way, she didn't think it was up to her to request they stay in a hotel.

At the bunks, he motioned for her to get in first; she slipped off her flip-flops and climbed up. He followed suit, and as she turned on her side facing him, he had climbed and turned so that his back was facing her. Paige scratched her nails lightly along his t-shirt and Jack had moaned appreciatively. It wasn't long before Paige heard his breathing become slow and steady. Jack was asleep. She closed her eyes, enjoying the warmth of him and soon nodded off as well.

It was Tony's voice calling up the steps that awoke them. Apparently, it was time for Jack to head to the stage for soundcheck. He stretched awake, then rolled to face her. They were both still quiet, coming awake. He kissed her forehead, "I could stay here for a few more hours."

Her eyes were now open, and looking into his, an exchange of agreed desire. “Sounds perfect.” They kissed until they heard again Tony’s voice. Jack gave her a squeeze. “I’ll see you after the show, babe.”

***

If he’d forgotten that they could stay off the bus, she didn’t know. Perhaps she should have called him back to see if she should make arrangements. Paige hadn’t done that. Now she was sitting out in the dark, her ears still ringing from the acoustics of the concert. Jack appeared at the door of the theater, Theo was with him, Trent close behind. The three men were laughing. She smiled at the scene. Theo seemed to fit back in well, the audience had given him a standing ovation when he was introduced.

Jack seemed to see her for the first time, and she could read the conflicted expression that passed over his face. He said something to the other two then moved toward her. Trent and Theo stopped where they were, waiting for Jack. Paige frowned suspecting where this was going.

“Hey, Paige.” He leaned in for a quick kiss.

“Great show tonight, Theo was fun to watch. You really hit those high notes,” Paige was laying it on thick, hoping to avoid his coming words.

“Um,” Jack nervously scratched the back of his neck, “Back in the day we used to have heavy competitive dart games. It was a tradition after a show. There’s a place around the corner that has darts, the guys want to see if we still have it.” Paige felt dread at having to sit at a dive bar while Jack threw darts with the others.

She was completely caught off guard when he said, "Do you mind if I go with them?"

He wanted her to stay behind? On the bus? Paige stood, anger and rejection filling her, "You're going out with the guys?"

"Yeah, just for tonight. We haven't done that for ages."

Her emotions were threatening to take over and Paige didn't want to make a scene. She turned to head to the bus, "Okay, I'll see you later."

Jack grabbed her arm, "Wait, I can't go without a big kiss." He seemed oblivious, and she was steaming.

"Be careful," was all she could muster as she moved toward the bus.

***

Three and a half hours later, Jack had shown up with Trent and Theo. Paige was in her sleeping attire of shorts and tank dozing in front of the big television in the second story lounge. Jed and Ricky were watching a movie and Paige had joined them. She saw Jack head toward the bunk. She was tempted to stay where she was and let him find her, but then again, she didn't feel like having Jed and Ricky hear them. Instead, she got up and moved to the bunk hallway.

"There you are," he was drunk as he struggled out of his jeans, which he dropped to the floor. Jack reached for her, but she rebuffed his hands.

"Go brush your teeth, please." She climbed up into the bunk. Before long he ungracefully pulled himself in beside her.

Paige sat in the dark, tiny space and tensed as Jack rolled towards her. “I missed you baby.” He attempted to kiss her neck, she pulled away.

“Yep,” her voice was curt. Now she turned so that her back was to him.

“Are you mad at me?” his voice was not a whisper and Paige was certain she heard a snicker from another bunk.

“Jack, be quiet.”

Now he turned his back against hers, “Don’t be nasty about it.”

That was the end of her rope. Paige sat up in her anger and hit her head on the slow ceiling. “Dammit, Jack!” she hissed. “I’m not being nasty. I didn’t say a word when you sent me back here for a night alone after I sat and watched you play for three hours, preceded by having you set up for two and a half. You can’t accuse me of that when you roll in here drunk from a night with your friends. In case you haven’t noticed we’re on a fucking bus not at home. You leaving me here sucked, but I said nothing.”

Jack sighed and even in the dark, Paige swore she could see his eyes roll. She moved again to face the wall, out of words. Soon his even breathing let her know he’d nodded off. How dare he! After perhaps a half an hour, she climbed over him and got out of the bunk.

Now she lay staring at the lights of the parking lot that glared in at her like silent judges. Paige had no idea what result she wanted. At one moment she wanted him to apologize, to realize that she was bored most of the day and it was his job to entertain her in the evening. On the other side, she was an adult. There was not an easy solution to this. He was on this tour working, and his downtime didn't need to circle around her. But dammit, it was dull. Could she stay?

Tears from her eyes rolled into her ears as she shivered under the thin blanket against the cranked air conditioning of the bus. Sleep eventually claimed her.

The sunrise glared against her eyelids. Paige awoke and looked at the pale pink sky. It was early. She stretched her sore back and stood up.

This vehicle was filled with touring musicians, she had hours before anyone else was up. Paige attempted near silence as she made her way back upstairs. In the bunk hall, she picked up Jack's jeans and shirt, more out of habit than affection, and placed them on the junk bunk. She then grabbed her duffle. Carefully she reached in the bunk to retrieve her phone off the shelf. Below her hand, she felt Jack's breath.

Paige looked at his peaceful face, rough with morning stubble, he was still beautiful. She had a momentary desire to climb up and place herself under his arm, her face against his bare chest. No, sleep would evade her and besides what would she say when he awoke?

Instead, she moved back downstairs with her bag. Squeezed into the tiny bathroom, Paige dug out jeans, a bra, and a top. She then washed her face, brushed her teeth and applied minimal makeup. Using water, she tousled her hair. She retrieved her small purse she kept in the duffle then shoved her feet into flip-flops. Looking around for a spot, she tucked her bag under the table. Her phone read 6:57. Paige pushed the button to open the door and exited the bus.

The city sun was already bright, and she popped on her sunglasses. Where to go? There was a guard at the gate of the theater lot where they'd camped for the night. Moving beyond the semi and buses, Paige approached him. Out of habit, she pulled out her ID tag. It was obvious from his smirk as he watched her approach, he thought this was a walk of shame. Just what she needed, another man acting stupid, "I'm with the tour." He straightened. "Can you tell me where I can get breakfast?"

"Oh yeah, there's a diner about three blocks down. But ma'am, let me call you a cab, it's early to be out there alone." He pulled a phone from his dark uniform pants.

"Is it unsafe?" Paige glanced out at the street, seeing a man walking a dog and another with a woman headed to a parked car.

"Not really, but it's a big city."

"Thanks, I'll be fine, can you give me directions?" It felt good to be moving in silence in the morning sun. The city was coming awake. Delivery trucks were stopping at businesses, cleaning crews were sweeping sidewalks and washing windows. She saw a few people heading from different directions to one storefront, the diner she guessed. Inside, she grabbed a booth. A server, a woman around her age, brought over a pot of coffee. Paige turned over the white porcelain mug and thanked her. She added sweetener and creamer, breathing in a sigh of relief. This was what she needed, space alone to collect her thoughts.

She opened the menu. As if in defiance of Jack's healthy smoothies, when the server returned, Paige ordered the *Good Morning* special which comprised of two eggs, hash browns, bacon and her bread of choice; wheat toast. Now she stirred the coffee then sipped it. It was bitter compared to the gourmet beverage she had the daily luxury of drinking most mornings. Still, it was peaceful sitting here alone. The steaming food came quicker than she would have expected.

An hour later, she glanced at her phone, just after eight a.m., no messages from Jack. He was still asleep from a show and then the drunken dart night with the guys. Paying her bill, she asked the man at the counter, "Is there a department store nearby?"

He considered, "There's a *Target* about a mile from downtown."

Target, that would be perfect. "Are there normally cabs downtown or should I call one?'

"Do you do Lyft? That's what most people around here do."

Paige thanked him and immediately pulled her phone out to request a ride.

Twenty minutes later she was happy to be walking into *Target*. It was such a familiar atmosphere; it felt like being home. She grabbed a cart, assuming this fight would blow over, there were plenty of things she could use. As she pushed the big red cart passed the women's clothing, Paige considered, was this going to work out? It was up to her unless he was over her after their fight.

Why would he be? Each moment of the day was on his schedule. Now she shook her head, admonishing herself. This was not a surprise, Paige knew she was entering his world. If she was going on the tour, she'd told herself to expect it to be like this. If she was unhappy, then it was on her and her option was to walk away. Unexpectedly she felt tears sting her eyes at this thought. Her heart wasn't ready to walk away.

She dreaded facing him. Paige despised confrontation. Determined to not let her ruminations ruin her shopping trip, she took a deep breath and moved the thoughts to the back. It was time to enjoy spending money.

Soon she had the cart reasonably full. She'd bought coffee, a few toiletries, new PJs, a giant bag of Kit Kats; Jack's favorite. There was a new paperback, the second in a series. In the craft section, she couldn't resist a new sketchpad and some fun pencils. This *Target* had a nice grocery section, so she bought herself some real dairy coffee creamer, more fruit, veggies for Jack and some snack food. These and other items filled her cart. She headed towards the registers and glanced at her phone. No new messages. It was 10:15 now; he was probably awake. She had no choice but to go back.

The store had a Starbucks at the entrance. After she checked out, she would get a coffee. The large array of items was traveling down the conveyor belt past the checkout clerk. Paige pulled a credit card out of her wallet and prepared to scan it. Fingers covered her hand and next to her a familiar voice said, "Let me get this."

Her tone was soft, "Jack."

The cashier gave him the cost, and Jack dug a couple of hundred-dollar bills out of his wallet, but looked at Paige, "Good morning, love."

"How'd you find me?"

Now he was pushing the cart to the exit, "It took some investigating. I showed your picture to the man at the counter in the diner, he led me here."

Where was he taking her stuff? Paige trailed Jack as he moved down an aisle of the parking lot. He stopped at a silver Lexus SUV, with a click of the key fob, he unlocked the hatch. They both tossed bags in the back, "Whose car?"

"I rented it."

"Just to come find me?" Paige asked, her face registering the absurdity of the idea.

"No," he closed the back door and leaned on it, "We're going to take a brief road trip."

"Look, Jack, that's not necessary."

He cut her off, "Yes, it is. I asked you to give up your summer and come with me. I'd have shown up at your door to get you to come with me. I have to consider your time too."

"All the same, I can't expect you to spend every moment with me."

Jack was moving closer as he responded, "If I have something to do that doesn't include you then I can be fair and give you notice. I knew all along that it was wrong, that's why I didn't get us a room. I thought if I did that, you'd really expect me to be there. Truth is, you'd have preferred being in a hotel room on your own. I was a jerk to leave you alone on the bus." Now he was in front of her, his pleading eyes looking into hers, "Will you forgive me?"

Paige smiled at his consideration, but then her expression changed to one of doubt.

He saw it, "What?"

She touched his arm, "I appreciate your thoughtfulness." Gesturing at the car behind him, "Driving around with just you sounds wonderful. But it's a band-aid." He looked ready to protest, so she rushed on, "I don't want to become the obligation that interferes with your life. This tour is a monumental decision you made, to come back to the fans and give them a great show. Along with the performances on stage comes all the little things; meet and greets, social time out with your bandmates, press events. If you quit doing those because you feel you must be with me, it will destroy what we have." Jack shook his head in disagreement, but she wouldn't allow him to interrupt. "The last few weeks have been unimaginably good. I've enjoyed every moment we've been together or when I'm watching you on stage. But we've both struggled. Last night was difficult for you and me. You because you wanted to do what a month ago you could've without thought, but now you felt guilty about it. Already you avoided telling me something because we would disagree. I struggled because my times without you on tour are not always ideal, sometimes downright boring. Other times I feel as if I'm intruding in your life."

"I wanted you to come. I still want you to be here," his voice was pleading, a sad little boy.

She felt a pain in her chest. Shoppers were wandering in and out of the store, Paige was afraid that someone would recognize him. "Let's talk inside." She went to the passenger's side and climbed in. Jack got behind the wheel.

Now he turned to her, "Were you leaving? Why'd you buy stuff?"

"No, I wasn't leaving." Paige looked down, avoiding eye contact, "At least not yet. I bought things for the bus. And some things to entertain myself with."

"You're really having a terrible time?" he sounded crestfallen.

"No, I'm not. And I didn't tell you anything because I don't want you to change how you're doing things. This is your tour that's the priority. Not me."

Now his voice was strong, "But meeting you has been the best thing that's happened in a very long time. I didn't expect it. The tour was all I cared about until that night, sitting on the stairs with you. It's changed my life." He paused then and smiled confidently,

"I will not give you up. When this tour is over, I want you to still be with me."

She inhaled and the air she blew out was shaky, "I feel the same way, but I don't' know how it's all going to work."

Jack started the car, and they moved out onto the road. "Let's make a plan. What can I do to make this situation better?"

"What can *we* do?"

"Okay, we." He was heading out of the city.

"Do you know where we're going?"

"A few miles in the country seems like a good way to talk."

"I won't react so childishly about your time with other people."

"I won't be selfish and take those times. I know I royally pissed you off when I stayed out half the night jamming with Tim."

"That's the problem, I don't want you to change your ways."

"Isn't that what a relationship is?"

Paige looked over at Jack, his eyes were on the road, but his smile was triumphant. "Yes, it is, in a way."

"What about staying on the bus, do you completely hate it?"

"No, Jack, I don't. It's okay, but I really appreciate our time in the hotels."

His eyebrows waggled, "Me, too."

Paige laughed, "When we have a few days between shows, I understand if you want us to go our separate ways."

"Is that what you want?" As he spoke Jack flipped on the radio.

"I thought so this morning, but then we're like this, alone and I don't. Please understand, I'm an old woman who lives alone. I'm set in my ways and used to not sharing my space."

"I live alone too, I get it. The bus crowd sucks. Only one night at a time on the bus, how's that?"

Paige smiled, she liked this; they were setting up a list of rules, a plan to make the time together better. The radio was playing The Beatles' *Here Comes the Sun.* Jack sang along. She loved his voice; he hit all the notes perfectly but kept the smoky tone that made it sound effortless. After a moment she joined in. Paige wouldn't set the world on fire with her voice, but she could carry a tune.

For a few miles, they didn't talk, just sang together, watching the road twist and turn in front of them. Their camaraderie reminded her of why it was worth the effort to try. His right hand was on the gear between them, Paige laid hers on top and their fingers entwined. This was it, the part that made it worth the effort. "It's alright," they both sang.

***

After their drive, Tony was on the phone looking for them. It was time to head back to the bus. Jack got serious again, "Trent and I were complete assholes last night. We should never have drunk. I can't believe I was that careless, tempting Theo."

Paige didn't console him, but said quietly, "I wondered about that."

"Please don't let me be so stupid again. Maybe I should make a no alcohol and drug policy on the bus for now."

"Would everyone listen?"

"They damn well better."

At the bus, Jack had kindly offered to keep the car, so they could be alone. Paige declined. All their things were still on the bus and she had groceries that needed to be unloaded. Jack had made exactly the right response to allay her concerns.

They put all their things on the bus. Rickie offered to take the car back to the rental agency, apparently, he'd been the one to pick it up for Jack. After a brief conversation with Tony about the day and night plans, Jack led Paige by the hand up to the second-floor lounge. Theo, Trent, Keely, and Joe were there playing video games.

Jack poked his head in the opening, "Hey guys, would you all scatter. I'd like some alone time here, with Paige." She began to protest, when without a word they all quit what they were doing and slowly filed out of the space. Was that rude of him? She kept forgetting that in his own way, Jack was the boss. He didn't demand too much, so when he made a request the others obliged.

They stretched out on the big sectional. Jack flipped on the television and together they chose a movie to watch. Soon they wrapped around each other watching a comedy. Jack kissed the top of her head, tucked under his chin. Paige squeezed his waist in response. "No one will come up here," he whispered.

Her hand trailed down to the fly of his jeans where she could already feel the muscle strain. "Are you certain?"

"Absolutely," his voice had gotten husky.

"Perfect."

***

Texas was stifling in the middle of the summer. To add to the discomfort, Paige felt lost in the shuffle before a show. Jack and Joe had both jumped down each other's throat, Theo had arrived a half hour late to set up. They pretended it was just inconsiderate, but Paige knew they were concerned that he'd been using.

She sat on a stool next to Cliff. At any moment, Tony might come over and kick her off. Gina was still in New York. Keely had cousins from Houston who were here for the night. She'd been gone since noon. Paige was lonely and in a foul mood.

Last night the air had been cranked so high on the bus that Paige had curled tightly into Jack for warmth. At breakfast, she'd come down in a hoodie and a pair of his sweats. Tony made a nasty remark about her finally looking her age. Paige had grabbed a coffee and a granola bar and gone straight back upstairs.

A woman of unknown origins was sprawled on the sectional in the lounge. Perhaps a conquest of Theo or Trent. Paige's wasn't sure. She didn't care. She switched on the television and watched the *Today Show*. Soon the woman opened her eyes, had the decency to look embarrassed and without a word headed down the stairs and out of the bus. Jack was still asleep.

It was 9:50. Paige began a texting conversation with Laurel. She and Pete were at Destin, Florida with his family. Laurel and her mother-in-law saw eye to eye on little. She was happy for the distraction.

So, how's Jack Corey's favorite fan bang?

Screw you! Paige replied but included a laughing emoji. *How's the beach?*

Destin is lovely, lots of fresh seafood. Working on my tan. If I could just stay away from the family beach house, I'd say it's great.

Try sharing a mobile home with a dozen spoiled musicians.

No thanks, that's the purgatory you put yourself in. Where are you today?

On the road in Texas.

Good lord woman, it's too hot to be in Texas.

Tell me about it. You can't walk barefoot on the pavement.

Is lover boy still sleeping?

As always. I have work to do for the Chamber of Commerce, but I'm feeling lazy. I scared a strange woman in the lounge.

And who was she hooking up with?

No idea.

Did you even think you'd do anything like this?

Never.

Is he still worth it?

Paige sent an emoji that matched the smile on her face. *Absolutely.* By now her coffee and granola bar were done. Her eyes looked toward the quiet bunk hall. *Just checking in. Drag Pete out for a romantic night of drinking by the water.*

Great idea. Have fun in Texas. Keep cool!

The women exchanged heart goodbyes.

***

Now hours later, she was once again on her own. The downtime was feeling tedious this week. She really didn't know a cure for it. Deep down inside was a nagging feeling that Paige couldn't live like this forever. The man, who was at this moment on stage thrilling a thousand people, had become the most important person in the world, but their lives were on different paths. Though she wanted to be with him, she couldn't continue the fall leg of the tour. When school started in a month, she would be back in her classroom. Would they be over? Right now, he was singing *Go Away*. She probably would do exactly that.

***

Paige sat next to Jack in a bus seat, the lights over the interstate shown in the windows. They'd agreed to only one consecutive night on the bus, but practical logistics had them here again. His hand was on her leg, holding her fingers in his. She could tell that his muscles were relaxing and soon he would be asleep. The bus was cruising down another highway, identical to the one last night and many nights before.

Out the window, there was a neighborhood beyond the road. In one house, Paige could make out the glow of a television screen. In another, she could see lights over a dining room table. Yet another, had people moving about. What would she be doing if she was home? It was nearly midnight, she'd be stretched out in her queen-sized bed. In the morning, she would jump into the shower then choose an outfit from her large walk-in closet. No need to dig through a bag, hoping to find something not wrinkled.

Jack's hand fell off her leg, he was asleep. Paige felt alone and very homesick. What was she doing here on this bus? Was this some crazy vacation adventure she'd tell her coworkers about in the fall? Would she reminisce about the insane life?

Next to her, Jack stirred and woke up. They were in a less inhabited area and no lights lined the road. "Hey babe," he whispered. Paige turned to him, his face familiar enough to be clear in the darkness.

"Go back to sleep, Jack."

His fingers ran along her cheek, "Let's go to bed." Paige forgot her feeling of homesickness as they made their way to the bunk.

Moments later, as they were settling into the tight space, he whispered, “The next bed we sleep in will be four times this size. We can open the doors and listen to the waves each night.” They were soon headed on vacation.

Chapter 18

Naples, Florida

Naples, Florida was a beautiful city. Paige loved the view of the palm trees as they landed at the Fort Myers airport. A driver was taking them to Jack's mother's home. Jack had his own car at the condo and was looking forward to driving. The warm air hit her instantly and though the temperature was in the mid-90s, the coastal area pleased her.

Mrs. Corey's condo was on Bay Colony drive. Paige was mesmerized by the panoramic Gulf view, immediately visible from the main living areas. The condo had floor-to-ceiling sliding windows, marble flooring throughout, and a chef's kitchen. Over two miles of beach stretched in front of the property. She thought she would spend her days just watching the waves. The community also had three beachfront dining clubs.

Margaret Corey was very welcoming. Paige saw the tears in her eyes when she hugged her son. She was friendly to Paige, stating that she had heard much about her. "I'm so happy you're both here, and I know this is a vacation from your hectic travels. I have my schedule, so there are no demands to entertain me. Jack, your car keys are in the dish by the front door."

His eyes lit up, "Has it been driven it at all?"

"Yes, Frank just took it out when you called and had the oil changed and the gas tank filled. We drive it once a month as you requested."

Her son's eyes twinkled, "Frank, huh? Are you still running around with that old geezer?"

Margaret playfully smacked her son's shoulder, "That old geezer is a year younger than me, watch what you say. He's a good friend."

Now Jack snickered, "A good friend. That's what you're calling it."

Ignoring him, she turned to Paige, "The master suite is this way," she motioned to the left.

"Oh no, that's your room."

"No, this is Jack's home, the master suite is his. My room is on the other side of the house."

Jack hugged his mom, "You know that's not how I feel." He led Paige to the bedroom. She was speechless at the view from the windows. An oversized sliding door led to the balcony.

"I'm never leaving this room!" she exclaimed, then walked out on the balcony. The sound of the water and the shrill of seagulls overtook her. She could see a stunning pool and wooden walkway to the beach. "On second thought, let's go down to the water."

They strolled along the shore, the water continually rolling up to their ankles. Paige found it comical that she felt self-conscious in a swimsuit with Jack. After all, she slept with him, had sex with him, had even been in the shower with him how many times? But being in daylight out in public and removing everything but her swimsuit had felt revealing. Naturally, as most men are, especially those in shape, Jack had little inhibition about stripping down to his starfish printed trunks.

She'd thrown her white gauze sleeveless cover-up over her suit. It didn't do much more than give her a little feeling of confidence. They both had on sunglasses. The sandpipers ran in the sand in front of them. Children were squealing, splashing into the water. Sunbathers stretched on towels or loungers, sounds of music coming from their phones or small wireless speakers.

"Have you ever lived on the beach?" Paige asked him

"I owned a home on the shores of Malibu."

"I haven't been to Malibu or any part of California."

"I think you'll love it. We had a house right near the beach. When JJ was little, he'd spend hours clamming and trying to surf."

"Oh, when you were married. That makes sense. Are you and JJ close?"

Jack shrugged, "As close as a father and son can be when they live states apart. We text and talk regularly. We don't see each other as often as I like. Both our businesses keep us away."

"Does he know about me?" Paige asked shyly.

"Yes, he does."

"Really?"

"We talked about you the week you joined the tour."

"That was nice you told him."

"He already knew."

"How?" Paige considered possible sources. "Who told him?"

"My guess is Tony. They may have crossed paths. Or his mother. Who knows who she keeps in touch with?" Paige silently laughed, leave it to a man to not ask details.

"Will I meet him?"

"I hope so. I mentioned that we'd be in California. He said he'd check his schedule." They walked on. Paige was amazed at the casual plans to see his son. She was already missing Hannah.

***

Jack's treasured car was a white 2010 Aston Martin Roadster. He spent an hour on the first morning, in the below ground parking area shining it up. Afterward, with the top down, he and Paige cruised down 951 to Marco Island. He was exhilarated as he shifted the gears and moved across the bridge to the island. Paige had to laugh at his once again boyish charm.

***

It was in this tropical paradise that Paige realized this might just be the real thing. She was still spending her days, and yes her very wonderful nights, with a beautiful man who showered her with affection and attention, but it was more. The aquamarine water that moved with a rhythm in front of the condo filled her soul.

They sat on the open-air deck, with the breeze blowing the salt up against their skin. One evening, Jack was stretched out on a lounger with his guitar and paper, softly playing chords and singing words. Paige loved the lines she was hearing, she knew it was a song about the summer and her. Moments like this had her flashing back to her young self, sitting in front of MTV watching Jack Corey performing in a music video. The video of *Go Away* had him moving all his things out of a woman's house, she was yelling at him. Finally, at the end, a loaded pick up was moving from the house, Jack was sitting on the open gate, playing his guitar and singing as the truck headed down the road until it was out of sight. The Paige that sat and watched that, fantasized about a moment like this one. How could this be real life?

She was sitting in a chair opposite of Jack, her small easel in front of her, painting a vista of the scene. A couple of dolphins leaping in the waves caught her eye. Paige grabbed the paper on the table and did a quick sketch, to remember the details for the painting when she got to that point. As she painted unaware, she was softly singing the chorus with Jack, "*The perfect summer began that day, your sun-kissed smile sent the loneliness away.*"

The music stopped, she looked over at Jack. He was leaning his guitar against the railing. He smiled at her and held out his hand, "Come here, baby."

Paige laid down her brush, wiped her hands on the rag and walked to his lounger. Jack pulled her between his legs so that her back was against his chest. He kissed her cheek and whispered, "Were you singing our song with me?"

She grinned and felt her cheeks pull tight against his lips, "Maybe. I love it, the words are beautiful."

"They are because it's true."

Just then the glass door slid open. Mrs. Corey and Frank stood there. "Look at you two lovebirds," his mother's smile was genuine. "We're going to the Boathouse for dinner, do you kids want to join us?"

Paige hadn't been there yet. Jack sat them both up straighter, "What do you think?"

"Yes, I'd love it."

***

They were at the pool when Jack got the call. He'd just stepped out of the water and was standing next to Paige, who was working on her tan. Draping his blue blended beach towel over his shoulders, Jack answered the call, "What's up?"

Paige guessed it was Tony. It was usually Tony. She wondered if in the past Tony had followed Jack around on vacations; he called so much. Or was this just how it was? He kept constant tabs on his superstar when they were on tour.

Jack's face formed a disappointed frown. "You're certain? Well shit. Where is he now?" She sat up, concerned. Was someone hurt? "What will happen? Is Jed aware?"

Paige leaned back in her chair, they were discussing Theo. Apparently, he'd relapsed. She listened to the one side of the conversation for more details.

"No, no more chances. I'm sorry to say it, but we can't. I agree with you this time." His voice took on a defensive tone, "I know what I've done in the past. Yes, you were probably right. That's not important." She saw him roll his eyes, "Theo's out, okay?" He clicked off the phone without a goodbye.

Jack sat at the foot of Paige's chair and put his face in his hands. She scooted close and patted his back. "Is Theo okay?"

"They found him passed out in an alley behind a bar in Brooklyn. The EMT's thought he was dead at first. He was loaded up on heroin."

"Wow, he really went off the wagon."

"At least he isn't hurt. They took him to a rehab center. If he stays, he'll be there for six months."

“Has he been to one before?”

“Three.” Jack stood up, “You dumbass, Theo!” She could tell it wasn’t anger but disappointment that caused him to yell.

“Do we need to head back to New York early?”

“No, Jed’s got the show down. I’ll call him, though make sure he knows he’s back on second guitar.” He picked up his phone again.

Paige stood up, “I’ll go take a dip, while you make the call.”

She stepped around him. “I can always call later,” Jack said as he scooped her up and jumped into the pool with her still in his arms.

***

Two days later they were back on a plane, heading to join the band. Paige admired her tan then looked at the man next to her, his golden skin enhanced his good looks even more. “I should have made you stay out of the sun. How can you get even more handsome?”

Jack kissed her, “Look who’s talking. I think your hair has turned the color of vanilla ice cream.” He pulled a lock between his fingers.

“As long as it isn’t a more silver tone,” she laughed.

Running his hand through his own hair, Jack said, “No, that would be me.”

“It gives you character, makes you seem distinguished.”

“Of all the things I’ve been called me, I think distinguished is new.”

Paige had loved every moment of the vacation. She was grateful that he’d suggested they go away. “Jack, thank you for suggesting this trip. I’m sorry that I nearly left New York. I’ve loved being here with you.”

"I'm sorry I nearly chased you away. This," he laid a hand on her leg, "between us is the priority. I know I'll still get caught in my old habit of music, but you are the most important thing." Now he was quiet for a moment, then a smile filled his face, "I love you, Paige."

"I love you too, Jack." At last the declaration.

Chapter 19

The Carolinas

Annabeth sat in the chair opposite of Jack, on the bus. He'd been strumming his guitar when she approached him. Paige was on the long bench across from them, her sketch pad in hand. Jack was friendly until Annabeth explained her purpose. Now he scowled at her, "No, I don't want this in the book."

"But Jack this is part of the story. Drug and alcohol addiction go hand in hand with the life you live. Every band has had their struggle with it. It's a good chapter to discuss how the rest of you can control your intake without falling prey to addiction."

"Not everyone is prone to addiction," Paige said from her seat.

Annabeth sighed impatiently, "No that's true, but there are more members who could easily have gotten messed up and addicted to heroin. How did they avoid it? Are there others who are recovering addicts in the band or on the crew?"

"This feels like a betrayal to Theo."

"It's not, and I will get his permission. I already have an appointment with him when we're back in New York."

Jack sat his guitar on the seat next to him and clasped his hands on the table in front of him, "Annabeth, I will not tell on anyone."

"How about you? How many drugs have you taken? Was there a time when you regularly got high before you went on stage?"

"I've never had the desire to do anything strong. Sure, I've smoked weed. In the first couple of years, we all had a lot to drink and smoke before a show. We were convinced that it gave us the courage to go out and perform. I realized quickly that it made me a sloppy musician. I also got damn tired of the hangovers. As you know, some guys hit the bottle hard." He gave her a pointed look, it was obviously regarding Trent. "How much do they drink? I don't know. It's been years since I had to talk to one of my crew about drugs or alcohol affecting their performance."

"Except Theo."

Jack eyed her sternly, "Look, we can talk about him, but you must promise that if he chooses not to talk to you, this conversation never happened."

Annabeth considered a moment, then shook her head, "Okay, agreed."

He sat back, recalling Theo and his problems. "It was clear early on that he was a heavy user. I let it go because when we got on stage or in the recording studio, he could play what he needed to play. The first problems were that he would show up late to things. Several times Carla and Ricky were walking the neighborhood around the venue hoping to find him and get him on stage before the show started. At least twice, he got belligerent and punched Ricky. When Carla found him and he smacked her, I suspended him from three shows."

Annabeth scribbled furiously even though she was recording.

"He was in rehab when we started this tour. Theo was the one who found Jed for us. We all thought the tour would motivate him to get clean. It motivated him, but he wasn't strong enough to stay away from it. This is a hard job when you're an addict. Everyone is drinking, it's part of the culture of both the fans and the workers.

The conversation went on for nearly an hour. When Annabeth turned off her recorder and closed her notebook, she held out her hand to Jack. He shook it surprised. "You have my word, I won't use this without explicit permission from Theo. But, it's a part of the Jack Corey band."

***

Annabeth left to head up to the lounge. Paige was checking the schedule on her iPad. This week they would be in Charlotte, North Carolina and Charleston, South Carolina. "I think I'll go home and miss the next two shows."

Jack's eyes grew wide then immediately narrowed suspiciously, "Just this weekend?" His words were accusing.

Paige pushed her bangs out of her eyes, "Just this weekend."

"What's so important that it can't wait until our three-day break on Sunday?

She took a deep breath, controlling her voice, determined not to take the bait and turn this into an argument. "You've got two major shows on Friday and Saturday, included is a line-up of media interviews, contest winner meet and greets and Saturday's show involves performing with Stonemaster. You guys toured together in the 90s. I know both bands will want to hang out more than just onstage."

"So, you don't want to be there to support me and let me show you off?" By now, Jack, out of habit, had picked up his guitar and though it was acoustic, was squealing his fingers across the strings playing the sharp notes of *Go Away*.

Paige spoke slowly, "Honey, thank you for wanting to show me off, but while you're busy, I can zip back home and take care of some of my art business. I can also check on the house. By the time all the excitement is over on Sunday afternoon, I can be back at the bus or we can meet somewhere to spend a couple of days off."

Jack turned the notes into Elvis Presley's *Are You Lonesome Tonight.* Paige slapped at his hands, "Stop it, you won't be lonely!"

Now he laid the guitar down and reached for her, "Yes, I will. Being with you every day feels like the most natural thing in the world."

She maneuvered, so she was leaning back against his chest. "I agree. It's crazy, I don't know about you, but even when I met the man I would marry it didn't feel this compatible."

He kissed her ear, "Well, I hope we feel better than a relationship that ended in divorce."

"That's a good point."

Now he turned her, so she was straddling him, and they were face to face, "You know that I am madly in love with you, right Paige?"

She grasped his face in her hands, "Yes, Jack, I am. And you know I feel the same way about you. I love you," she spoke against his mouth before taking a long kiss.

When the kiss ended, Paige ran her fingers through the hair at his temples, "Thank you for not being upset about my plans."

Jack tilted his head to the side, "Were you worried about that?"

"Well," Paige avoided eye contact and slid off his lap, instead sitting next to him, leaning on his shoulder.

"I'm a spoiled little child, aren't I? I'm sorry. Meeting you on tour doesn't show you the best me. When I get into the mode of the performer, I'm self-centered." She protested, but he wouldn't let her, "I promise, the Jack Corey post tour will be a different man with you."

And there it was, his confident declaration that this would not end after the summer tour. Paige was so happy to see this beautiful man smiling at her, reaching out to touch her. She refused to allow the doubt creeping in to spoil the moment.

By late afternoon, Paige had secured an airline ticket, a ride to the airport and a rental car to get to Findlay. She could have asked Kyle or Hannah to drive her home, but selfishly she wanted her presence in Findlay to be a secret. She was having fantasies about quiet solitude.

***

Though the temperature was in the eighties, Paige turned off the central air and opened all the windows. Time to air this poor museum of a home out. After a quick text to Jack that she'd arrived safely, she avoided engaging in chatter. Instead, she dumped most of the continents of her suitcase in the washer and moved through the house barefoot. Her toes touching the cool soft, wood floors were a treat. Paige didn't go shoeless on the bus. There were too many residents and not enough showers. Today she could enjoy that.

It was also a treat to curl up in her bed and take an afternoon nap. The slight breeze blowing in her window, and the homey sounds of a lawnmower and a barking dog, lulled her into sleep.

When she awoke, she saw that it was nearly six. No wonder her rumbling stomach had awakened her. The last bite of food she'd had was crackers on the plane. She got up and searched for her sandals. It would be fruitless to rummage through the cupboards and fridge. Without looking, she knew it was empty. She made a mental note to leave some food in the house. Whether she was here alone or with Jack next, having something quick to cook would be wise.

At the grocery, she realized that cooking was exactly what she wanted to do. She gathered the ingredients for lasagna, potato soup, and lemon bars. In the produce section, she added the items to make homemade guacamole. Now she returned to the chip aisle in search of lime tortilla chips. Well, lasagna and guacamole would require two different wines.

When she went to the wine section, she surprised herself by immediately going for his Cabernet. Paige hadn't realized it really was what she wanted to drink. That would do for the pasta and she chose something different for the guacamole.

At home, she put the pasta on to boil and browned the meat for lasagna, then got out her chopper for the guacamole. She might as well cover all the dishes at once.

She pulled a wineglass down from the cupboard and turned on some music. It wasn't long before one of his songs came on. This inspired her to send him a text, wishing him well for the evening. Paige realized after she sent it, he was already on stage. She had a moment that felt almost like sadness; she was missing out on a show.

By the time the lasagna was ready for the oven, Paige was no longer hungry for the heavy pasta dish. She decided to freeze it for another time. Instead, she turned to the guacamole and chips.

With her feet planted on the coffee table, Paige flipped through TV channels, munching on the fresh avocado mixture. Nothing held her interest. What was going on? Why did she feel depressed being in her own home?

Hours later, she enjoyed a quiet sleep. Paige awoke to morning sunshine, a good day for a bike ride. She frowned, she didn't own a bike at home. Would Jack ride without her? The clock showed that he wouldn't be up for hours.

***

While she was home alone, Paige took the time to call her family in Germany. All previous communication with them from the road had been texts. Her explanation as to how she was spending her summer had been vague. Now she spoke to Krista and her mother.

Krista's initial reaction had been like Hannah's, skeptical. After Paige continued to share details on where they had gone, her visit to both Jack's home and his mother's home, her sister warmed up to the idea. To her surprise, her mother was much more open to her daughter's spontaneous decision, "Darling, I am so happy to hear you're having an adventure this summer."

Paige balked at this, no reproach? "Thanks, Mom," she responded slowly.

"I think we've all learned that there are no guarantees on tomorrow." This was about Doug, Paige was starting to understand her mother's meaning. "Enjoy life to the fullest."

"Thank you, Mom. That's exactly what I'm doing. I appreciate your reminder of why I should enjoy myself. How's Germany?"

"Your dad and I are adjusting nicely. He's even learning some phrases in German." The conversation continued pleasantly. Paige hung up, grateful to have her family's support.

***

Lunch was the remaining guacamole, this time accompanied by a diet soda. On Paige's laptop screen was the airline website. She had accomplished all the errands she had set out to do and now she wanted to head back to the tour. A late-night flight would get her to Charleston at 5:45 a.m., that would be perfect. She would be at the hotel before Jack was even awake. What a good surprise.

***

Jack's time alone wasn't relaxing, other than some moments composing *The Perfect Summer*. If it came together as he thought, he'd perform it a few of their shows.

Trent appeared in front of him, "Did the old ball and chain go home for a couple of days?"

Jack frowned, "You're hilarious man. What's up?"

"The guys from Stonemaster are coming in later, thought maybe we could get onstage and do some practice now."

"Okay, let's go." The two bands were performing for an Autism Awareness Benefit. Both would play for a half an hour of their own. The finale would be their combined bands performing a number. After a lot of talk back-and-forth and interfering managers who were trying to make their band look the best, they created a plan.

Trent sat down next to Jack. "So, have we got this figured out who's doing the guitar and lead bass?" Jack smiled, this was why

Tony and Trent got along so well, both wanted to be the superstars. Both had pushed Jack when he needed that more competitive edge. He could get lost in the music and not care about that stuff, but those two men kept on him. He knew they had a lot to do with his success. Trent had never begrudged them being the Jack Corey band. He'd used that in his reasoning to Paige the last time they'd argued over Trent's infidelity.

As he considered this, Annabeth climbed up on the bus. "Hi guys," she said. "What are you working on?"

Jack spoke up before Trent could make an inappropriate comment or some suggestions so that the two of them would disappear. With Paige gone, Jack almost felt the need to stand in for her and keep the two apart. He knew what she'd been doing lately. He knew how important Gina was to her and he was seeing it her way. "Not much, now's your chance to talk to both of us. Didn't you say you needed to do that? We've got a few minutes before we go to the stage."

Annabeth's eyes lit up, "I sure did. Let me grab my bag."

Trent groaned, "I don't want to do this."

Jack laughed, "Too bad sport, we're both here, we'll talk to her." The conversation was good. Together they shared many stories about the good days. Trent had a lot of things to add. Annabeth soaked up their words. The tales of utter chaos when filming music videos would make great copy.

It had been nearly an hour and a half when Trent stood up, "I need to smoke." He looked at Annabeth, "How about you?"

Annabeth glanced at Jack to gage his reaction. He was frowning. "No thanks," she said.

"Come on, Trent, you can smoke while we walk." Jack grabbed his guitar, they headed to practice.

***

They were performing *Light My Fire* the sixties hit by the Doors. The two bands greeted each other with enthusiasm backstage. Between them, there were eight original members, which was statistically good for a profession that was so notorious for drug and alcohol problems, disputes and dramatic exits.

Callen Badger, the lead singer of Stonemaster was married to Deanna. They were a rarity in the business, a marriage that had lasted. It hadn't always been a perfect marriage, but they never divorced.

Now as Jack saw Deanna walking in, a small equipment crate in her arms, he flinched. A million years ago, he had crossed a line that to this day shamed him. The two bands had done a four-month tour in 1989. Jack was a year out of his divorce and feeling down on himself that his time with JJ was so limited. By now his ex was already remarried to her current husband, they were creating a little family unit. He felt it was distancing him from his son. He had no desire to even try to find another wife, but he was lonely and bitter.

Callen and his band had just released a smash album that had taken them well over a year to complete. A big problem was that Callen was fighting an addiction to prescription medication that he'd gotten hooked on while recovering from ACL surgery. Not only had the band suffered but so had Deanna. She and Jack found themselves outside of the post-show circle most nights. The bands were still partying heavy, Callen had once again fallen off the wagon. His use of pills was being replaced by large quantities of whiskey.

Jack never shied away from a drink, but after too many nights of seeing the whole group get sloppy drunk, he'd gotten bored. He would get two beers and sit outside of the bus to wind down after the show. Deanna joined him and after the second night, he had beers for them both. By the third night, Callen was on a real bender and he announced he, his drummer, Joe, and Trent were heading out to find a billiard bar.

It was almost embarrassing how easily Jack and Deanna had ended up in bed together that first time. It wasn't romantic or great passion; it was more an act of mutual comfort. Whatever it was, it lasted for the rest of the tour. During the moments they saw each other before the shows, they ignored one another. She focused on keeping Callen sober enough to perform. Jack kept his attention on his music and the band. Each night, though, after the show it would be the same routine. Everyone else would go party and they would end up alone together. At the end of the tour, they walked away from one another with little fanfare, just an acknowledgment of what it had been, companionship and sex.

Now nearly twenty years later, there she was. Jack suddenly regretted not convincing Paige to stay. As he walked up the steps to the stage, Deanna noticed him and smiled eagerly. When she turned toward his direction, Jack considered moving away and ignoring her. How childish was that? Instead, he smiled back and faced her. She sat down the crate and reached out for a hug.

"Hello stranger," her voice was intimate, he knew he'd have to say something quick.

"Deanna, so nice to see you after all of these years. Callen looks good." They both glanced toward her husband, who was at the soundboard.

"He's sober and ready to play. How are things with you?"

"Excellent. Having a good time on the tour." How did he mention Paige without looking foolishly obvious?

Keely did his work for him, just at that moment she approached, "Jack, will Paige be back for tonight's show?" He put his hand on her arm and gave a grateful squeeze, though she looked at him quizzically.

"No, not until late tomorrow." As he was turning to tell Deanna who they were talking about, he saw Joe a distance away over her shoulder, he was giving his friend a thumbs up. So, his old pal had known what was going on. He owed him one.

"Are you married?" Deanna raised an eyebrow.

"They might as well be," snorted Keely as she walked away. Jack felt relief flood through him.

"Jack Corey in a relationship? It's been a while."

He laughed, "I've dated."

"But nothing serious. Isn't that how you usually like it? No strings attached."

It surprised Jack to see a spark in her eyes that may have been resentment. Had he been the only one who thought the affair was just sex? Deciding to avoid talk of the past, he focused on the present, "Paige is different."

"A musician? A crew member or your old favorite; a model?" the bitterness in Deanna's voice was new. The years of helping Callen through his addiction had taken its toll.

"She teaches art at a high school."

This amused her and he was fine with it. Her face relaxed, "How you met must be some story."

"It's kind of sweet." Before the conversation continued, Callen approached, arms stretched happy to see his old friend.

***

The bands got into their groove together quickly. Callen and Jack bounced back and forth on lead vocals and side by side played the guitar solo parts. The crowd went crazy screaming the lyrics. It was a great way to end the dual concert.

Afterward, Jack showered and put on clean clothes. There was a gathering in the venue's party room. Media, contest winners and some people involved in the research foundation would be present. Once again, he felt the absence of Paige strongly. He wanted her next to him in all this. A nugget of resentment grew as he enjoyed a glass of wine.

Annabeth had stood nearby as he shook all the right hands, signed autographs and posed for photos. That was good material for the book. When it was down to social time, she had wandered nearer to Trent. Seeing them flirting added to Jack's irritation. That too increased when he thought of Paige. It was her fault he even cared about that. Trent had behaved like this for years and Gina had let him. It wasn't his place to judge because Paige looked at them disapprovingly.

Next to him, a familiar voice spoke, "It was a great show tonight."

Jack turned to Deanna, "It was. Stonemaster sounds great. Our number together went well."

"It's so nice to see you after all these years," her voice was low and flirty. Jack had the urge to step back. "What're you drinking?"

"Cabernet."

"Would I like it?" Jack wanted to ask how he would know, when she gave him a smile and said, "You know what I like."

"Let me get you a glass," Jack spoke and went to retrieve one from the bar. By now she had found a table.

"Do I get to hear this sweet story?" she asked.

Jack poured her a glass, "Do you really want to?" He recalled the unhappiness that seemed to fill her earlier in the afternoon.

She stopped mid-sip and raised her eyebrows, "Good point, not really."

There didn't seem to be a response to that, so Jack just focused on his drink.

Deanna was pouring another when she blurted out, "I was kind of hoping we'd pick where we left off." She saw his shock, "It was nice, I could use some adventure."

He felt pressured to agree, "It was fun, but I shouldn't have. Callen's a friend."

"How many times did you say that? Why isn't your girlfriend here?"

Jack couldn't help frowning, his irritation coming to the surface, "I think she's getting tired of the road show."

"Well, then this won't last. It's a fact that if you want to be with a rocker, you must get used to the life. Hasn't Gina Crosby told her that?"

"Yes, she has." Now he got angry, "I thought she understood all that. I'm wondering if she's really in it."

Deanna laid a hand on his bare arm, her long crimson nails scratching lightly, "A woman needs to know what a man like you needs after a big show."

***

The flight was uneventful. Paige had slept for most of it. Her communication with Jack had been intentionally vague. He was very excited about how the duo concert performance had gone. Someone had filmed it and he couldn't wait to share it with her. A perusal of social media led her to some glowing reviews of the Jack Corey band and Stonemaster doing a remake of *Light My Fire* together. Jack was still touted as the premier guitarist of his time.

She felt reasonably rested by the time she reached the hotel. Paige wasn't certain what room Jack was in but as always, the identification around her neck resulted in the information. It was only 15 minutes after six in the morning; she knew he'd still be sound asleep. She requested that her large suitcase be kept downstairs. The caravan was headed out this afternoon and there was no need to lug that up to her room, especially when she expected Jack to be asleep. Grabbing only her carry-on and her purse, she tipped the young man and headed into the elevator.

***

The room was nearly pitch black as Paige entered. There was only the light of the bathroom left on with the door slightly ajar. She could see that Jack was in the bed. Surprisingly, the other side of the bed seemed to be occupied as well. She circled around to it, curiosity getting the most of her. Someone was definitely in there. Paige felt her chest tighten. This couldn't be.

Now she was just a few feet away. Her eyes had adjusted to the dim lighting. Paige took a closer look, her pulse beating in her ears. She suddenly recognized the familiar curve and slender form. Unable to control it, she gave a shaky laugh. She should've known.

Jack was in bed with his first love. His guitar was at his side. Paige carefully reached over and picked up his Gibson acoustic. She set it both gently on the chair. Then she removed her sandals, her jeans, her t-shirt. She pulled the covers back to climb in next to Jack.

He was warm, she knew she was cool to the touch. Paige let her fingers run lightly across him, starting at his collarbone and down to his belly. Jack shivered and then groaned in pleasure. Her hand had just reached one hip bone when his eyes flew open in alarm. He turned his head and looked at her. It was a moment before Jack realized who it was. His face broke into one of the biggest grins she'd ever seen.

"Hello beautiful," he said, and he wrapped his arms tight around her. "What the hell are you doing here already?"

Paige leaned in and touched his face, "I know I'm crazy, but I missed you so much. I wanted to go home and get time to myself and then I didn't want it."

Jack gave her a long kiss. "I know exactly what you mean. Last night's party was awful. I missed you."

"I watched the duet online on the plane, you guys were incredible. Tell me all about it." Paige had sat up, her hands moving in excitement.

Jack had other ideas, he sat up too, and reached around to her bra strap, "I will darling, but not right now." He swiftly removed the unnecessary garment. Then he laid her back on the bed and slid off her panties. His kisses began at her neck and moved down. Paige knew showing up this early was the best decision ever.

***

They were headed to the elevator hand in hand when Annabeth stepped out of her own room. Her eyes could not disguise her emotions; a mixture of shock and relief. "Paige, when did you get home?"

Paige adored that phrase, for she was feeling that this unique collection of individuals was a kind of family. She did not understand Annabeth's expression, "Just this morning. I found Jack sleeping with his first love."

Annabeth made a choking cough but before she could say anything, Jack intervened, "That' what she calls my Gibson. I fell asleep working on the bridge for my new song."

Recovering, Annabeth responded, "That sounds like you. I didn't see you leave the party."

He understood and felt the need to explain, "I left Deanna Badger," Now he turned to Paige, "Callen's wife, with a bottle of wine. After my second glass, I was ready to call it a night. She deserves a good drink occasionally." To Paige he added, "Callen is once again trying to sober up, so Deanna never gets to have a drink."

"That was nice of you." Jack hadn't felt very nice when he had rejected Deanna last night, he'd felt guilty.

Chapter 20

Columbus, Ohio

At last, the tour had taken them back to Ohio. The show would be in Columbus on the weekend, so Jack and Paige headed back to her house for the days off. There was a sense of familiarity with the two of them being in her house. This was his third visit, and he treated it like home. She wondered if she should try his place again, in hopes of better results.

She happily pulled the lasagna and potato soup out of the freezer. They'd eat home cooked food for two meals. Jack opened the fridge, looking for something to drink. He pulled out a bottle of water and took a swig. "I love lasagna. Are you going to cook for me again?"

She remembered the surprise visit he'd paid in May. It seemed years ago, their relationship had advanced at lightning speed. "Sort of, I made these."

Now, he seemed content to be watching daytime television on her couch while she caught up on unpaid bills and took care of some emails.

"Is there anything you'd be doing in New York, that you need to do here?"

Jack ran his hands through his hair, "I'd like to get a haircut."

Paige considered her own salon. There were usually four or five stylists in at a time, so it was fairly populated. "I can see if there's an opening at my salon. There may be a few people there."

He reached up and clasped her fingertips, "Are you trying to keep me a secret?"

"No, I thought maybe you didn't want to be recognized."

Now he pulled her down beside him. "It's no big deal. I really think nothing about it."

Paige leaned into him and pulled out her phone. She sent a text to Morgan, her stylist, asking if she had any openings. Fortunately, she did late that afternoon. "Okay, we'll go grab lunch in a couple of hours. Then you can get a haircut and I can get groceries."

Jack moved close and kissed her, "Playing house, I love it." That decision made, they sat back and watched the rest of the HGTV show he had on, each choosing which beach house was the best.

***

At the salon, he held open the door then placed his hand on the small of her back. This was normal for Jack, but today in her hometown it felt different. Anyone who's eyes watched their entrance knew they were a couple. Did they also recognize Jack?

It was the middle of summer, so she'd encouraged him to leave his jeans and recognizable boots in the closet. Jack looked good in grey shorts, a black t-shirt with a Corvette logo on it and black slip-on Gucci sneakers on his feet. Paige realized that even in this style of clothes, Jack stood out. He was so damn handsome.

Once inside the salon, Jack pulled off his sunglasses. Several pairs of eyes were, in fact, looking at him. She wasn't sure if they recognized him or just saw how good looking he was. Morgan turned around from her station and squealed, "Paige!" She then smiled when she saw who had accompanied her, "I wondered if you were my next client." Apparently, Paige's personal life was no longer a secret.

Jack gave her his megawatt grin, and his identity was clear "Thanks for fitting me in."

Morgan gave Paige a brief hug, "I've been seeing you on Instagram. One of my customers follows the Jack Corey band. It looks like you've had a good summer, so far."

While she talked, Morgan led Jack to her chair and fitted him with a smock. She ran her fingers through his hair, Paige thought she detected a tremble. She sat in the unused chair next to him. "Just a trim?"

"That'd be great," he was using his nicest, huskiest voice. Paige realized he was playing the crowd a bit. When she looked in the mirror at the patrons behind her, she saw photos being taken with phones and fingers flying with messages. She only hoped that no one else would show up.

"So how did you two meet?" Morgan asked as she clipped his hair. Jack told the story, smiling at Paige. Morgan turned to her, "Then you left with him?"

"No, I finished the school year. It took a couple of weeks for us to track each other down."

"I think *I* was looking for *you*," Jack grinned.

Paige could almost guarantee that the next person to sit in the chair would hear this story. Morgan finished Jack's haircut. He readily agreed to a picture with her. As they left the shop, he also signed a few autographs.

***

The next night, they agreed to a dinner party at Laurel's house. Laurel held her best friend in a long hug. Jack stood back patiently. Paige was nearly tearful, feeling the familiarity of her friend at her side. She now moved to Jack, "Laurel, I would like you to officially meet Jack Corey."

Laurel smiled, then for the first time that Paige could ever remember, was at a loss for words. Pete came up behind her and rescued her. He held out his hand, "Jack Corey, I'm such a big fan. So glad you could come over with Paige. We're big fans of hers too."

This immediately won Jack over. The four of them were moving from the foyer of the attractive split level when suddenly there was the feeling of movement and a large dog nudged between Laurel and Pete. "Roger!" squealed Paige. She leaned down to the massive mop of gray and white fur and gave him a hug. Roger, an English Sheepdog, responded with a big, wet kiss. Jack laughed and leaned down to scratch the big dog who enthusiastically licked Jack too.

Jack laughed, "Roger?" They all moved with the dog, into the living room. Pete directed the group out onto a magnificent deck that was partially covered by a roof. Roger raced through the yard at an imagined rabbit.

"Yes, I'm a big *Who* fan. I couldn't resist."

Jack nodded his head, "I get it, Roger and Pete! It's perfect." While they talked, Pete led him to an outdoor bar.

"Do you like Kentucky Bourbon?"

"Yes, I do." Pete handed him a tumbler of golden liquid.

The four couples sat at a glass-topped table. Laurel jumped in, telling Paige some work gossip. They'd discovered two middle school teachers having an affair. The women laughed over the tale, both speculated on the chance of it lasting.

Roger, back from the yard, joined them on the patio. He laid his large head on Jack's knee. Jack smiled, "I wonder if there are any dogs named after me?"

"I'm sure there are," replied Laurel.

Paige joined in, "I'm certain. Look how many little girls are named after the Disney princesses of their mother's childhood. Somewhere, a woman is yelling at Jack to get off the couch."

"Or, Jack quit pooping in the neighbor's yard," Laurel joined into the joke. It pleased Paige that they were all getting along.

"Where's Liz this weekend?" she turned to Jack. "Liz is Pete's 15-year-old daughter from his first marriage."

Jack gave them a solemn nod, "I have a child with my ex-wife."

"Me too," Paige chimed in.

"Liz stays with us every other weekend and more times in the summer and on holidays. It's getting trickier now that she's old enough to make her own choice," Laurel explained.

"I admit that I spoil her just to see her," Pete shrugged. "You're damn right you do, last weekend we took her shopping, she maxed out his card."

"I get it, man." Jack shook his head, "You should've seen the car JJ convinced me to buy when he turned 16." The night continued to flow well. Jack invited Pete and Laurel to come to the show in Columbus.

***

Hannah's work schedule didn't coincide with their time in Findlay. She would have to wait until Saturday in Columbus to meet

Jack. Paige was very disappointed. Jack consoled her by getting the kids a room at the same hotel as they were staying. The four agreed to meet for lunch at the patio restaurant in the hotel.

Jack gave Hannah a hug the first moment he saw her. Paige squeezed both kids tight. It had been a long time.

Halfway into lunch, Jack was called away. There was a problem at the venue. He gave Paige a kiss, and they agreed to meet before the show.

***

Just two hours later, they headed out of the Express Live building as Pete and Laurel approached from the area next to the busses and trucks. Pete was looking at the tour bus. "Do we get to go in this?"

Paige moved toward it, "Of course. Let's go now, it'll be empty." She had rushed around all morning, making certain it was clean on the bus. Assistants came in every morning to do actual cleaning, but the band could be messy. Paige had felt like a mother hen, forcing everyone to pick up their clothes, do their dishes and make their bed. The plug-in air fresheners she'd picked up at *Target* were placed in four corners on the bus. Her friends and family climbed up the few steps.

She felt almost a proud ownership as they oohed and aahed at the luxurious traveling accommodations. Only Laurel whispered to her, "How can you stand to be in these tight quarters every day?"

"Believe me, I can't. We get a hotel whenever we aren't going directly from one venue to another."

"Good idea." Now they were at the sleeping quarters . "Where's your bunk?" Laurel was pulling back each curtain.

Paige led her down the row and pulled the curtain back on the last one.

Laurel elbowed her. "Ooh, close quarters"

Paige pushed back. "Stop it!" she protested, her head tilting to show her daughter was listening.

But Hannah jumped in, "No doubt, Mom. This looks like my dorm bed."

Paige closed the curtain, "And I don't want to hear who you shared it with." She shooed the group out of the bunks.

The lounge area impressed Pete. They all sat for a moment. Keely appeared in the doorway. "Hey."

Tonight's outfit was a tiny frayed denim skirt and a rhinestone-covered hot pink tee that drew dangerously low over one shoulder. The hoops in her ears nearly reached her bare shoulders. On her feet were sandals that snaked around her calves. The skinny spiked heels looked impossible to walk on. "Want to grab food?"

Paige stood up. "This is Keely. She's Joe Casto's girlfriend."

Pete shot up and held up his hand. "I'm a huge fan of Joe's. Best drummer ever."

Keely gave a half smile and rolled her eyes. Pete was probably her dad's age but then again so was Joe. "Thanks. So, do you?" She directed her gaze back to Paige.

Paige turned to the group, "Let's go eat."

The group headed out.

***

Paige stood with her friends and family at the side of the stage. The band was in full swing, belting out *Find Me*. She felt so proud, which was a funny response as those closest to her watched and cheered in amazement.

Afterward, they circled around Jack as if he'd just won the Superbowl. In his world versus theirs, it was similar. Jack didn't mind, he loved getting to be around the people important in Paige's life. He touched her back, enjoying that in the halter jumpsuit it was bare. She turned and looked at him. Her eyes shone with pure bliss. He kissed the top of her head and spoke to the group, "I'll go clean up then let's see what kind of trouble we can get into."

Tonight, Jack dressed more like the crowd he was with. He stepped out of the building in white jeans and a pale blue linen buttoned shirt. On his feet were light loafers. Seeing Paige in the sexy one-piece thing had inspired him. The effort paid off in her expression as he approached the group. They headed by foot down the street. In his outfit with this group of six, he felt safe he wouldn't be recognized. He held Paige's hand as they walked to a rooftop bar a few blocks away.

He was glad he'd already spent an evening with Pete. He was asking a lot of questions about the other musicians and some questions about sound; his electrical engineering curiosity kicking into overdrive.

They snagged a table that showed them the expanse of Columbus. He ordered a bottle of his favorite Cabernet. Kyle and Hannah declined any, choosing instead to be beer drinkers. Laurel reminded Pete that they had to go home later. Jack offered to get them a room for the evening. Laurel thanked him but said they had Roger waiting for them. The conversation flowed as well as the drinks. Jack loved the feeling of being just one of the group, not a celebrity.

Kyle turned to Jack, “I love JJ sportswear.”

Jack’s eyes lit up proudly “Oh yeah? Me too.”

“I’m on a golf league for work and the shorts and shirts are the best!”

“Have you tried the golf shoes? They’re rated number one this season.”

Kyle looked embarrassed, “Not yet. Out of my price range. But I have some of his workout clothes.”

“Me too, that’s all I wear. I can’t believe how soft they are.”

Laurel turned to Paige, “So did you hear we have two pregnant teachers in our building?”

Paige replied, “When doesn’t the elementary? Will they start the year?”

“Yes. They’re both early. Bill Dodge left the history department.”

“Why?”

“He’s going to some high paying academy in Cincinnati.”

“I heard from Mike in the middle school. It looks like they messed up our supply order again,” Paige lamented. “Next time I’m home, I must get together with him and sort it all out. I don’t want to wait until it’s time for school to have my supplies unpacked.” This statement caught Jack’s attention.

Later when they were in bed, Paige was looking on her phone. Jack spoke, “I heard you talking about school tonight.”

She was distracted, “Yes.”

“When does it start?”

“August 26th.”

“That’s too soon.”

“Don’t I know it. The summer always flies.” Paige plugged her phone in on the nightstand and turned to Jack.

"You don't have to go back to school."

She rubbed his cheek. "Yes, I do. I'm under contract. I can't stay on tour forever."

"The tour doesn't last forever."

She leaned in and kissed him, "Let's not worry about it tonight. Thanks for hanging out with my gang."

"I loved it."

"They loved you. It was such a normal night with them, and the bonus was having you with us. Hannah really likes you. I think she's finally convinced that I'm not a middle-aged groupie forcing myself onto your bus or that you're just a figment of my imagination and I'm really hiding out on the crew bus."

Jack smiled at that. "Hey, get me Kyle's shoe size. I want to send him some of JJ's golf shoes."

"That is sweet."

***

The next morning found the four of them wandering the counters at the North Market. Paige discovered that Jack had a passion for macarons, and they bought two of all fifteen flavors. She loved the barista who created a design on her latte. Though she showed no signs of recognizing Jack, when she handed over the mug to Paige, she shaped the foam into a guitar. Paige grinned, whispered *thank you* and then held up a finger to her lips begging her to keep the secret.

They parted ways with Hannah and Kyle in the parking lot. As she held her daughter close, Paige was tearful; a mixture of joy and sadness. It had been a wonderful 24 hours. Hannah got along well with Jack. She felt that her daughter supported her decision to spend the rest of the summer with him.

She was saddened to be leaving again. Though Hannah was an adult, the miles between them as she toured with the band seemed significant. Hannah whispered in her ear when she felt her mother squeeze tighter, “I’ve never seen you this way. I love it. Enjoy this time, Mom.” By the time she pulled away, Paige was all smiles.

Chapter 21

Denver, Colorado

For weeks now, Annabeth had plugged along on her manuscript. The tour was uneventful in some ways. She'd figured out the routine. The material for the section of live performances was very detailed; notes on that part of Jack Corey and his band. When the time came, these notes and the many photos and videos she'd taken would lend itself to strong chapters. Musicians, as well as fans, would enjoy reading it because she was certain she could capture the essence of a concert with her words.

Jack's past was explored as well. His life held little secrets. He'd been forthcoming about his childhood, the early years of the band and the history there. The band, itself, was a positive story. She'd interviewed Theo for an extensive amount of time. Sadly, her need to stay on the tour was quickly ending. Annabeth would miss this group of people.

There was another reason she was still around, one she wasn't willing to face. Trent Crosby was her own personal hell. Their relationship, if you could call it that, had been many things. They'd had sloppy drunk sex behind the bus, in the bathroom at bars, even in the dressing room at a venue. They'd had more affectionate trysts in his bunk on the bus where half the thrill was being so quiet that no one knew what was going on. Her favorite times they shared were in hotel rooms. After sex, they would stay in bed and watch a movie; usually while eating outrageously expensive room service.

They spent no other time together. If Annabeth thought she could fool herself into thinking it was a relationship, she was wrong. He didn't acknowledge her during the day, especially in front of the band. They'd never gone to lunch together, or sightseeing. Those romantic movie moments were all experienced by Paige and Jack. Their relationship made Annabeth beat herself up even more over the times she snuck around with Trent.

At home in New York, she wasn't in the habit of regular hook-ups, but they happened. She'd dated a few guys, had a man or two live with her for extended amounts of time. The sex thing with Trent was its own entity. First, he was a star she'd admired for decades. Second, he turned her on when he was on stage. She'd watch him with his bass, pounding out that sexy deep rhythm and she was hot all over. Finally, being on this trip was lonely. The hours of travel usually lent itself to writing time, but not always. When she'd see Jack and Paige jump on their bikes and head out to explore the next city, something felt empty inside. It was laughable to even consider she and Trent strapping on bike helmets and following the paths through a city, that was neither of their styles, but at least she had close human contact.

Paige was a nice woman. She was also a hell of an artist. Annabeth considered that if she stayed with Jack and ended up in New York, she might really make a living at it. Why wouldn't she stay with Jack? He was the hottest man that Annabeth had ever seen, hands down. He kept that fifty-year-old body in top, muscular condition. Jack also knew, or his stylist knew, how to fit jeans to show it all off. Add a snug fitting t-shirt and boots and he was every woman's fantasy. Annabeth had to admit, he'd been hers a time or two, sometimes even when she was in the bunk with Trent, knowing just yards away was Jack asleep in his.

It thrilled Annabeth to see the two of them; Paige and Jack. They were unaware she'd also been documenting their story. She kept a log of their activities and took her share of stealthy photos and videos. If they progressed and appeared to be lasting, it would be a great final chapter to the book. Jack Corey took the band back out on the road to give his fans what they wanted, and in return, he found true love. This stuff was practically writing itself.

She wasn't finding true love. Annabeth hadn't even particularly cared about that. Her career kept her occupied. Earning a living as a writer was work that required a lot of self-discipline. Pursuing romance was more than she had time for. Besides, she considered herself a person who lacked what it took to be that loving. She wasn't much into personal appearance, clean but with little effort towards hair and makeup. In her opinion, a little mascara could go a long way. The tour had forced her to wear more than jeans occasionally. Jack and the band were very accommodating, including her in everything. She suspected that Tony had made this the rule when they agreed on the book. He saw it as a big money maker and something that would bring the Jack Corey band back into the limelight enough to convince Jack to do a new album.

Attending some of the better shows, after parties and charity events had forced Annabeth to purchase dress clothes. She wished she could take Paige with her. Paige's own style was quickly evolving into what a rock star's classy girlfriend should look like. She was wearing dresses that accentuated her body and sexy strappy sandals. Annabeth opted for black pants and tops.

Gina Crosby had re-appeared like a bad egg. Annabeth dreaded having her join the tour. Trent was so rude about it, he'd treated her as if she was chasing him. He'd warned that his wife and family were coming so she better not even look at him sideways. It was humiliating and worse were the hot tears that filled her eyes and threatened to spill out. Annabeth had been so furious that she'd left the band bus and gotten on the crew bus. The atmosphere was nice back in that bus. No one was above anyone else. She joined in on a euchre tournament with two roadies and the wardrobe assistant. They were drinking coffee with Baileys and eating from the biggest box of donuts she'd ever seen. The music playing in this bus was country, no egos in here about who's music was crap compared to the Jack Corey band.

An hour or so into the game, the buses stopped for a bathroom break and to fill up the tanks. Annabeth and her card buddies didn't move. The door opened and Trent climbed on. "What the fuck are you doing in here?" he looked at her companions and dismissed them as not needing acknowledged.

"I'm playing cards," she didn't make eye contact.

"Well, come on, let's go back to the bus." It was more of a demand than a request. Annabeth wanted to tell him to go to hell. These people were nicer. These people hadn't just told her that when his family arrived in 24 hours, she had to get lost. Dammit, though, she laid her cards down.

“Thanks, guys, this was fun. Ricky, will you take my hand?” The others said nothing, but she saw a look exchanged, it was something between disgust and pity. Hating herself, Annabeth followed Trent off the bus.

***

Page heard Gina’s tone on the phone and got the message. Gina demanded, “What’s going on with my husband?”

Page winced, “What do you mean?”

“He’s been sweet on the phone and you’re being evasive. This tour is not my first rodeo, you know. Does he have a woman with him? Has some 20-something joined the tour with him?”

Paige’s intake of breath was audible, she attempted to sound casual, “No, he hasn’t brought someone with him.”

“Don’t act so surprised. It’s happened before.”

“Oh, Gina.”

“Spit it out, if that’s what’s going on, just tell me. I want to know before I get to Denver.”

Paige took a deep breath, “I promise you, he didn’t bring a girl.”

“So, then what’s going on? Come on, you were dying to tell me in Cleveland. What changed your mind?”

“Jack told me you don’t want to know.” Now there was an awkward silence.

Gina spoke, “It’s true. It’s something I’ve overlooked and accepted. Now listen, Paige, it’s embarrassing for me to ask you this. Before we get to Denver, especially with my kids, I need to know who my husband is sleeping with.”

Paige couldn’t believe she was in this situation. She’d been around people who had affairs. Hell, her ex-husband got married so quickly, it was obvious he had an affair. Everyone had told her to stay out of it, and now Gina was asking for details. It put her in a spot. She considered all the angles and as much as she respected Jack, she also counted her friendship with Gina important. "All right, I'll tell you." Gina was silent waiting for the answer. "Trent and Annabeth."

Before she could go further, Gina said, "Thank you, Paige. How long has it been going on?"

"I think it must have begun shortly after Cleveland. It's been going on since I've been on the tour."

Gina's voice sounded disappointed and surprised, "Annabeth, seriously?"

Paige tried to explain, "Well I guess she's always available,"

"Are they together every night?"

"I honestly don't know. On the bus, I don't see her in his bunk."

"But when you're at hotels?"

"Probably. I know for a fact at least a couple of times. But they're not living like a couple. To be honest, Gina, I think she hates herself for it. We had a confrontation when I first joined the tour and she told me she didn't want to do it. I think she gets lonely. I'm sorry, I'm not sticking up for her. You know I'm the one who's wanted to tell you everything."

Gina spoke up, "You're right. I'm not mad at you. We both know I should be mad at myself. This has been going on for so long."

"Why do you put up with it? I'm sorry, I know it's not any of my business. I need your friendship. I'll be clear here, I want your friendship. I care about you and I hate what's going on, but it's not my business. Every marriage is different. Every relationship is different," Paige was talking quickly, stumbling over her own phrases.

"It's okay, I get what you're saying. You will not lose my friendship. You'll gain my friendship by caring this much. I married him like any starry-eyed young girl ever does. He was everything; he was rough and gruff and sweet and talented and the life on the rock tour was so fun. We had Reed, and we loved being parents together. He was so wonderful. Trent would put Reed in one of those packs on his back and take him with him on stage to warm up. Reed loved the music. To be honest, I think it's when Callie came along that it became too much for him. I had to be the mom and not just the fun partner. I didn't want to travel all the time with them. Trent's ego was so big that he had to be first in everything.

When Callie turned one, I walked away. We were apart for almost a year and he made the papers. The tabloids caught with multiple women in his hotel room. Groupies were also giving him what he needed right there behind the venues. The problem was that when he came home to see the kids; it was like Christmas. It was too damn easy to fall into it, way too easy when the father of your children travels. You get no time, there's no split custody. And I was feeling pretty ripped off.

He decided he wanted us back; I took him. I never had the nerve to say, 'no more women' and I think Trent to this day uses that as an excuse. I have an ideal lifestyle, I can do what I want. He's good to the kids when he's around them. I see my friends in New York who have regular marriages. At our age, they're bored. The people on the bus like Keely and Joe, I think they care about each other, but obviously, the girl has daddy issues. Then you appear and watching you and Jack at our age and being in love. I must tell you, it's pissed me off. It pissed me off because I sold myself out 15 years ago and I hate it. The only reason I wanted to know about Annabeth was that I need a reason to reconsider my choices. I don't know if I can do it, Paige. I don't know if I can deal with all of it, but it's what I want to do."

"You want to leave him?"

Gina hesitated, "I do."

Paige's voice was gentle, "I've been through a divorce, I know what it's like. I waited until my daughter was older and that helped. You deserve more."

"I really do."

"Jack will kill me."

Gina responded, "No he won't. He's such a good guy."

"Then why did he let this happen?"

"About every two years, he would tell me I should leave."

Paige was secretly pleased, "Then why was he so tough on me when I wanted to say something?"

"Because we're family and you weren't yet. But as of today, we have a new family member."

Paige gave a relieved laugh, "Then hurry and get to Denver!"

"I will enjoy my time there with the kids and the week in California. I will soak in all the celebrity status and the fun things we get to do. You'll love the places we go. The life we live when we're in California is amazing. I will live it as his wife. Please, I'm begging you, don't say a word to anyone, not even Jack. Let me do this my way because that's the worst part. If I walk away, I won't get to do any of this again. I may have the money, but I'll never have the celebrity status. For this week, let me be Trent's adoring wife; happy to be back with him. It will be our secret and I'll show you how to live their high life. Is that a deal? Will you do that for me?"

***

Gina came up the ramp from the airplane, two teens behind her. The girl was tall and lanky like her dad, her long chestnut hair resembling what his hair looked like on those long-ago album covers; thick and shiny. The boy had taken most of his looks from Gina. He stood an inch taller than the girl, his hair was the rich dark chocolate tone that Gina had told Paige was her natural color. His eyes were a matching shade, just like his mom. Gina got to Paige and grabbed her in a hug.

Paige was surprised at her own response, it felt like she was reuniting with a sister she hadn't seen for a while. The past weeks had made her so eager to share some tour time with Gina. Now here she was for a while. They released each other and Gina introduced her to the teens

Reed looked at his mother, "Where's Dad?"

Paige answered for Gina, "There was some issue with the stage, so I offered to meet you guys. He was disappointed not to do it himself." She wasn't certain what the kids' exchanged expression signified. Was Trent an absent father even when he was home? Were they aware of his constant infidelity? It pained her to think they might.

***

The three women, Paige, Gina, and Keely were back where they'd first formed their friendship; offstage during a show. The kids were at the board with Tony. Like Jack, they treated him as if he was a familiar uncle. Paige saw more compassion from the man with these two than she'd ever witnessed. He was animated in his conversation with them. The boy apparently was showing him some video footage of a baseball game because Tony was pantomiming hitting a ball.

Gina turned to Keely. "Tell me about Theo."

"So far he's staying in rehab. Everyone was glad to have him back on stage."

"Damn him, I wanted it to work out for him this time," as she spoke, her eyes were following Annabeth, who was snapping pictures on stage.

Keely rolled her eyes, "That bitch."

"No," Gina said pointedly, "that son of a bitch." Her head moved toward her husband. "Now back to Theo, did he seem fine?"

"Yes. Trent and Jack took him out on his first night and like total assholes, they both got wasted in front of him," Keely was livid.

"It was poor judgment," Paige agreed.

"Idiots," Gina added. "He didn't fall off the wagon?"

Keely glanced out at the musicians they were discussing, "Lucky for them, no. But it didn't take long."

"Sadly, it's Theo's fight alone," Gina said. "His life's been a disaster for years."

Keely changed the subject, "Our girl Paige, here, is getting to be a regular rock chick. She and Jack even kicked us all downstairs the other day so they could have the place to themselves."

Paige looked embarrassed, Gina gave her a thumbs up, "You sleep with the big dog, you take advantage of the perks." She glanced at Keely, "This one took to the tour life like it was what she was used to. How about you?"

"Oh no, the close quarters with everyone has been a challenge, not showering first thing in the morning hasn't been ideal either. But I'm learning."

"Glad you two are still getting along so well."

"There've been some bumps."

Keely laughed, "She took off while everyone was asleep. Jack rented a car and found her filling a cart at *Target*."

Paige nodded, "It's true."

"He rented a car to find you?"

"I'd gone for breakfast down the street and after that needed some retail therapy."

"That's so funny. Did he think you were mad at him?"

"I was, that was the night he and your husband took Theo out. It was all good, he even showed up in time to pay for everything." The three women laughed.

***

When Gina arrived, she brought with her two beautiful teenagers. It hurt Annabeth's heart to see how much the tall, thin girl resembled her father. The kids were thrilled to see their father; she saw his genuine pleasure as he held them both tight. For the first few days, Annabeth stayed away from the family.

The entire band was staying in a mansion in Denver. The home boasted seven bedrooms. Annabeth had been paying her own expenses with the advance she'd received for the book from the publisher. This time she was grateful that she did because she secured herself the smallest but still luxurious private bedroom and bath a floor away from the Crosby family.

The days in Denver allowed her to spend time talking to Tony. He had excellent stories of his own about Jack. It was a great perspective coming from someone who managed the band, got to see their move to stardom. They spent a couple of hours sitting by the pool, Annabeth with her notepad. When the Crosby kids appeared, dressed for a swim, she nearly took off. Fortunately, it was just the teenagers, she could continue her time out there.

***

Jack gave Paige a quick kiss as he left their bedroom. From the window, she could see Carla and Ricky bringing in black crates. The band was meeting in the basement room for some planning practice. She knew she'd be without him for at least two hours.

Going to her portfolio case, she pulled out her latest canvas. The piece was coming along nicely. Though normally she wasn't a fan of landscape drawing, the lake house was spectacular. The photos of a dozen different angles gave her the unique challenge of bringing not only the house to life but the feel of the moving waves of Lake Erie. After a few strokes on the chimney, Paige found herself uninterested in sitting in a quiet room, with only the sounds of a distant guitar to keep her company. She packed the project away and wandered down to the main floor.

Seated on different ends of a mammoth leather sectional were Gina and Keely. Paige sat in the middle, "Where are the kids?"

Gina was looking at a *Denver Life* magazine that had been on the coffee table carved from a slab of oak. "They're hiking with their dad."

"You didn't want to join the family adventure?"

Gina tossed the magazine back on the table, "They're here for quality time with him. I'm with them all the time. It's good for Trent to spend these precious moments with them both." Because they were typical teenagers, her tone on the last line was sarcastic.

Paige spent her working hours with teens and laughed appreciatively. Keely was glued to her phone, as always, but added, "About damn time he took his turn."

Annabeth walked into the room and Paige felt the temperature change. Had the two had it out over Trent? The women exchanged a brief look, Annabeth seemed to try for some conciliatory action. "Ladies, can I fix someone a drink?" She moved to the large bar in the room's corner.

Gina shook her head. Paige spoke, "No thank you. I'm only drinking at the shows. Otherwise, I'm drinking too much."

Keely said, "Hey we're in Colorado, we need more than alcohol."

"I've got just the thing." Annabeth moved toward the sectional and sat between Keely and Paige. She pulled a large joint from her jeans pocket. "How about this?"

Keely clapped her hands, "Now that's what I'm talking about."

Gina slid closer to Paige, "Why not?"

"I haven't smoked for years." The other three women stared at Paige. "I'm a teacher, we get drug tested."

Annabeth lit the joint, she handed it to Paige first, "Happy summer vacation."

The four women shared the weed and watched the panoramic view of the mountains in front. Keely was telling them a story about her grandmother eating a bag of marijuana gummy bears she found in Keely's book bag from high school. They were giggling when Carla appeared from the basement.

She took a sniff and walked toward them, "I smell a women's weed party. If it's a BYOJ, I want to join." At that, she produced one from her jacket pocket. "Ready for more?" Carla sat at the right of Gina and they passed her joint around.

The stories were silly and light. Paige was not only feeling the giddy relaxation of being stoned but enjoying the shared intimacy with these women. Even Annabeth and Gina were at peace for the moment. Carla had her own story about being caught with a bag by her mom and they were laughing together.

Suddenly, Jack stood in front of them. Paige looked up at him, delighted to see he was done in the basement. She was unaware when the guitar and drum sounds had quieted. He, however, wasn't smiling. "Paige, if you're done getting stoned, can we talk?"

Keely stage whispered, "Busted."

Paige stood up, "Thank you, ladies, for a lovely afternoon." She was still smiling as she followed Jack to their room.

Once inside, he turned to her. "What were you doing?"

His tone surprised her and feeling the effects, she didn't really care for his disapproval, "Just passing the time with my friends."

"Oh, so it's okay for Gina and Annabeth to be friends when you say?"

"That was a little bitchy."

Jack turned, surprised. "I didn't know you'd start getting high."

Her laugh was an angry bark, "Start getting high? I smoked a little weed. Jack, you were busy. I was sitting around, again, with the women and we did it. What's the big deal?"

He leaned against the back of the loveseat and shrugged. "I don't want that to become a habit."

"Oh, you don't want that to become a habit? Are you making my rules?" She was standing directly in front of him, "Do I need to be down on my knees asking the great Jack Corey what rules I'm to follow when I'm here as his guest?" Paige turned her back on him. She grabbed her swimsuit and cover up then locked herself in the bathroom. When she emerged, Jack was sitting on the edge of the bed with his guitar.

He opened his mouth to speak, but she held up her hand, "Not now, I'm going to go for a swim, alone." She closed the bedroom door firmly as she left.

The water felt good as Paige climbed into the sparkling pool. With just her head above the water, she could see the sun, a yellow kaleidoscope. Sinking below it muffled all sound as she sat on the bottom of the pool. When she surfaced, she saw Gina standing at a table nearby.

Annabeth approached, a tray loaded with food in her hand. "I guess we all had the same thought." Behind her, the house cook followed with a pitcher of iced tea and frosty glasses.

Climbing out of the pool, Paige heard Gina speak, "I guess it's time we talked." She was looking at Annabeth. Paige grabbed her towel and looked as if she would leave the pool area. "Please stay," now Gina addressed her. The other two women both sat.

Paige poured them iced tea. Annabeth seemed very interested in the contents of her glass. She stared intently at the slowly melting ice.

"For too many years, I've ignored Trent's infidelity. I'm sure you've heard the rest of the band's creed *don't tell Gina*. I thought that was fine. Before this tour, my husband was home most nights. For years he wasn't. The band and their family just got used to the idea that I didn't want to know details. Now I'm feeling differently. I'm certain you and any other woman who was keeping my husband company," the suggestion that there could be more hit its intended mark, Annabeth was offended, "were told that I was coming to Denver and would be around for the California week and therefore back off." Annabeth still did not reply.

"Trent is right. When I'm around, he is to behave like the married man he's been for nearly twenty years." Her voice got thick. "Apparently it's too much to ask that he always act like that. Dammit, I'd accepted that until Jack found Paige." Now she looked at her accusingly, "You changed it all. You two walk around in this absurd cloud of love and it makes the rest of us feel like garbage."

Annabeth nodded. "It's true, it feels like that."

"Too soon," Gina rounded it back to her. "You don't get to have that
with my husband. You never get to have that with my husband. Stop sleeping with him. This isn't a request."

Annabeth was silent for a long moment. Just when Paige thought she wouldn't answer, she looked up and directly at Gina. "I'm sorry. You're right. I don't want to do that to you or myself."

To Paige's surprise, Gina smiled with satisfaction. "No, you don't. He's not worth it."

"Gina, I'm sorry. My actions were entirely selfish. I respect you for being direct. I will never come near your husband again."

***

Paige was pacing in front of Jack. "It was such a great moment. Gina said it was because of us she changed her mind." She had returned to their room.

At least an hour had passed, he was still there. Apparently, his anger hadn't completely abated. Jack gave her a half look from his guitar, the ever-present extra appendage to his body.

"She said what we have is an example of what they should all want."

Jack continued to strum his guitar and mumbled, "Trent will light into me after he gets that speech from both of his women." This outraged Paige that he'd say that even in jest and it didn't sound like he was joking.

"Jack, it's a good thing. "

Still, he focused on the guitar, stopping to adjust a fret. He said, "I thought they were both happy with the marriage they had."

"How could Gina be happy with him and his infidelity?"

He shrugged absentmindedly, "It's been that way for nearly twenty years."

Paige watched him, trying to tamper down her frustration, "Maybe they're all being premature about the fine example we are."

That got his attention, his hands dropped from the guitar and Jack looked up, "What?"

She dramatically shrugged her shoulders, "After all your mistress is with us 24/7."

His eyes focused on the instrument in his lap, "This is my career, my livelihood."

"I'm aware," she responded flippantly. "I'm not holding onto paint brushes or colored pencils every moment of my day." Paige knew she'd gone too far, but she couldn't stop. "Your career is at its peak, you no longer have to be honing your skill and writing new music to stay successful."

His eyes showed complete shock. In a moment of fury, he shoved the legal pad from the couch; it sailed across the room. "Well, it certainly seems like I don't need to be writing about a perfect summer." They'd crossed a line that neither could come back from. "I've spent my entire life with this guitar, I didn't realize that I had to give it up to have a relationship with you."

"I never asked you to do that, but I wasn't aware that I had to come in second place. I gave up my summer to be around you, but only when you aren't focused on that," she gestured at the instrument with disdain.

"Give up your entire summer? Spending this time with me is a sacrifice?" They were now both standing, facing off.

She backed down a little, "You know what I mean."

Jack wasn't ready to stop, "No Paige, I don't think I do. Why don't you explain it? Giving up your free time to get to travel the country with me and live the life I'm living is some sort of courtesy?"

"Oh, I see, I should submit to superstar Jack Corey because he has allowed me into the inner circle." They stared at one another, faces a mixture of anger and hurt. "Is this about the fact that I'm living at your expense? I'd be happy to pay my way."

That really annoyed him, "I don't give a fuck about the money. Don't you dare throw that back in my face! You started this!"

"No, I didn't. I came in here to tell you that Gina and Annabeth were discussing our relationship as if it was the finest of examples, one they both would like to follow. Somehow that annoyed you because it was breaking your boy code with Trent that has had you turning a blind eye to his regular cheating on his wife."

He held out his arms in exasperation, "They didn't need or want me to interfere They've stayed married. It was none of my damn business. It was none of your business either, but I'm guessing you told Gina all about Annabeth."

The accusation was a knife inserted, "I didn't go to Gina. She knew there was someone and finally asked me to tell her who it was. Then, and only when I got her promise that she wanted to know, did I say it was Annabeth." Paige turned away from him, "I have no place in this world that's yours. My presence here is causing more irritation than fun." She'd moved a few steps away and turned back to him, tears beginning to course down her cheeks which infuriated her, "Jack, I'll go."

He stood alone in the middle of the room, his eyes squeezed tight. Finally, he took a deep breath, his own voice was low and ragged, "Shit, Paige, you can't go. I don't want you to go. I'd lose my mind if you left." He was moving toward her, "I love you, baby. I'm sorry."

They embraced, she laid her head on his shoulder until her tears stopped, saying nothing.

He moved away just enough so that they were still holding hands and looking at one another. "What the hell just happened? We both exploded. Is something going on?"

She let go of his hand and used hers to touch his cheek, "I think I was full of adrenaline because of the conversation with those two. I came in here pumped to talk about it. Our moods just clashed."

"Do we need to discuss my music, your time here?" his eyes were still serious.

She shook her head, "How about the money part?"

"Never." Jack pulled her close again and said, "Everything is perfect."

Paige smiled, but in her mind, she was telling herself to lower her expectations and hold on to this. The time together was brief. She kissed him and reached her hands under his shirt and caressed him.

***

She woke up an hour later, naked on top of the sheets. When she opened her eyes, she could see the mountains outside of her window. An eagle soared near the clouds. Though her back was to him, she knew Jack was also awake, his hand began a slow trail of circles across her shoulders. She sighed appreciatively.

"Paige, is the tour boring you?" His fingers continued their movement. "I don't want you to hate our time together. I didn't mean to leave you this afternoon, we wanted to try something different on the intro of *Swept Away*."

Now she turned to face him and placed a hand on his bare chest. "Jack, I'm not unhappy being on the road with you. There are moments where I feel aimless, but I knew this would happen." She traced his jawline with her fingers, "I won't spend my time getting wasted, it was just something fun. I haven't smoked pot for years. Those women are the people I spend every show with. I won't sit up here in our room."

"I'm sorry I was a jerk. I feel like I'm always apologizing."

Paige pulled his mouth to hers and kissed him slowly. "You don't need to apologize. I'm getting accustomed to your schedule. We'll adjust."

***

The phone pulled her out of a deep slumber. Blackout curtains blocked the sun, Paige had no idea what time it was. She fumbled to pull her phone off the charger and answer. “Hello?” her voice was thick with sleep.

“Mom?” it was Hannah. “Are you asleep? It’s one o’clock in the afternoon.”

Paige saw Jack turn as if to avoid being woken up. She crawled out of bed and moved to the bathroom. The light made her flinch as she turned it on and closed the door. Sitting on the edge of the tub, she spoke, “It’s only ten here.”

“You sleep in?”

“Hannah, we had a show last night, with a meet and greet to follow. It was late when we got back to the house.”

“Listen to you, ‘we had a show’ like you’re part of it.”

“I am a part of it.” Her voice was terse. Paige took a deep breath to regain her composure, “How are you, dear? What are you doing on a Saturday afternoon?”

“I’ve got a surprise for you.”

Paige came fully awake, “Did you get engaged?”

“Now there’s my mother. No.” Hannah laughed.

“Are you pregnant?” this was said a little more cautiously. Paige glanced at her surroundings and the fact that she was only wearing an oversized band t-shirt. *Grandma?*

“No, but we got a new family member, a little gray kitten named Eleanor.”

“And what does Elliott think of this?”

Hannah launched into a tale of the two cats meeting. “I can’t wait for you to meet her. She’s so tiny and sweet. When am I going to see you, Mom?” This time her tone was reminiscent of the little girl she’d once been.

Paige felt a clutch of her heart, "I miss you too. We have a few days next week. I think I'll come home for a bit."

"That'd be great. Still want to stay on the tour, huh?"

"Yes."

Hannah redirected the conversation, "So how is Jack?"

"He's great. They did some new things at the show last night. It was amazing. The amphitheater is built into the rocks, so are the rows of seats. It was the coolest experience. And cool is the perfect word because up here in the mountains you need a jacket even in the middle of summer."

"How are you two?"

Paige thought about the last twenty-four hours. Would her daughter even believe her if she talked about getting stoned, the fight, the makeup sex and then the two of them dancing below the stars at the amphitheater after party? Probably not. "We're having a great time together."

"I can tell, you sound happy. I really hope I get to see you next week. Denver sounds nice. "

"The past few days we've all rented a house. Honestly, Hannah, it's the biggest place I've stayed in."

"So how many people are in it?"

Paige named the group out loud.

"There are enough rooms for everyone?"

"Yep."

"What's your room like?"

"It's the master suite, it has a panoramic view of the mountains and a great jet tub in the bathroom."

"You get the master?"

"Jack is Jack Corey. We even have a cooking and cleaning staff."

"I can't even comprehend half of what you're saying. Mom, this is a different world for you. You like it?"

"Yep, I'm acclimating quickly, you don't have a choice. We move at the speed of lightning."

When they hung up, Paige considered what she said to her daughter and the disastrous fight with Jack yesterday. He was wonderful and he loved her. Her focus needed to be making the most of these short weeks. Paige felt a pain in her chest when she considered that most likely the fall would find her back in Findlay, alone.

***

It was soundcheck time. Paige was with her regular crew. They'd sneaked over to a local restaurant for food that was more fulfilling than the guys' green room healthy spread. They'd found a steak place. Now working on their salads and enjoying a cocktail, Paige told them she'd had quite a row with Jack yesterday afternoon.

"What did you guys fight about?" Gina plucked a small tomato from her bowl and popped it into her mouth.

"I told him you complimented us when we were talking with Annabeth."

Keely interrupted, "You two talked to Annabeth together? What about?" She was eyeing Gina.

Gina rolled her eyes at Keely, "You know exactly what it was about." She turned back to Paige, "How did that turn into an argument?"

Paige had just swallowed a taste of her drink, she set the glass down. "It started about us getting stoned, that's why I was at the pool. Then I said he was too focused on his guitar and I made a reference to me being second place."

"Oh shit, you did not mention his precious guitar." This was Keely. "I've only been around for a year, and I know that's his holy grail." Gina nodded in agreement.

"Exactly why it turned into World War III."

"So, is it all worked out now?"

"Did you apologize for your mistake?"

Paige laughed at the two women, "We both apologized. It's fine. This whole thing is just a lot of adjusting. We barely knew each other and threw ourselves into a full-time relationship on the road."

Keely agreed, "When I hooked up with Joe, they were just doing a two-week stint for summer. It was better after the shows. By the time this tour started, we were solid. This would be a crazy way to start a relationship."

***

When Gina pinned Annabeth by the pool with Paige, it had come as something akin to a physical blow. Gina's questions had been direct, as had her command that it must end. It surprised Annabeth to discover that what she felt inside was mostly relief. She'd needed someone to decide for her. They had formed a fragile truce.

She couldn't be as friendly with Gina as she was with Paige and Keely. Keely was easy to get along with. She was young and felt as if she'd won a coup by ending up with Joe. The rocker girlfriend was as much of a fantasy life as a young woman at 26 from a poor Philly neighborhood could dream of. She was not the least bit bothered by his old age and seem to overlook it. Good for her, the wild way Joe had lived, he'd be lucky to survive another twenty-five years, then Keely could enjoy his money.

Paige was true to herself, she came into this group of people with no preconceived perceptions that because she shared the bed of the band's namesake she deserved more. As the weeks went by, she no longer looked guilty when they got the best suite or bedroom. Paige was intelligent enough to adjust quickly to it and not appear the country mouse living like a city mouse, but she was a nice person. She had not only been fascinated with the stories Annabeth had told her about Jack's earlier life; she found Annabeth's life interesting. To her, a *Rolling Stone* journalist was also a bit of a rock star. They had a rough moment when Paige confronted her about Trent with her own opinions. Annabeth knew she was going against Jack's wishes. The part she hated about it the most, was the more it upset Paige, the more she saw the disappointment in Jack's eyes when he caught her pushed up against the back of the bus, Trent's hands up her shirt. She was relieved that Gina had forced her to stop this humiliating behavior.

Chapter 22

San Francisco, California

The flight to California held many new experiences for Paige. She'd never sat in the executive lounges at the airports and been treated to so much pampering. This was compounded when they sat in first class, another new thing for her. The seats were huge, as recently as last month, she was squeezed into a row of seats with two other strangers whose knees knocked her own.

They landed at SFO, San Francisco's airport. A car was waiting for them. The crew had traveled with the busses and trucks. It was just the band, Tony and a couple of assistants who traveled by plane. The hotel they were taken to was a historic gem and had Paige's artistic instincts awed. Inside, their suite was palatial; as open and expansive as Jack's New York apartment, but furnished with elegance. Chandeliers hung above them. There was a fireplace. The bedroom's furnishing felt as if she was sleeping in the queen's bedroom.

Brooklyn made some calls, and they secured a table at Che Fico for lunch. This was a luxury that many couldn't easily obtain. Jack promised her that the rustic Italian meal would be memorable. Paige was not disappointed. She indulged in squash ravioli while Jack splurged on potato gnocchi. They ate early and then walked through the city. Jack needed to walk off the carbs to be ready for the night's show. Back in the hotel, a nap was in order. Together they climbed into the massive, ornate bed.

***

Two hours later, Jack's cell buzzed, Brooklyn was letting him know a car was waiting to take him to Monterey to the Golden State Theatre. He didn't need to change clothes, his performance outfits stayed on the bus. All Jack needed was his faithful companion, his Gibson. He smiled when he thought about the trouble the guitar had caused last week. Paige really tore into him over it. Was she right? The guitar had been a part of him for what felt like his entire life. He couldn't imagine not always having one with him. He guessed it was like what a smoker felt; to calm him or to unwind, he liked to play his guitar. Was he doing that too often? Would it even be possible for him to leave the Gibson on the bus tonight and spend time in this hotel with just Paige?

After a tender goodbye, and leaving her still in bed, Jack headed to the elevator. When the door slid open, Tony and Trent were already on. One more floor and Joe joined them. The men arrived in the posh lobby. They passed a corporate giant who spoke a friendly hello. An Oscar-winning actress was just stepping away from the desk with her movie executive husband. Tony greeted them. Jack simply gave a wave. Outside a sleek black SUV and driver waited as the parking attendant opened the doors for them to enter.

"None of the women are coming?" Tony raised an eyebrow in surprise.

Joe spoke up, "I think they're all coming together, later."

***

The stay at San Francisco was followed by a trip to Malibu. The band, once again, got a large house together. Annabeth was pleased to be invited, but Trent was a problem. He was having difficulty believing that they were through. He kissed his wife goodbye at LAX in the morning. They had one more day at the Malibu beach house before they jumped on a plane to Clarkston, Michigan. The busses had been gone for days and the elite of the group had enjoyed their playtime with the wealthy of California.

Annabeth was sitting by the pool, her iPad in front of her, working on the manuscript. Suddenly an exotic-looking cocktail was in front of her. She smiled at what she thought was a bartender. As her eyes focused under her sunglasses through the glaring sun, Annabeth realized it was Trent.

"Hey sugar, want to skinny dip?"

Of all the nerve, his wife could still be sitting on the runway. Annabeth accepted the drink and slowly took a long swallow of the fruity rum mixture. Trent saw that as an invitation and spread his legs over both sides of her chaise, in preparation to sit down. She held up a hand, "I'm working Trent. I want to get this chapter done."

"You can work when we're done," he was lowering his body.

In a quick maneuver, she jumped out of the chaise, drink intact just as he sat down. "Enjoy the sun for a while. Maybe you should take that dip and cool off. Our playtime is over, Trent. I meant it when I said it in Denver." She heard a string of profanities as she moved across the patio and into the house.

***

Putting on new guitar strings was something that Jack rarely did for himself. Now, he was sitting in the living area that faced the beach. In this peaceful spot, alone, he didn't mind the task. Solitude ended quickly as Trent pushed open a French door. Jack could see a scowl on his longtime friend's face.

"Well, I hope your god damn nosey girlfriend is happy!" Trent spat at him.

Though he knew what this was about, Jack feigned ignorance, "What?"

"She had to tell Gina about something that was none of her fucking business."

Placing his guitar on the table in front of him, Jack ran his fingers through his hair, "Trent, I don't think you can blame Paige for what Gina said to Annabeth."

His friend had stalked over to the bar and pulled a beer out of the fridge. He was just twisting off the cap when he heard Jack's words. "Gina talked to Annabeth?" Trent let off a string of curses. "Why the hell did Paige get her fucking nose into it?"

Jack stood up, "Don't blame Paige. It's your fault you got caught. Gina said she knew you were seeing someone, and she asked Paige to tell her who it was."

"The way I live my life is nobody's business!"

Joining him at the bar, Jack retrieved a beer for himself. After a swallow, he said, "Sorry bud, it was going to catch up with you someday."

"Gina and I have been doing things our way for years. Did your self-righteous bitch of a girlfriend tell my wife it wasn't okay?"

"You can shut your damn mouth about Paige, this is on you." Jack was getting angry too.

"Fuck you," Trent said and stalked out of the room.

***

"Is this how you're accustomed to vacations being?" Paige asked Jack as they climbed out of the limo. They were attending a movie premiere. Cameras were flashing around them, some directly on Jack. He smiled comfortably and held out his hand for Paige. She stepped out, making sure she was balanced on the narrow heels of her shoes, straightening her midnight blue sheath that sat just above her knees. It was very flattering with its form fit and crossover neckline.

"Technically, I'm not on vacation."

"But you're used to this atmosphere?"

"I've done this many times. You'll love it. Ready to get out?"

Paige's eyes were taking in the people milling about. While many of the cameras flashed as the stars stepped out of the cars and walked the red carpet, they focused mostly on the platform in front of the immense lit movie banner. The celebrities took their turns standing in front of the banner for photographs. With his hand at the small of her back, Jack edged her toward the line. "You want me to get my picture with you?"

He laughed, and she thought it might be more for the photo op than for her, "Of course, darling." Together they stepped in front of the camera. A few of the paparazzi called out a hello. One asked who Jack's date was. He held her at arm's length, their fingers entwined,

"This is my beautiful Paige." He then pulled her close for more pictures. Paige was delighted at his flattery and realized later that Jack was professional enough to know that was how he could get her to smile her brightest.

Later, as Paige stretched her sore toes, happy to be released from the tall, skinny heels of her shoes, she thought about the Jack she'd been with. He was so friendly to everyone but held himself at a reserved distance. It made him seem incredibly polished. This was such a contradiction to the reputation of a rock star. They mingled with movie stars she'd been watching for years. It was clear that he was not only well liked from these big names in Hollywood, but that they'd been friendly for a long time.

Other famous musicians were also there. Jack got into one lengthy conversation with a guitarist from a 90s band that was more pop than the Jack Corey band. Paige didn't mind being quiet in the shadows for that time. They were seated near so many celebrities she was happy to simply sit and watch.

The ride back to Malibu by limousine had been nice too. Seeing the many car lights shining, traffic seemed to always be heavy in California. Jack was relaxed sitting back in the seat holding her hand. "Did you enjoy the evening?" he asked.

"Yes, it was something I never imagined doing." She was scrolling through her phone surreptitiously looking for photos of them on social media. There were a few on his fan twitter pages, fan Instagram and on a couple of entertainment sites. Paige looked at herself, she didn't stick out as an outsider. In one photo, Jack stood confidently, looking delicious in a suit, his hand possessively around her. Paige was turned slightly toward him, a radiant smile on her face. The dress fit wonderfully and made her legs seem extra-long. The biking she did regularly with Jack had helped too.

Paige screenshot the photo and quickly sent it to Laurel and Hannah. Laurel responded first, gushing with praise. She teased in her text she couldn't believe her famous friend even remembered the little people. Hannah responded that she looked beautiful.

Chapter 23

Chicago, Illinois

Chicago was the trip the entire band had been waiting for. They would perform Friday night and then take part in the big 80s Rock Festival in Millennium Park on Sunday afternoon. The excitement was building as views of Lake Michigan appeared out the tour bus windows. The four-hour ride from Detroit had passed quickly.

For the first leg, Paige and Jack had sat on a loveseat. They talked, watching silly YouTube videos on his phone. Gina joined the band in Detroit. Paige guessed she'd decided to soak up more of the perks of being Trent's wife. She'd moved up to a chair across from them, Keely at her heels. "So boring upstairs," Keely complained.

"They act like children over *Mortal Kombat*," Gina added.

Jack's eyes perked up, "*Mortal Kombat*?"

Paige playfully smacked his leg, "Go play, little boy." He flashed a grin, gave her a quick kiss and took off.

Gina was smiling when Paige looked over, "You guys act like young love."

Keely responded, "Don't Joe and I act like that?"

"No, you act like horny teenagers," Gina showed her distaste, but Keely took it as a compliment. "Seriously Paige, I've never seen Jack so happy."

Paige smiled but shied away from the compliment. "So, what does everyone do in Chicago?"

The other women volleyed their answers. "Eat," said Gina.

"Party," Keely answered.

Together they gushed, "Shop!"

***

Paige sat on the balcony, her bare feet against the metal rung of the patio chair. Thirty floors below her the city of Chicago raced. Bicycles moved alongside cars. Trucks sounded their warning as they backed up to delivery doors and unloaded goods. People filled the sidewalk. Residents walked small dogs, cellphone at their ears. Tourists, just off the train at Union Station, dragged luggage behind them.

The door behind her slid open. She could smell the rich vanilla scented coffee before Jack handed her a mug. She looked up at him, his hair still damp, wearing only athletic shorts. *How the hell had she ended up here*? "Perfect," she said in a low voice, clarifying that she could be describing the coffee or him.

He grinned, understanding, and leaned down for a kiss. They sat beside one another, sipping coffee. As much as she hated mentioning plans, knowing Jack would move into work mode, Paige reluctantly asked, "What's on the schedule today?"

To her surprise, he reached his hand across the glass table towards her. She set down her mug and grasped his. "Us."

She was pleased, "Really?"

His fingers trailed a circle around the top of her hand. "Yes. I told Tony to reschedule all my appointments. I want to spend the day with you."

"What shall we do?" She looked out at the big city, the possibilities were endless.

"Want to go shopping?" he looked like he meant it.

Paige nodded, "I would never turn down a shopping trip."

Jack was reaching for his phone, "Perfect." In the next moment, he was speaking to someone, Brooklyn presumably. "Set us up at the Gold Coast. I want to do some shopping. Let me know."

As he clicked off, she looked at him inquiringly, "Set us up?"

***

The Oak Street experience was beyond anything that Paige could have imagined. Jack had a personal shopper take them from store to store where they had scheduled appointments to be shown items of interest. Jack was trying on leather sneakers that cost more than Paige's mortgage payment. He had them both trying on gorgeous, but outrageously expensive fashions. He ignored her protests and added four outfits for her to his own growing pile. She was even more stunned when he insisted on buying her luxurious diamond earrings.

Near the end of the spree, they wandered into a unique jewelry boutique. He pulled her over to a display of delicate necklaces with colorful gems on them. She was stroking a stunning gold bangle with a circle of diamonds in the middle when he asked her, "Isn't Hannah's birthday coming up?" Paige was pleased that he remembered that from their meeting.

"A month from now," then she looked at what he was holding.

"Absolutely not, Jack."

"What?"

She tried to put the necklace back on the display. She could see the four-figure price tag.

Jack wouldn't hear of it. "Tell me the color, or I'm going to buy the red one."

Paige sighed, "Blue."

He laughed and lightly pushed her away, "Go explore the shop and let me have fun in peace. I'll be quick and then we can go eat."

Soon he was at her side with a lovely little bag. They headed to an outdoor restaurant. As they sat sipping chilled wine and enjoying steak salads, Jack reached for her arm. She cocked her head questioningly. He slid the diamond cuff bracelet on her wrist, "This is for you, darling. I can't tell you how much fun you've made my life."

Paige's instinct was to protest, but she saw the myriad of sparkling diamonds and knew that was not the appropriate response. "Jack, it's beautiful. Thank you."

***

On Sunday, Jack was brushing his teeth at the sink. Paige found him distracting, standing in the open bathroom door in jeans, the ends of his hair damp. She was on her phone, checking that her bills were paid. The everyday upkeep of her other life was easy to forget in the whirlwind of the tour. There was an email from school, she opened it. "Oh, I can't believe it!"

Jack was drying his mouth off with a towel, "What?"

"Our opening meeting for school begins three weeks from tomorrow."

Now he was standing in front of her, "You're going back?"

Paige, sitting on the hotel couch, set her phone on the side table. "Yes, Jack. It's my job."

"I thought we talked about it."

"We did talk about it. You suggested I quit my job and stay on tour with you for the next four months."

He sat down next to her, "After next week, there's a three-week break."

Paige shook her head, "I have a home and a job."

Jack sighed heavily, leaning back on the couch, momentarily staring at the ceiling. He sat back up and turned to her, "This was just fun for the summer?" She opened her mouth to respond but his next words were increasing in volume, "I thought we had more going than that. Am I the only one that thought of this as a relationship? You were just screwing the rock star for the summer?"

Paige stood up and walked away, "Stop it, Jack!"

He leaped up, moving in front of her again, "Isn't what we feel real? I put my entire self into this and you're just going to leave?" Jack dramatically shrugged his shoulders and used a high-pitched voice, "Oh well, summer's over, play time with Jack is done."

"What do you expect me to do? Give up my life and spend my days on the tour bus?" Paige was angry.

Jack put his hands on his hips, "Do you want *me* to cancel the tour and stay at your house while you're at school?"

"No, Jack. That's ridiculous, and that's the point. Our lives are completely different and one of us must walk away from their life for us to be together. And, it's obvious it has to be me." Tears rolled down her cheeks.

Jack held on to her waist, with one hand and with the other brushed at her tears. “Oh baby, don’t cry. I’m only upset because I love you.”

Fresh tears squeezed out, “Jack, I love you too, but it still solves nothing.”

“I don’t understand why you won’t stay with me. I’m not asking you to give up your friends and family. We can fly into Ohio whenever you want or have them come to us.” He sat down on the couch, Paige returned to where she’d been so that they were sitting side by side.

Jack continued, “You won’t have to work, so that gives you time to do that.”

“I like my job,” her voice was quiet. Paige was feeling the frustration of having a conversation that could go nowhere.

“You can do your art anywhere.”

“This sounds so nice, but Jack, we hardly know one another. For Paige, the real reluctance was because it was risky. How could she leave her job and go with him? The stakes were high for her if it didn’t work out. She signed a contract, and once she broke it, there’d be no going back.

“Technically, we’d both be sort of employed, think how much fun that’d be.” When Paige didn’t join Jack in smiling, he rested his head on the back of the couch and closed his eyes. She remained silent. Finally, he stood up, “Apparently, I’m the only one in this relationship who thought it was real.”

“That’s not true.”

He turned toward her, “Nope, from where I’m standing it seems clear. I’m not asking you to move away and never see Hannah again.”

She stood up, her own ire rising, "Leaving my job is drastic, Jack."

"I can support you."

"That's not the point."

"The point seems to be that even though we've been together all this time, it seems perfectly okay to you if now we live thousands of miles apart."

Paige closed her eyes, "It's not perfectly okay."

Jack's phone laying on the table buzzed. "They're waiting for me downstairs." He glanced at the screen then stuffed it in his pocket. After he picked up his guitar, he turned to her, "Are you coming to the show?"

She went to him and put her hands on his upper arms, "Of course I'm coming today. I just said school is in three weeks. Not now. Do you want me here?"

Jack kissed her hard, "That's not even the question. I guess I'll try to make the most out of three weeks." With that, he slammed out of the hotel room.

Paige sat on the couch for quite a while, not moving. She tried to imagine herself back home again. She pretended that a week from today she was back in her house. What did she do on a Saturday afternoon? During the school year, she would first do things around the house. After getting groceries she would run any other errands. On a Saturday night, she may have plans with friends or a date. If neither of those was going on and she wasn't seeing Hannah and Kyle, Paige would probably just sit at home and watch television. She usually had something to work on in her studio. It sounded painfully boring. How long had she lived her life that way?

With a glance around the all too familiar layout of a hotel room, she saw her suitcase, shoes and Jack's bags. A second guitar, her laptop bag and art portfolio were strewn about. The truth was, that when they weren't on the bus, those things were rarely touched. They had explored so many new places this summer.

Jack had also been generous in taking her to some popular tourist spots in cities that were new to her. Of course he was generous, Jack was the most giving person she'd ever met. It wasn't just about the incredible wealth he seemed to possess, he was giving in his time and attention too. His only distraction was his guitar as it should be. If this ended, she would truly treasure this summer as a rare gem in her life.

Paige's eyes stung as she reconsidered the thought of the relationship ending. Why was it foolish to stay with him? She considered her own life in Findlay. Paige would have to break her contract, or would she? Perhaps she could take an unpaid leave of absence, then investigate retirement.

The school district wouldn't hold her job, but if things went south with Jack, Paige could still get a good recommendation and find another job. She wouldn't have to put her house for sale just yet, but eventually, she would. He said she could fly in for visits when she wanted. Would there have to be some agreement on her financial situation? If she could retire early for a smaller percentage and sold her house that would give her some of her own money. Was she really considering this? Picturing the man who had just left her and the anguish on his face at losing her, she realized that yes; she was truly considering it.

Long before she met him, he was a superstar. His world came first. It had to. Jack wasn't just performing songs, he was creating emotions and memories in other people's hearts, into their souls. Paige should've realized this all along. Her own life was filled with song lyrics and notes that would trigger other moments in her life. Jack, himself, had played a part in her own past. She could remember a time in college when she and her roommate had shouted his lyrics when a boyfriend had broken up with her. His work stayed with millions for life.

Trading her own world for his would not be a compromise, it would be a gift. They loved one another. The love between them was more than she had ever felt in her life.

Her smile brightened the room. Though her hands shook as she went to dress for the show, Paige was excited. She would tell Jack as soon as she got the chance that she would stay with him.

***

The band and crew had squeezed onto one bus. Parking was scarce at Millennium Park. The women had called an UberLUX to get them to the concert. Paige stood with Gina and Keely in the lobby waiting for the black Range Rover that was to be their ride to the park. She was wired because of the decision she made and prayed that she would have the opportunity to let Jack know before he went on stage.

Gina sensed her mood, "What's up with you? Excited for the show?"

Keely spoke up, "I love this city. I think it's my favorite. Three years ago, my friends and I took the train from Philly to see Lady Gaga on the same stage. Now, I will be back there with my boyfriend. Life is so fucking cool!" She was decked out in a fuchsia, spaghetti strap spandex dress, perfect for the heat of this hot August day.

Paige laughed, a bark of emotion, "You're right Keely, life is fucking cool!"

Gina gave her a sideways look, "All right, spill. You never talk that way."

Paige took a deep breath. "Jack and I had a big fight before he left."

Keely snorted, "That's what you're amped about?"

"I told him I was going home when school starts in three weeks."

"Paige," this was Gina, "I bet you broke his heart."

"Well," she was in the middle of the two women, and squeezed each of their arms, "I decided to give it a chance and be with him. It's insane. I must quit my job and everything. But I want to take the chance."

Gina spoke, "He doesn't know?"

"Not yet."

"I hope we get there in time for you to tell him before they go on stage."

***

The band was in the green room surrounded by other famous musicians. Once through a throng of celebrities, Paige searched out Jack. He had just picked up a bottle of water and twisted off the cap when they made eye contact. She gave him her biggest smile and headed toward him. He didn't return the smile but gave her a brief hug.

"Jack, we need to talk," she stood on tiptoe to whisper in his ear.

"Aren't those always the fateful words," his mouth was grim, and he didn't make eye contact.

"No, not in this circumstance." Before she could continue Tony waved the band forward. With barely a kiss to her cheek, Jack moved with the other men.

All the performing musicians had agreed to use one sound system. The drummers of each band had gotten together to agree on one shared drum set. This way, as one group exited the stage, the time between would be minimal. Only guitars and headsets were personal.

The Jack Corey band hooked up wireless microphones, just as the eighties girl group, *Exhibition*, was preparing to head on stage. The two bands greeted each other as old friends, having crossed paths many times. The lead singer hugged Jack and whispered in his ear. He turned and motioned to Paige. She stepped up, feeling plain next to him in his show attire; fitted black jeans, boots and his tight black shirt. *Exhibition*'s lead singer was wearing a splashy silver micro mini dress with matching tall boots. In just white shorts and a black silk tank, Paige felt unremarkable.

The other woman gave her a half hug, "So you're the one." Her smile seemed genuine, "I've been waiting for Jack to decide to be in a relationship for decades. You must have swooped in at just the right moment." Paige laughed nervously. Before she could come up with a reply, someone was leading the other woman to the stage. She reached over and kissed Jack right on the lips before being led away.

The crowd cheered as the ladies launched into their number one song. Jack rolled his eyes, "She's always been a bit crazy." He was still barely making eye contact.

Paige reached up and wiped scarlet lipstick from his mouth. "Crazy for you, I'd say."

The gesture softened him, and he kissed her fingertips as they moved over his lips. "Too bad. I love you." Jack looked at her meaningfully.

"I love you, too."

Just then Tony appeared, she lost her chance to share her decision. "Be careful out there," Tony warned, "I guess the cords are a mess. Joe Walsh nearly sprained an ankle tripping over a couple."

Jack nodded, "I can see it's a poorly done." The girl group was maneuvering some of their signature choreography in high heels. "I guess if they can manage, we'll be okay."

Paige was eager for the two men to finish the conversation so she could tell Jack her decision. The time didn't happen, Jack and Tony moved toward the band. Jack gave her an air kiss as he moved away. Paige was crushed.

Gina caught her expression, "He didn't like your news?"

"I didn't get to tell him."

The girls' group was exiting off stage. Jack's roadie ran ahead for some quick adjustments. Joe was the first on stage. As he hit the beats of *Go Away,* the crowd went wild. The other members appeared as their instruments joined in. An assistant was helping Jack with a last-minute adjustment to his headset. Now the vocals and lead guitar would begin. He walked out on stage. The city of Chicago reverberated with screams and applause.

Paige stood off to the side and looked at the thousands of people spread across the lawn surrounded by the stately buildings of downtown. Every eye was on Jack. Even before he sang a word, cheers and whistles were heard. He stretched out the opening guitar notes, teasing the audience. His fingers slid along the strings, each note building the anticipation. At last, he opened his mouth to sing. As the first words came out, the fans joined in. This was everyone's song. Paige felt tears at the back of her eyes, it was magical. How could she have ever considered walking away from this?

Jack was in the moment and moved closer to the crowd. Customarily he would shake hands with those in front. Today, they held the crowd back by a railing, only the security staff stood on the concrete directly in front of the stage. A man lifted his date on his shoulders. She leaned her body at a precarious angle, her hand stretched out for Jack's. A security man put his arms up to push her back. Jack reached his own arm out, trying to make contact with the fan. As he stretched out his upper body, his foot caught on an unexpected cord taped to the stage.

Time moved in slow motion as Jack and his guitar suddenly went airborne. His body did a near complete flip before it landed on the bare concrete. There was a splintering sound and a screech of a guitar string amplified for everyone. The other band members stopped mid-note. For a split second there was silence, then the audience screamed.

Paige realized that she too had screamed. She instinctively pushed forward, repeatedly yelling, "Jack!" Stage personnel tried to hold her back and prevent her from moving on stage. Undeterred, she pushed and scratched her way through, until she could climb down the steps that led to the concrete where Jack lay.

They cleared the front of the crowd while the emergency crew, there on standby, raced to Jack. Joe and Trent had jumped down as well. Tony flew from off stage, down to the concrete floor. Paige saw

Jack's body, twisted and unmoving. She knelt beside him. His eyes were closed, there was blood on his face.

"Jack, honey," she whispered, her voice choked with sobs. A security guard reached in to grab her, but Joe stopped him. Tony knelt beside her, touching Jack's shoulder.

Paige looked down at his chest, it was moving; he was breathing. She felt hands at her shoulder, a woman in an EMT uniform spoke gently, "Please step back so we can get to him." Paige stood up, Tony moved beside her. Unaware, they were holding hands. She heard an uproar behind her and turned to look. The fans were being led away and the members of the press were trying to push their way up to the rail. Television cameras aimed at Jack on the ground. Paige and Tony both tried to move their bodies to shield him from view.

Joe and Trent were at the rails. "Get the fuck out of here!" Trent was yelling, attempting to grab cameras.

"Have some respect!" Joe shouted.

They all made a path when a stretcher arrived. Paige could see they had a board to stabilize his body. Finally, he was lifted onto the stretcher. Now she rushed close, hoping to touch him. His eyes were still closed. The EMTs allowed her and Tony to stay with them as they snaked a path to the squad. At the door, an attendant addressed Tony, "Only one of you can ride with us."

Tony looked at Paige, tears blinding her, "She will."

Paige stumbled to get in and another attendant helped her up. She sat next to Jack, afraid to touch him. There was blood on his forehead. Under the sheet, she couldn't see any limbs sticking out at odd angles. She looked at the attendant monitoring his vitals. "Where's he hurt?"

The attendant was about to respond when Jack moved. The other man lightly placed his hand on Jack's shoulder, "Mr. Corey, you're in an ambulance. You've been in an accident Try to stay calm."

Jack groaned and started to rise. Paige touched his cheek, "Jack it's okay. Honey, stay still."

With difficulty, his eyes opened. First, he looked at the young man on his right, and then to Paige. "What happened?" his voice was hoarse.

"You fell," she stroked his hair.

"Oh yeah," he tried to smile but winced. "How did I fall?"

"Your foot got caught on a cord."

"Mr. Corey," the attendant interrupted, "Can you tell me what hurts?"

Jack seemed to take stock. "Damn near everything. Especially my hip and leg." He moved it to show and gasped in pain. The attendant took out swabs and cleaned the blood off Jack's face.

Touching her cheek, Jack spoke, "It'll be okay."

She kissed his hand, "I'm supposed to be telling you that." Paige decided it was the time to tell him she was staying, but Jack coughed.

"Ma'am, can you move back a moment? I'll hook him up to some oxygen." After that Jack wavered in and out of consciousness. Paige never got the chance to speak to him.

Chapter 24

Chicago, Illinois

It turned out that Jack was lucky. He had survived his fall onto concrete with a bruised spine, dislocated shoulder, fractured hip, four cracked ribs, and a broken ankle. They had permitted Paige to stay with him through his first examination by a doctor and that day's subsequent procedures.

Once he was moved into a room, Paige was no longer on the top of the list to be present with him. The line of celebrities that had stopped in would rival a red-carpet event.

She sat in the uncomfortable tweed and chrome chair in the hospital waiting room, alone. Gina had left to pick up some "real coffee". Five minutes ago, J.J. Corey had arrived. He had been ushered right into his father's room by Tony. There was no question who he was. Jack Corey, Jr. was the spitting image of his father; similar build, same hair color. Neither man acknowledged her though J.J. wouldn't have a clue who she was.

The elevator dinged again; it was Gina. She handed Paige a Starbucks. After a reviving sip, Paige informed Gina of the arrival of Jack's son. Before she could say anything else, the elevator opened. Mavis Corey-Steiner stepped out, Jack's ex-wife. She was a former supermodel, and she still carried herself like she was prepared to move down the runway. Jack said their marriage had lasted only three years. She'd been with Gerald Steiner, the name was synonymous with ski gear, for eighteen years, but she refused to give up the Corey name and hyphenated them.

Mavis made an entrance into the waiting room, a cloud of white linen and rows of silver bracelets. A fog of jasmine-scented perfume filled the small place. Gina smiled, "Mavis!" The other woman rushed to her and air-kissed her.

"Gina dear, it is so good to see you. Is J.J. already in Jacky's room?" Paige raised her eyebrows at the name "Jacky".

Gina could only nod before Mavis continued, "The press has been hounding me for two days. I could barely get to the airport. I'll give J.J. a couple more minutes with his dad."

Paige surreptitiously studied the only woman that Jack had ever married. Now in her forties, she was still model thin. Her trademark tawny mane of hair was cut shoulder length and tamed into submission with what must be a powerful straightening iron. She was still lovely as she clasped her long fingers around a chandelier earring.

Gina motioned towards Paige, "Mavis, this is Paige, she's..." Mavis' eyes flitted dismissively over her.

Cutting in, Mavis spoke, "I'm going to go in and be with my family."

Gina looked embarrassed as she turned to Paige, "She always was a drama queen." From down the hall, they could hear the woman utter a loud, "Jacky!"

Paige wanted to rush into the room and claim her man. Her man? Doubt was creeping in. "I can't imagine her traveling with the band."

Gina swallowed some coffee, "She didn't travel with us. She'd just show up when we were in big cities." Without thinking she laughed, "Trent always referred to her arrivals as conjugal visits." Now Gina looked up chagrined, "I'm sorry."

"Oh, don't be, I'm a grownup. I've read about Jack's life long before I ever met him."

The elevator sounded once again. Tony ushered in some members of the press. Cameras, microphones, and reporters poured out of the elevator. Gina grabbed Paige's elbow, "Turn around, don't let them recognize us." Not to worry, Tony was leading them straight to Jack's room. Paige heard him use the phrase, "Family reunion."

Had Jack okayed this? He had been adamant about not allowing cameras in his room. She suspected this was more Mavis and Tony. Her instinct was to stop and protect Jack. But who was she? She was impotent around his manager, son and former wife. The feelings of this relationship ending were once again gaining roots. Paige's dream summer with Jack Corey wouldn't last.

Gina spoke, "I'm going to head back to the hotel. Trent and I are flying home in a few hours."

"I'll walk you out." Once in the elevator, she added, "I'm considering heading to the hotel."

Gina touched her arm, "Oh hon, don't let all of this scare you away."

"I'm not," though her insecurity was getting the best of her. "It's just a good time for a shower.

***

Back in the hotel, Paige wanted to climb into the freshly made bed and cry. She was concerned for Jack and his recovery. Looking at the bed reminded her that only a few nights ago, they had crawled under those cool sheets together.

Paige ran her hand along Jack's pillow. Now his head was on another pillow and she wasn't certain she had a place there. Jack hadn't called for her to meet his son. Then, there was Mavis. Paige scowled when she remembered her saying, "Jacky."

Tony was a traitor too; bringing in the press and referring to it as a family reunion. He was the band's manager and would jump on such an opportunity for publicity. There were probably news alerts out already. Paige clicked open her phone to Instagram. Sure enough, there was a picture of Jack in the hospital bed, his son stood at his right and Mavis sat beside him at the left, her hand over Jack's. Was he holding hands with her? His expression was grim, which the post referred to as pain. Paige wondered if it was more annoyance? She was familiar with that expression.

She clicked off her phone, what did it matter? After her shower, she dressed in clean clothes retrieved from her suitcase. Jack's things were hanging in the closet next to hers. She realized that he wouldn't be back in this room. Paige ran a hand along his shirts, she'd come close to losing him. The thought made her more determined to get to the hospital and finally tell him she was staying with him.

She was preparing to call for a car when her phone buzzed. It was Jack. "Hello?"

His voice sounded tired and weak, "Where are you?"

"Just ran to the hotel."

"Are you coming back? We need to talk."

"Of course. I'll be right over."

***

A few media vans were still milling about as she climbed out of the cab. None of them paid attention to her, with the appearance of Mavis, her identity wouldn't even register.

Jack was alone and sleeping when she entered his room. Paige silently walked up next to him and looked at him. With several days of whiskers on his face, decidedly gray whiskers, and an IV tube traveling from his arm, Jack was still so beautiful. She felt her heart squeeze. Had she really gotten to share these past months with him? He wasn't just the musician, Jack Corey, he was a loving man who had focused all his affection on her. They had traveled and explored many places together. She inched closer as she thought about this.

Paige traced her fingers across the side of his cheek, pushing hair behind his ears. Jack opened his eyes and looked up, a frown on his face. "Are you in pain?"

"No. The pills are working."

"Can I get you something then?"

"I thought maybe you were leaving," He moved his head toward the wall.

She turned his chin to look at her, "Jack, I'm not going anywhere. I'm staying with you."

He turned back away from her, "That's not what you said the other day. I don't even know what day this is."

"I tried to tell you on Sunday, before you went on stage, that after you left our room I decided to stay. I don't know how I'll work it out with my job, but I will," Paige squeezed lightly on his upper arm. "Jack, I'd never leave you now."

"Now," his tone was accusatory.

"I promise you, I wasn't going to go. You can ask Gina or Keely."

Before he could respond, Tony swept in, "I just got off the phone with NBC. They want to do an hour special on you; your life, career and surviving the accident."

Jack scowled, glancing down at the bandages and tubes on his body. "I'm not going to appear on camera like this."

"Not now, when you're back in New York. It will be a few weeks before they get to that part."

"Will I even be out of here by then?"

"Mavis and I talked to your doctor. In another week, you'll be released to fly home. She and JJ are headed there now to get the place ready for you." Paige could tell from Jack's expression that he wasn't any more pleased to have Mavis involved than she was.

A nurse walked into the room, followed by an orderly with a gurney. "Mr. Corey, the doctor has ordered an MRI on your shoulder." She looked at Paige and Tony, "This will take about 45 minutes."

Tony said his good byes and headed out of the room. Paige watched them maneuver Jack's body and the tubes attached onto the gurney. She reached over and touched his face, "Ill be up here when you're done."

Jack reached for her hand. She savored the touch. His words didn't match the affection she felt, "Just go back to the hotel and get some sleep. I'm going to want to do the same."

Paige wanted to protest, but instead kissed his cheek. "I love you," she whispered as they rolled him out the door.

***

She resisted texting him that evening, respecting his need to rest. Paige was restless in the room. It was late when sleep finally claimed her. Now she was up and showered, eager to head back to the hospital. Her phone buzzed, it was Brooklyn.

Jack wanted you to know that he went into surgery about an hour ago.

Paige felt her pulse quicken in alarm, *For what?*

His ankle, it was scheduled yesterday.

Is he still down there?

No, he's in recovery.

Paige was frustrated to be texting, she called Brooklyn. "He never mentioned surgery."

"Sorry, I think they were just trying to repair the break, possibly with a pin. Jack said you would probably be flying home today?"

Paige was surprised, "To New York?"

Brooklyn paused, looking at notes most likely, "No, Toledo, Ohio?"

"I'm not leaving him here."

"He thought today or tomorrow and wanted me to get the ticket."

"Brooklyn don't get me a ticket. I'm not going anywhere."

***

Within a half an hour, she was at the hospital. Jack had just been brought back to his room. He looked even paler under the white sheet. Now his ankle was bandaged tight and propped up. Paige moved to him, running her hand across his forehead. Jack slowly opened his eyes, squinting against the bright light.

"Hi darling," Paige whispered as he looked at her.

For the slightest moment, Jack flashed his grin. In another instant, she saw a cloud pass his face. “Paige,” he croaked, his voice rough and dry.

She picked up the water jug and placed the straw to his lips. He took a sip.

“You didn’t tell me you were having surgery.”

“They didn’t have to put in a pin, which is good.”

Paige moved as if to pull up a chair, but Jack patted the bed. She gingerly sat down, careful not to hurt him. “Why did you tell Brooklyn to get me an airline ticket?”

Instead of answering, Jack just stared at her for a moment, his expression serious, “Beautiful Paige, I do love you.”

“I love you too, Jack.”

Now his eyes slid from her face to a spot just past her shoulder. “But you need to go home.”

“What?” Paige felt her heart stop.

“You were right to plan on returning to your life. It’s what you have to do.”

“Jack,” she touched his chin, forcing him to face her, “I’m not leaving you. I made the decision to build a new life with you.”

His expression was hard, “The life I’m going to have now? You want to sit around and watch me rehabilitate? See me struggle through physical therapy just to hold my guitar again?”

“Yes,” she said softly.

“Paige, listen to me, I’m a selfish man. That’s the reason I never settled down. My music comes first. I must give everything I have to get it back.”

“I’ll help you,” she reached to touch his hair, he tilted his head to avoid her touch.

"No, you won't. You're not leaving your daughter, your job and your home just to watch me struggle through rehab."

She didn't want to cry, but the tears escaped, "I have to be with you."

For the first time since she'd met him, Paige saw tears fill Jack's eyes. Something inside of her began to break. He was going to push her away. Paige was going to lose Jack Corey.

"I don't want you in New York with me," the last words cracked. His eyes were red, the tears were falling.

She couldn't stand to see him in pain. Paige stood up, "You're telling me to leave you, leave us?"

Jack attempted to take a deep breath, but it shuddered through his chest. "I love you, Paige, but please go. I don't want you to go through this with me."

"Forever?" her voice was a whisper as she openly cried.

He squeezed his eyes tight, tears spiked his lashes. Finally, he looked up, "I don't know."

Paige moved across the room, her sobs uncontrollable. Jack lifted his good arm, "Come here."

Beside the bed, she leaned gently against his shoulder. He kissed the top of her head. "I love you. I'm sorry it has to end this way."

"I love you too. I'm not going to leave."

"Please, if you love me, then go." His words were broken. Paige looked up and saw that his skin was gray. This was draining an already injured man. Forcing herself, she stood up.

"Will you keep in touch with me?"

"Yes," Jack whispered. "Please baby, go."

Paige backed out of the room.

Chapter 25

After the Show

At the hospital, Annabeth stayed in the background. Though she felt true fear for Jack's life and grave concern for his recovery, she also knew for her career this was a gold mine. Not only was this storyline material that writers dream of, but she was also here before it happened. Normally, when a celebrity as big as Jack is in an accident such as this, he receives offers to have a book written about him. Annabeth was in the middle of one. She had immediately contacted her agent to decide if she should send press releases out. Her inside take would be big. Annabeth was scrambling to get her manuscript completed as her agent was being pushed by the publisher. They wanted it quick. Everyone was suddenly interested in Jack Corey again.

The real dilemma was the separation of Jack and Paige. Annabeth had not been expecting that. Her final chapter was already in outline form. It was a great conclusion. Superstar finds love at last. Now she couldn't decide if she should even include it. She also didn't know who to ask for advice. She would never bother

Jack with it. For one, he was busy with physical therapy. Also, reminding him of his broken heart seemed a poor way to get him to open up.

She hadn't figured out what happened. She'd heard Gina and Keely pushing Paige to tell Jack of her decision that afternoon at Millennium Park. They were all smiling so she couldn't believe her decision was to leave. But then suddenly Paige was gone before they even released Jack from the hospital.

Tony would also be a bad choice to ask. He had often considered Paige his competition, someone getting Jack's attention over him. He was certain to say Paige and that relationship be left out of the book.

Though Annabeth had ended things with Trent, she wasn't sure Gina would talk to her. Gina and Paige seemed close. She would know the truth. Could Annabeth contact Gina?

The answer came to her easily. She had gone to the network studios where they were putting together the pieces of Jack's special edition. Annabeth has volunteered to share footage of the green room moments before the band went on stage that fateful day.

She was headed toward the elevator when Keely approached. She greeted Annabeth eagerly, "I was being interviewed about what happened after Jack's accident. I hope I did okay."

"I'm sure you did. How's Joe?"

"Oh, he's good. To tell you the truth, he was tired of the tour and is happy to be home."

"How about you?" Annabeth walked alongside the other woman. Even if she had to retrace her steps, it was worth it to pick Keely's brain.

"Hell yes. I love having a real bed and bathroom." She pushed the button, and the elevator opened. They both got in.

"Have you guys seen Jack?"

"Joe goes to see him a few times a week. I haven't."

"Do you know if he's living alone?"

"I think so. Man, I can't believe Paige left. I thought they would last." Keely headed to the parking garage, Annabeth stayed at her side.

"You don't think they'll get back together?"

"I don't know. I guess Jack told her he wasn't worth giving up her life for, hurt and all."

"And she listened?"

"He sort of pushed her out."

"Think it's over forever?" They were now stopped in front of a flashy red Audi that Annabeth guessed must be Keely's.

"I don't know. I talked to Gina just yesterday, she doesn't think so. But how are they ever going to work it out?"

***

Her cell phone was ringing. Paige was still in her classroom, checking her students' collages and making comments on a rubric. The building was empty at her wing. There were others in the school; volleyball practice was going on, the marching band was rehearsing, but in the education wing, Paige was alone. She glanced at her phone and back at the multicolored creations in front of her. She didn't want to answer. Finally, the call clicked off; she sighed in relief.

Walking to the car, the brilliant red and orange leaves went unnoticed by her. Most things that brought joy went unnoticed. It had been six weeks since that fateful day that Paige had gone into Jack's room after his ankle surgery.

At the hotel, she discovered that Brooklyn had been in the room and packed up all of Paige's things. Jack's stuff was completely gone. On the bed was a first-class ticket to a plane that departed in ninety minutes. Paige left. What else could she do? The flight home was something she couldn't recall a single detail about.

She spent the next four days, holed up in the house talking to no one. Her phone was turned off. When she finally was overcome with hunger, and discovered an empty kitchen, Paige forced herself up and out. Her charged phone revealed that she'd been contacted by everyone important at home and her friends from the tour, except for one. No calls or texts from Jack.

Sadness rolled into bitterness and anger. By the weekend, she was back at school organizing her supplies. In her mind, Paige had turned the entire summer into a fling for Jack. She now told herself that the accident was the perfect way for him to end the relationship. When she ran into coworkers at school, she took on a casual tone. They, of course, knew of the accident. Paige promised that he was fine.

Two weeks later, she couldn't stand it. She sent Jack a text, asking about his health. His response was quick. The recovery was going well. He made small inquiries about her return to work. After a few exchanges, the communication ended without a good bye. Paige spent another night crying herself to sleep.

The phone buzzed again as she climbed in the car. "Fine," she said aloud and reached for it. "Hello?"

"About damn time," the voice attempted to sound stern but was warm.

"Hi Gina," her own voice was soft, fragile.

"How are you doing?"

She shrugged, but realized that Gina couldn't hear her response, "I'm fine. How are you and the kids?" The two women had text a few times, but Paige was trying to force an end to all people that were from Jack's life. It hurt.

"We're good. Callie got her license, I despise her driving in New York. Trent bought her a BMW, at least it's a solid car. Reed is being looked at by a couple of colleges for baseball."

"Trent's home now?"

"Not in my home. Have you talked to Jack?"

Paige gripped the steering wheel, giving herself a moment to steady her voice, "No. We've exchanged a few texts."

"That's too bad."

"How is he?"

"I wish you knew because you were with him." Gina threw out the remark. When it went unanswered, she continued, "He's doing okay. Keely says physical therapy is very painful. Joe's gone with him when Tony couldn't."

"So, Mavis and JJ didn't stick around?"

"You knew they wouldn't," Gina's tone was accusatory.

"How's Keely doing?"

"She's great. Joe made her go back and finish her cosmetology license. Now she's been working backstage at a tv show. She loves it."

"That's perfect for her. Can we get back to my first question?" it was Paige's turn to ask pointed questions. "How are things for you?"

"It sucks, Paige," her friend's voice cracked a little.

"What does, sweetie?"

"I can't continue to play house with Trent. I know he's still fooling around."

"With Annabeth?" This surprised Paige.

"No, definitely not, but any little trash that's available. I don't know how I'll do this, but I don't want to live like this."

"You don't have to. You were married long before he needed a pre-nuptial agreement. The kids are older, and they won't mind. Have you found a good lawyer?"

"I meet with one in two days."

"I'm proud of you."

The women were both silent, emotion filling the space. Finally, Gina spoke, her voice was deadly serious, "So if I can get my head out my ass, why don't you do the same thing?"

By now, Paige had pulled into her garage, the door closing silently behind the vehicle. She leaned her head against the steering wheel. "What is there for me to do? He ended it, remember?"

"Do you still want to be with him?"

"I'm not sure if I even know who he is." Paige forced herself to get out of the car and walk into the house. She dumped her bags and went straight out the back door and onto the patio. She sank onto the wicker sofa and even that was painful. Jack had first composed T*he Perfect Summer*, their song, right on this seat.

"Yes, you do. The man you love is the man Jack is. He was crazy to send you away. I know he did it because he thought it was best for you."

"Why couldn't he have let me make the decision?" Paige told herself to get past that. "I hate that he's in pain."

"Of course he's in pain, look at the injuries he sustained. But he's working hard to recover."

"Is the press still hounding him?"

"Yes, and Tony loves it. His TV special comes out in two weeks and the biography is being rushed through by the publisher. Everyone wants to make money from his accident."

Paige couldn't answer. She was crying now. Gina sighed, "Oh honey, I didn't call to upset you. I miss you and I want you to still be my friend."

"I am."

"We'll figure this out. You two should be together."

They said their goodbyes and hung up. Paige sat without moving for a moment taking in all that she'd heard. Then she picked up her phone and sent Jack a text. *Hi.*

Though he'd said he'd call that day at the hospital, he never had. They'd exchanged texts exactly three times since then.

Less than two minutes passed, and he answered. *Hi. How are you?*

Good. How's therapy?

Going well. My leg is really getting stronger. I've regained a lot of flexibility in my shoulder.

That's good news. She didn't know what to say.

He sent more. *How're things with you?*

Going fine. She still couldn't ask the bigger questions or show any emotions.

How's Hannah? It touched her.

Thanks for asking, she's good. She's taking a new position at a children's hospital. It's her dream job.

She'll be good with kids.

Yes, she will. Has JJ been back?

No. He calls.

There was a lull, was he satisfied with the polite inquiry or was he, like her, unsure of what to say?

I thought I'd check on you. She watched the screen bubbles that showed he was responding and then it disappeared. What had he been about to say? She didn't know what else to text and sat staring at the phone for a few moments, imagining all she'd like to say. Paige knew Jack preferred to talk not text. When she'd given up on any more texts, she held it longer hoping for a call to come in. One didn't.

She called Hannah. Her daughter was a reminder of why it was good she was in Ohio.

Hannah answered on the first ring, though her voice sounded in a rush, "Hey Mom, what's up?"

"Are you busy?"

"Well, I'm just getting ready to go out. As soon as Kyle gets home, we're going to Cleveland. He surprised me with Mumford and Son tickets."

"That's wonderful." Paige thought wistfully of her own time in Cleveland. It was when she'd fallen for Jack. "I won't keep you."

"Did you call for anything or just to chat?"

"Just to chat. You can call me when you have time."

"How're you doing, Mom?"

She tried to swallow her emotions, "Fine. Gina called today. She's splitting up with Trent."

"Good for her. How'd she say Jack is?"

"Still struggling through physical therapy."

Hannah's medical knowledge kicked in, "I bet it's a tough regimen. He'll probably need therapy for at least another six months. Have you talked to him?"

"We text a little. He asked about you."

Paige heard the smile in her daughter's voice, "That's sweet. Mom, do you want to go see him?"

"I don't know what I want." It was a lie, but he hadn't invited her.

"You don't?" Hannah sounded doubtful.

"I'll be fine, honey. You get ready for your show. Have a wonderful time."

Hannah wasn't fooled. "Mom, how about I come down this weekend? We can spend the day together."

"Perfect. Have a good time tonight. I love you, honey."

"I love you too, Mom."

***

Jack walked carefully back to his bedroom. Mobility was improving every day, but the hurt he was feeling inside, increased the physical pain that was still accompanying each step. He set his phone on his nightstand and sat down hard on the mattress, then winced at the sudden movement. He looked at his feet, he still had on shoes. Which would be the easiest way to remove them? Finally, he used the opposite foot of each to kick out the heels and when he was at last barefoot; he stretched out on the bed. His eyes scanned the ceiling as if searching for answers there.

Why had Paige texted? His response at one point had been spontaneous declarations of love. Fortunately, he'd deleted them.

He'd had a setback at the hospital after he sent her away. That day he had become ill, most certainly an emotional reaction. They'd worried about his heart. Jack felt he'd had no choice but to make her leave. Life was unbearably lonely, but he'd adjust. He'd been alone for a long time, he could do it again. The problem was that he didn't want to do it again. Dammit, this summer was supposed to be the beginning. That fateful day in Chicago had ruined so much.

He didn't remember much after the fall. Tony told him he'd allowed Paige to ride in the ambulance. He'd told Jack with remorse. He wouldn't have if he'd been aware that Jack was going to end things with her. Tony fully supported those actions. When she'd been on the tour, he had felt she'd cut into his territory. Jack knew how Tony was, it was his job to play all things to his advantage. He was more than happy to paint her as a deserter now.

Jack felt only heart-breaking sorrow and loss. He'd been intentionally rough at the hospital. She didn't deserve to give up her life and spend time with him when his own was such a mess. It was best to send her away.

***

Too many weeks had passed, and Annabeth was at a standstill on her book. She decided the best way to get the answer she needed was to go directly to the source. Jack answered on the first ring. After greetings and asking for an update on his health, she jumped right into why she'd called. "I'm getting close to being done with my first draft."

"That's great news, Annabeth."

"I wanted to know about some content I want to put in." Jack didn't answer but just waited for her to go on. "I want to put Paige in your book."

Silence was on the other end for a moment. "Well, I can see that."

"So, it's okay with you?"

"I figured you'd want to, but I don't know."

"We agreed to it, previously." She stopped, not sure how to continue.

"Okay. What did you have in mind?"

"I don't know how to conclude that part. To be honest, I thought it would end a lot differently."

His voice was grim, "So did I. I guess there was a lot I thought would go differently." Jack was silent for so long that she thought perhaps he'd hung up. When she heard him sigh, she was expecting him to tell her to remove Paige completely. That would be very disappointing. She was surprised when he finally spoke. His voice was stronger, "I think I know what you should write. I'm certain I can explain the end. Let me tell you." For the next half an hour, Jack shared with Annabeth all that was on his heart about Paige and their relationship. When she ended the call with him, she rubbed her hands together. She couldn't wait to write this chapter.

***

Paint brushes were spraying spatters of red and yellow paint on her apron. Paige stood at the utility sink after a long day. School had been in session for a month and she was struggling to enjoy it.

Pam peeked in her room, "Tonight's the Jack Corey special." Her principal seemed nearly as disappointed as she that the relationship had ended.

Picking up a clean rag, Paige wrapped up the wet brushes and turned, "I know."

"Are you going to watch?" Pam's expression was sympathetic.

"I'd love to say no, but I can't resist."

"Are you going to be alone?"

Paige nodded, "Laurel wanted to be with me, but I think this is something I need to do alone."

"You may need a drink to get through it." As she backed out of the room, Pam surprised her when she added, "If you want to talk, you can always call me."

***

Paige filled her largest wineglass. On the couch, she crossed her legs and got comfortable. With the wineglass in one hand and the remote in the other, she clicked on the show.

After a few commercials, the theme song began. The host spoke, "Tonight we are premiering a special on rock legend Jack Corey." A photo of him on stage appeared in the corner. The host discussed his career, hits, and awards. Clips of concerts and music videos replaced the photo.

"That all changed on August 8th." Now the host faded to actual news footage from the night of the accident. Paige felt cold chills through her body. They ended with a dire prediction of his possible death and headed into a commercial break. Her phone buzzed, it was Laurel *Are you watching?*

Yes, I feel sick.

Like it's happening all over?

Yes.

Drink your wine. Laurel knew her so well. She took a long swallow of the Cabernet. The dark fruity taste carried her back to his presence. This was a bad idea.

The show was back on. A brief repeat of the first part, then it moved to the hospital. Paige thought she saw a glimpse of herself by the hospital waiting room as a parade of celebrities stopped in to see Jack. Laurel's next text verified it.

The show followed J.J. and Mavis. J.J. didn't speak to the reporters. Mavis did. Paige's wine nearly came back up when she said, "Jacky". The show continued with the "family" at the hospital and a brief history of their marriage. There were old clips of the two as a couple at Hollywood events. Photos after the birth of J.J. Paige couldn't believe how upset she felt over young Jack holding Mavis' hand or giving her a kiss while cradling infant J.J.

Soon, another host, a young, perky woman, perched on a chair next to Jack's sofa. He was in the middle of Mavis and J.J. It was the same sofa that Jack and Paige had spent time on; eating Chinese food, stretched out together. Paige drank more wine.

After another commercial break, in which Laurel text to comment on how gorgeous the place was, and didn't it look like Mavis had work done? The show was back on. Now, Jack was alone on the couch. Paige watched him. His voice as familiar to her as her own. He looked good, strong in fact. She imagined the hours he must be spending at the gym. Jack talked about the tour that he referred to as the best one ever. Did she add to that? He then described the accident. The host asked about his plans. Was the delayed fall tour going to be rescheduled?

Jack looked serious, "I need to examine my priorities." He struggled to stand up. It looked as if he was still in some pain. How long ago was this filmed?

The camera followed him to the white baby grand. Jack gestured above it to something hanging on the wall. "See this," his voice was slow, Jack was carefully choosing his words. The camera zoomed close. Paige let out a loud exclamation. The picture was the drawing she had made last spring of his hands on the guitar.

The reporter walked to him and near the picture. "Jack, that's beautiful. Did you draw that?"

"No," he smiled, years of training allowing him to know just where to focus his eyes. Paige felt as if he was looking right at her. "Someone incredibly important drew this. When I didn't even know I was being watched, this person was taking in all the details of me doing what I love to do." He sat down on the piano bench, abruptly. Paige thought he must be exhausted. His face looked up at the camera, but as he started to speak again, he shook his head and looked down. The show went to commercial.

What was he going to say? Did he choke up? And was that really her picture? Paige grabbed the remote and hit rewind. There was her drawing on his wall. She hit fast forward, just as the show was coming back on. The interviewer was in front of the camera. "Jack Corey has a special surprise for all of us. For the first time since his accident, he will perform." Paige sucked in her breath, could he?

The camera moved to Jack still on the piano bench, but this time with his guitar. Seeing him in that familiar position made her smile, tearfully. There was the man she loved.

"My life changed on the tour. Before my fall, it was all for the good. Since my accident, I've been a fool to let the most important things go. Now, I'd like to share with you tonight, *The Perfect Summer.*"

As he sang the words, his voice was still as strong as ever. His tone was deep and clear. Paige watched closely at his shoulder as he played the guitar, Jack looked like he always did, it was just a part of him.

The Perfect Summer

By Jack Corey

I went out on the road,
Just to share my song.
Never expected to find,
Something so strong.
I traveled endless miles,
No one caught my eye.
Saw millions of smiles
But life was moving by.
Didn't know I had it in me,
To fall this deep.
Didn't know I even wanted
Someone to keep.

CHORUS
The perfect summer began
That day.
Your sun-kissed smile
Sent the loneliness away.
Take my love and travel
The road with me.
This perfect summer
Is our destiny.

Baby, when I found you
Sitting on the stair,
My whole world changed,
Right then and there.
My love songs were words,
For others to hear.
With you the lyrics,
Are finally real.
I thought love was not meant
For this old man's soul.
But in your arms,
My heart is full.

His performance of the song was the conclusion of the show. *Swept Away* was playing in the background as the credits rolled.

Paige sat frozen and stared. What now? Her phone rang. Laurel would have an opinion. "Hello?" she realized tears choked her voice.

"Did you watch?" it was Jack, not Laurel. Paige nearly dropped the phone.

"Yes."

"What did you think?"

She scrambled for coherent words, “You looked good. How are you feeling?” There was a knock on the door. Paige groaned. She said, “Someone’s at the door, I’m going to ignore it.”

“You better answer.”

“No, I want to talk to you.”

“It could be important, I’m not going anywhere.”

Hurrying across the room, she yanked open her front door, Jack stood on the threshold. “You shouldn’t just open the door at night without checking who it is.” He was still speaking into the phone. Paige looked at him and clicked hers off.

For a moment she just stared at him. “You sang our song.”

“Can I come in?”

Paige mumbled an apology and stepped out of his way as he crossed the threshold. She led him to the couch, watching him move stiffly. “How’d you get here?”

“I drove from the airport.”

She eyed him suspiciously, “Were you sitting in the car until exactly ten o’clock?”

“Maybe,” he gave her the grin she’d missed so very much.

Paige didn’t trust herself, she still felt that her heart was too fragile. She would not fall for his smile. Her voice was suspicious, “Why?”

“I love you, Paige. That’s why I’m here.”

“I love you too, but I’m unsure what you’re doing here.

“You’re the priority that I mentioned. I made you go because I didn’t want to ruin your life by making you watch me get better.”

“But you did by sending me away,” Paige felt her nerves building inside of her. She was afraid to hope.

Jack looked down, when he tilted his face back up, his expression was solemn. "I think I handled it wrong. I should've at least let you stay until school started."

Her face was serious, "You should have let me make my own decision."

Now he smiled again, a bit of his former confidence showing in the light of his eyes, "Once again, this is why I have to keep you with me. You tell me exactly what you think, and I should always listen. Its one of the many reasons that I love you."

Taking a deep breath, ready to accept his words, Paige spoke, "I love you, too Jack." She reached out, needing to touch him. He pulled her in for a hug. Paige lay her hands against his chest, "I've missed you so much." They kissed. When they stopped, she looked up at him, "So how do we do all this?"

Jack gave her another smile, "I don't know, and I don't care. We'll make it work because life is nothing without you, Paige Baxter."

Epilogue

Annabeth opened the box that had just been delivered to her door. She hurriedly ripped off the tape and pushed past the bubble wrap. In her hand was the product of the summer. This was good. The biography was her best so far; she was certain. This had been a smart idea. A rock star book would sell in a big way. And who could've imagined that Jack Corey would have an accident that caused him to be a media sensation while she was there in the field with him? The gods were looking down on her in August.

She had a moment of feeling bad for looking at Jack's misfortune as her fortune, but she shook it off. His body would recover and so would the rest of him. She would make money off this. Her agent and publisher were already discussing new projects. The three of them had just met yesterday. Her agent wanted her to write a book for a female politician who was changing things in Washington. After her summer with the rock band, she wasn't certain the DC life was where she wanted to spend half a year.

Annabeth thought of those months. Going over to the counter, she fixed herself a cup of coffee. Dammit, she missed those people, living in close quarters they were a family. That bus world was like summer camp. Despite some moments over her poor choices, those women had been friends.

She'd been foolish enough for some time to think she might have been in love. What she had done with Trent Crosby for those months was far removed from love. He'd used her like he used any woman. Annabeth had been dumb enough to allow him. She could still recall her final rejection of him in Malibu. That had felt good.

When she thought of the house in Malibu, Annabeth considered the money her agent was convinced she would make. She wanted a nicer place to live, maybe it was time to move out of Queens. Thinking for a moment of the lavish lifestyle she'd partaken in this summer, she decided to look carefully at her next project. Which subject would sell the most copies?

Annabeth had been standing at her window, watching the city below her. Now she picked up her phone. She should call Tony. He'd be pleased to know the book was printed. Instead, she called Jack. She was certain she'd never liked a story subject more than she liked Jack. In fact, she'd had to be careful to stay objective in her writing. It would have been easy to write the book as a tribute to a truly good person. Readers didn't want it to be all of that. Fortunately, the world around Jack gave his story more color.

"I'm looking at your face," this was how she greeted him when he answered the phone.

"Can you see in my window?" Jack laughed.

"I'm holding the first copy of your book."

She could hear his smile through the line, "Congratulations, Annabeth! It's more yours than mine."

"Fair enough, it's our book. How are you feeling?"

"Good. I rode my bike this morning."

"That's incredible. Your effort to get in shape has inspired me. I joined a gym."

"Good for you! Now if you'll just drink my kale smoothies."

They both laughed, "That's asking too much."

"So, what's next for Annabeth Muldoon?"

"I don't know. There's already some talk about my next project. I'm trying to decide where I want to spend my time. You guys spoiled me. I've traveled the country, now I want to be selective."

"I'm glad you were with us."

"Me too. I'll always remember this summer."

"Annabeth, don't worry, you haven't seen the last of me."

"Oh, I know," she chuckled. "Don't forget, our book's promotions are just beginning.

***

The lights, cameras, and monitors on the television stage were a change, but as Paige stood off to the side, she felt the familiar exhilaration. The Jack Corey band was performing on The Tonight Show. As part of the book promotion, Jack had agreed to a few appearances with Annabeth. For this late-night show, the band had accepted the request to do a performance.

At this moment, Jack was standing before an appreciative audience singing Swept Away. His arms were strong as they held onto the guitar. The notes were fire as his fingers flew across the strings. The small stage gave him an excuse not to strut around, but the rest of the performance was pure Jack Corey magic.

He was recovering from his accident, steadily making great improvements. At fifty, he told Paige he couldn't say he was completely better, but he was gaining flexibility. It was enough.

There were no more tours planned in the foreseeable future. Jack said he couldn't imagine there would be. When they lay in bed at night, they would reminisce about the summer. He shared that for many reasons, he wouldn't trade the past year on the road. It had been sublime to be back on stage several nights a week doing what he loved most; playing his music. It never got old to hear the crowd sing the lyrics he'd written. It was like going home to be on stage with Trent and Joe. For that brief period that Theo was with him, it felt like they'd traveled back in time and were once again those young men who were kissed with luck and became superstars.

It saddened Jack to consider that Theo's addiction demon was preventing him from the life that Jack got to enjoy. Jed, who'd been with them, had successfully filled that void on stage. For that part, Jack appreciated him.

Now they were all back in front of adoring fans; live and across the nation. Paige stood with Keely and Annabeth. She was also in a spot that she loved. The absence of Gina was felt, but now they could see each other regularly.

Paige had taken a leave of absence through the month of December. When the semester ended at the first of the year, she would be officially retired. This was without regret. The night Jack showed up at her door, she knew what she wanted most.

Now she had moved her things to the New York apartment. Her life as an artist was just beginning. Jack had one of the rooms turned into a studio for her. Never would she have believed all the high-end tools and supplies were for her. She still had clients in Ohio and word was catching in New York. Paige wasn't certain what she wanted to do with her art, but the possibilities were endless.

For now, Paige was enthralled in the sound coming from the band in front of her. Jack's voice pulled her in. He had been worth every chance she had taken this summer. They'd struggled through small things and fought through bigger things. After the show, Jack would walk off the stage, and she'd be waiting for him with open arms.

Jack Corey had come into her life and offered her all the love she'd ever needed. She would treasure it. The night in Findlay, when he'd joined her on the steps, she'd looked up at him, and Paige had seen her future.

Linda Van Meter is the author of *Worth Losing* and *Whispered Regrets*. She is a mother of three and grandmother of three. Linda lives in Ohio with her husband, where she teaches Language Arts, Creative Writing and Communications at Pleasant High School.

Follow Linda on Facebook @ldvanmeter
Twitter: @lldvmeter
Instagram: lindadvm81
Email: lindadvm81@gmail.com

33092381R00162

Made in the USA
Lexington, KY
08 March 2019